WHY DID THE KLINGONS LOOK SO DIFFERENT IN THE STAR TREK MOVIE?

HOW DID THE ANDROID, NORMAN, MANAGE TO LEAVE MUDD'S PLANET AND BOARD THE *ENTERPRISE*?

WHAT FORCES, OTHER THAN STAR FLEET, DOES THE FEDERATION HAVE AT ITS COMMAND?

WHY IS CAPTAIN KIRK SO POPULAR?

These are just a few of the questions examined in this brand-new collection about the universe of Star Trek. You'll explore the careers of the characters; find out the reasons behind the differences and similarities in the TV series, cartoons, movie, novelizations, and comics; and learn more about Federation history, special effects, aliens, and everything else that has helped to give Star Trek so much meaning for fans of all ages.

THE BEST OF TREK #3

SIGNET Books of Special Interest

☐ **THE BEST OF TREK®: From the Magazine for Star Trek Fans** edited by Walter Irwin and G. B. Love. A collection of articles that will delight every Star Trek fan, covering the TV show, cartoons, comic books, and characters. Complete with photos and original artwork, *The Best of Trek* tells it all, from what makes Mr. Spock tick to a history of the Klingons and Romulans. (#W8030—$1.75)

☐ **THE BEST OF TREK® #2: From the Magazine for Star Trek Fans** edited by Walter Irwin and G. B. Love. Whether Kirk, Spock, McCoy, or a Klingon is your favorite character, you'll find lots of new information about them all. Span the farthest reaches of time and space as you turn the pages of this latest great collection of fact and fancy.
(#J9131—$1.95)*

☐ **FROM *THE BLOB* TO *STAR WARS*: The Science Fiction Movie Quiz Book** by Bart Andrews. A fantastic new collection of science fiction trivia that contains 1001 questions on everything from heroes and villains to filmmakers and special effects. Also features a wealth of trivia on *Star Wars* and a special 16 page photo quiz. (#W7948—$1.50)

☐ **TREKKIE QUIZ BOOK** by Bart Andrews with Brad Dunning. Here are 100 quizzes, 1001 questions to test you and your friends for the post of honorary crew members on the U.S.S. *Enterprise!* (#W8413—$1.50)

☐ **THE UFO MOVIE QUIZ BOOK** by Jeff Rovin with an Introduction by Robert Wise, director of the movie *Star Trek*. From the first invasion of Earth by aliens to the incredible meeting at "Devil's Tower," here are Hollywood's most amazing close encounters on the cinema screen—titles, plots, stars, directors, producers, writers, and everything else you could possibly remember about these globe-spanning movies.
(#E8258—$1.75)

* Price slightly higher in Canada

Buy them at your local bookstore or use this convenient coupon for ordering.

THE NEW AMERICAN LIBRARY, INC.,
P.O. Box 999, Bergenfield, New Jersey 07621

Please send me the SIGNET BOOKS I have checked above. I am enclosing
$_____ (please add 50¢ to this order to cover postage and handling).
Send check or money order—no cash or C.O.D.'s. Prices and numbers are subject to change without notice.

Name _____

Address _____

City_____ State _____ Zip Code_____
Allow 4-6 weeks for delivery.
This offer is subject to withdrawal without notice.

THE BEST OF TREK #3

FROM THE MAGAZINE FOR STAR TREK FANS

EDITED BY WALTER IRWIN AND G. B. LOVE

A SIGNET BOOK
NEW AMERICAN LIBRARY
TIMES MIRROR

NAL BOOKS ARE AVAILABLE AT QUANTITY DISCOUNTS
WHEN USED TO PROMOTE PRODUCTS OR SERVICES. FOR
INFORMATION PLEASE WRITE TO PREMIUM MARKETING DIVISION,
THE NEW AMERICAN LIBRARY, INC., 1633 BROADWAY,
NEW YORK, NEW YORK 10019.

Copyright © 1979, 1980 by Walter Irwin and G. B. Love

Copyright © 1980 by TREK®

All rights reserved

TREK® is a registered trademark ® of G. B. Love and Walter Irwin

SIGNET TRADEMARK REG. U.S. PAT. OFF. AND FOREIGN COUNTRIES
REGISTERED TRADEMARK—MARCA REGISTRADA
HECHO EN CHICAGO, U.S.A.

SIGNET, SIGNET CLASSICS, MENTOR, PLUME, MERIDIAN AND NAL BOOKS
are published by The New American Library, Inc.,
1633 Broadway, New York, New York 10019

First Printing, January, 1981

1 2 3 4 5 6 7 8 9

PRINTED IN THE UNITED STATES OF AMERICA

ACKNOWLEDGMENTS

Thanks, as always, are due to the many people who have made this third collection possible and support the continued existence of *Trek:* Sheila Gilbert of NAL, who is patient with lateness and lost mail; Jim Houston, John Murphy, and James van Hise for helping out; Elaine Hauptmann and her gang for support (sorry, still no *Starsky and Hutch* articles!); Leslie Thompson, Woman of the Night; Hal Schuster, distributor *extraordinaire;* and, of course, all of the writers, artists, subscribers, and advertisers. You all make us very proud!

And special thanks to Pat Mooney, who sent a copy of *The Best of Trek #1* all the way to England to have one of my favorite authors autograph it as a Christmas present. Wow!

—W.G.I.

CONTENTS

INTRODUCTION 1

1. MORE STAR TREK MYSTERIES SOLVED 3
   by Leslie Thompson and our readers

2. COMMAND DECISION CRISIS:
   A STAR TREK FAN FICTION PARODY 12
   by Walter Irwin

3. THE STAR TREK MOVIE NOVEL
   AND COMICS ADAPTATIONS 32
   by Van James

4. THE KLINGONS (?) IN STAR TREK:
   THE MOTION PICTURE 38
   by Leslie Thompson

5. WALTER KOENIG: AN INTERVIEW 44

6. PARALLELS IN STAR TREK:
   THE MOTION PICTURE VS. THE SERIES 55
   by Lynn Adams

7. A SAMPLING OF TREK ROUNDTABLE 61

8. A LETTER FROM JUDITH WOLPER 78

9. BRIDGING THE GAP:
   THE PROMETHEAN STAR TREK 91
   by Joyce Tullock

10. SULU'S PROFILE 106
    by Colleen Arima

11. A BRIEF LOOK AT SPOCK'S CAREER 117
    by Leslie Thompson

12. STAR TREK:
    THE MOTION PICTURE—A REVIEW 134
    by Walter Irwin

13. THE PSYCHOLOGY OF CAPTAIN
    KIRK'S POPULARITY 143
    by Gloria-Ann Rovelstad

14. CHANGES IN STAR TREK:
    THE MOTION PICTURE 150
    by G. B. Love

15. THE OTHER FEDERATION FORCES 161
    by Walter Irwin

16. VULCAN AS A PATRIARCHY 168
    by Rebecca Hoffman

17. A TREK INTO GENEALOGY 179
    by Linda Frankel

18. ALTERNATE UNIVERSES IN STAR TREK 186
    by Mark Andrew Golding

THE BEST OF TREK #3
FROM THE MAGAZINE FOR STAR TREK FANS

INTRODUCTION

Thank you for buying this third collection of articles and features from our magazine, *Trek*. We are sure that you will enjoy this edition just as much as—if not more than—you did our previous two collections.

You will note that a large number of the articles and features in this volume concern *Star Trek: The Motion Picture*. The reason why is obvious. No single event in the history of Star Trek fandom has caused so much excitement, discussion, and controversy. The fact that the motion picture exists, is a rousing success both critically and financially, and has garnered so much comment is the best proof we could have of our contention that Star Trek has now become an integral and lasting part of our fictional heritage.

If you enjoy the articles in this collection and would like to see more, please turn to the ad at the back of this book for information on how you can order and subscribe to *Trek*. And if you have been stirred to write an article or two yourself, please send it along to us. We would be most happy to see it, as we are constantly on the lookout for fresh and exciting new contributors. Artists are also welcome to contribute to *Trek*.

We want to hear from you in any case. Our lines of communication are always open. It is only through *your* comments that we know if we are doing our job.

Again, many thanks, and we hope you will enjoy *The Best of Trek #3*.

WALTER IRWIN
G. B. LOVE

1.
MORE STAR TREK MYSTERIES SOLVED

by Leslie Thompson and our readers

The publication of Leslie's article "Star Trek Mysteries—Solved" drew a flood of mail into our offices, almost all of which challenged our intrepid correspondent to solve even more "mysteries." So Leslie started listening to tapes, reading books, and chewing her fingernails—the result of which is this second "Mysteries" article. And if it draws even a fraction of the mail the first one did, a third will be on the way very soon.

The explanations which I offered to some of the "mysteries" and loose ends in various Star Trek episodes proved to be one of the most popular articles to appear in *Trek* thus far. Many readers agreed with my speculations, many more challenged them. But in each of these letters, and in dozens more, came queries about other mysteries—and a "challenge" to me and our staff to explain them.

Some are simply unanswerable. As I mentioned in the first Mysteries article, a thousand and one details go into the production of a weekly television series, and in the pressure of time to get the show on film, it is a virtual certainty that inaccuracies and inconsistencies slip into finished episodes. Star Trek was even more prone to this, as the writers were working with what was essentially a newly created universe. It is a tribute to Gene Roddenberry and the Star Trek staff that as much continuity was preserved as possible, and that none of the episodes (even in the slipshod third season) were destroyed by a major and glaring mistake.

But minor mistakes abounded. Any number of them can be pointed out by even the most casual fan. The sad part of this is that these minor errors cannot be placed in the continuity of the series by any stretch of the imagination. They are errors in scripts or casting, and remain unanswerable to those who demand that everything fit nicely into an intricate Star Trek pattern. We have to learn to live with them, just as we have had to live with some of the weaker and more ridiculous episodes.

Here is a good example of an unanswerable query. Mary Jo Lawrence asks: "What is the relation between Dr. Anne Mulhall and Dr. Miranda Jones, both played by Diana Muldaur?"

Skipping the impulse to say they are a paradox, this is probably one of the best examples of casting errors. The excellent Ms. Muldaur was hired to play two separate roles at two separate times without someone taking the time to think about the consternation it would cause to fans. This happened with William Campbell (Trelane in "The Squire of Gothos" and Koloth in "The Trouble with Tribbles") and Mark Lenard (The Romulan commander in "Balance of Terror" and Sarek in "Journey to Babel").

It is a compliment to the abilities of the actors that they were chosen to appear on Star Trek more than once, and in reality, Gene Roddenberry and his staff had no idea they were creating a legendary series. It is a truism of television production that the viewing public in general doesn't have a very long memory, so casting directors see little harm in using the same actors in different roles if a sufficient length of time has passed. So we can forgive the action. But wow, doesn't it drive you crazy?

These casting duplications were mentioned in many letters, mainly because of my contention in the first article that Number One and Nurse Chapel (both played by Majel Barrett) were sisters, thereby explaining their uncanny resemblance.

One letter especially took me to task for this. "Are Sarek and the Romulan commander first cousins? Are Trelane and Koloth clones?" It would be damned difficult and probably downright silly to attempt to form any kind of relationship between these people. I only did so with Number One and Chapel because the role of Christine is so pivotal to Star Trek (and the personality of Spock), and because it was a reasonable and natural assumption—especially in light of the fact that we were never given a proper name of any sort for Number One.

Several letters spoke of one of the greatest Star Trek mysteries: the "grounding" of the Klingon fleet by the Organians in James Blish's novel *Spock Must Die!* and their subsequent reappearance in the animated episodes and fiction. In general, fans want to know, "How?"

In my article on the Klingons (*The Best of TREK*), I pretty much offhandedly dismissed the entire story of *Spock Must Die!* as not being part of the established Star Trek canon. It seems I was a little too quick in doing so. Not only does it set a bad precedent—why not dismiss "Spock's Brain"?—but it is a disservice to the talents and memory of a fine writer. Blish wrote the novel in all sincerity, and did not arbitrarily decide to get rid of the Klingons. It was a suitable and logical conclusion to the book, one which the omniscient Organians would do under the circumstances.

So the book as written stands. Now how did the Klingons regain starflight capability and why did the Organians allow it to happen?

My contention is that the Organians not only allowed the Klingons to regain their former status, they caused it to happen. After the events of *Spock Must Die!* the balance of power in our portion of the universe was so upset that a major upheaval of some type took place. What it was is sheer speculation. Perhaps the Romulans, now fearing Federation dominance, started a preemptive war, and that war threatened to tear the civilized portions of the galaxy apart. Or perhaps a powerful foe from outside our galaxy attacked, and without the added might of the Klingons (who would have fought a common foe with the Federation), the defenders of our galaxy would have fallen.

The possibilities are endless. In any event, the Organians saw that they had made a mistake, and using their great powers, set things right. In the process, they obviously removed the knowledge of the energy shield the Klingons had placed around their planet, or arranged matters so that such a device would never again be able to operate against them. So once again, our favorite villains are free to wreak havoc and cause trouble all over the galaxy, much to the delight and consternation of Star Trek fans.

The character of Spock has prompted many questions, some about actions of his in various scripts which seem radically out of character, and others on the nature of Vulcans and Vulcan society.

One of the most interesting of these comes from Joanne Philagios. She wants to know why Spock, in "The Cloud Minders," is "bandying about, in a social context, information he was not willing to give either his doctor or his commanding officer." This is, of course, a reference to Spock's discussing the mating habits of Vulcans with the immaculate Droxine.

It is no secret that Spock was attracted to Droxine, if only in an intellectual way, and the uncharacteristic frankness he showed on this occasion must have stemmed from his wish to convince Droxine (and himself!) that the attraction did not—and must not!—be on a sexual basis. Spock was being frank with Droxine to avoid being frank with himself, and thereby avoid the admission that he could feel a physical attraction to a female without the onset of *pon farr*. This is an excellent instance of Spock's denying his emotions, instead of merely controlling them.

Allison Perry supplied us with a partial answer to the question of Vulcan society which fans have debated for years—is Vulcan patriarchal or matriarchal in makeup? The debate stems from the fact that T'Pau officiated at Spock's "marriage" ceremony, and that she was offered a seat on the Federation Council.

Allison sees Spock's deference to T'Pau simply as a gesture of respect and admiration for her rank and achievements: "[Vulcan] leaders deserve their positions more due to the fact that they are chosen logically."

So Vulcan leaders deserve to lead. No arguments there; such a system fits right in with all that we know about Vulcan customs and mentality. But if their system is *neither* patriarchal nor matriarchal, then why does Amanda show such deference to Sarek in "Journey to Babel"? And why would T'Pring become "the property of the victor" of the battle in "Amok Time"? Sounds pretty much like a male-dominated society on Vulcan from these examples.

To explain this, we have to go back into Vulcan history. We know that Vulcan was once a warlike and savage world, one on which women would naturally be considered property and spoils of war. After the Reformation, women were given their rightful stature as equals, but the ancient rituals controlling

Vulcan life could not be changed. As the males were drawn to *pon farr*, so the women needed to have a controlling instinct to protect the fabric of society. As we saw with T'Pring, Vulcan females are affected very little at amok time, so the instinct must take a different form.

This form is a compulsion to defer completely to the male at the time of *pon farr*, and to defer ritually to the male at all other times. As the male is relatively helpless at *pon farr*, the women must be submissive and meek so that they cannot gain either a physical or intellectual advantage of any sort. This is why T'Pring was willing to become the property of the victor. She had no other choice, no more than Spock had to attend *pon farr* or die, or to battle his best friend to the death.

So Vulcan women defer to their mates at all times simply as a continuing assurance that Vulcan society will continue, along with the sanctity of *pon farr*, and not because the males are considered superior. Although Amanda does not feel the instinctual need to act in this way toward Sarek, she would probably do so anyway because she loves him and respects him. And above all, she would not want to cause him embarrassment.

Pamela Rose wants to know how the android Norman managed to leave "Mudd's Planet" in "I, Mudd" if the androids had no spaceflight capability and needed the *Enterprise* to venture out into the galaxy to serve humans. This is relatively easy. Harry Mudd arrived on Mudd's Planet on a damaged ship. As this was a small ship, probably designed to carry only a few passengers, it would be unsuitable for the androids' purposes. It is also probable that the androids' resources, having never developed spaceflight, were unable to duplicate the mechanism of the ship, and were only able to repair it for one flight. So Norman got to the *Enterprise* in Mudd's ship.

But that is not the rub. The mystery in this episode is not how Norman got off his planet and to the *Enterprise*, but how he got *on* the *Enterprise*. He couldn't have transported on, as small ships like the one he borrowed from Mudd do not contain transporter equipment; and it was never stated in the episode that he was transported on by the *Enterprise* equipment. Even if he had been, he would not have been allowed to wear a Starfleet uniform, or have free run of the ship.

So if Norman didn't just beam aboard the *Enterprise*, then he must have been allowed to come aboard, and in the guise of a Starfleet officer assigned to the ship. But again we run into a problem: When his sabotage is discovered, no one on board seems to have ever seen him before.

Had he managed to make his way to a starbase, take over the identity of an officer due to be assigned to the *Enterprise*, and then boarded in a routine manner, then certainly Spock, if not Kirk, could have identified him.

The only answer is that Norman, being the only model of his series, had abilities beyond the norm of the other androids. In this case, he would have had to be able to change or disguise his features to the aspect of a new or current *Enterprise* officer, and thereby board the ship during a shore leave or some such. As he would have appeared to the crew and probably the instruments to be a known person, he would have been above suspicion until he made his move.

Another puzzler which bothers many fans is the method by which episodes are listed according to stardates. Some feel that the stardates should be sequential—that is, following in the order of their number. With this method, stardate 2715.1 would follow stardate 1151.6, regardless of when the episodes so numbered were filmed or aired. But this would place some of the animated episodes within the live series sequence, and if stardates correspond to solar years, cause the length of the *Enterprise*'s five-year mission to be over 16 years!

Obviously, this cannot be the case. But this is one instance in which we have the word of Gene Roddenberry himself to solve our mystery. In *The Making of Star Trek*, Roddenberry states that stardates are based on a system of galactic location, not on a simple time basis. So stardate 2356.9 might be correct on, say, Delta Vega while it would be stardate 1213.7 at the exact same instant on Earth. The confusion surrounding stardates is understandable, as it would take a computer to be able to utilize them in relation to one another. And many fans are further confused by the common practice of Trekkers using current dates in stardate fashion, for example 7912.26.

Many readers have wondered about the fact that most of the inhabited planets visited by the *Enterprise* have but one culture. There were major exceptions to this in the series, of course, but the point was usually only made when it was necessary to the story. This practice, like so many others in television, was due primarily to time and money considerations, but it also reflected the old writer's adage: "Tell the reader all that he has to know, and nothing more than he has to know."

But we are concerned with the Star Trek universe here, and not with problems of scriptwriting and production. So when we know that Kirk and company visited so many single-culture planets, there must be a good and logical reason for this sort of planet to exist.

The answer lies in the humanoid condition. It is basic to the nature of a humanoid species to be aggressive and warlike. This is true not only of Earth, but of Vulcan and many other planets mentioned in Star Trek. What makes Earth almost unique among the planets of Star Trek's time is that the many and varied Earth cultures remained separate and distinct during the long road upward to civilization and peace.

Most other planets did not (or could not) achieve stability while allowing differing intraplanetary cultures—you can usually read "nations" in place of cultures—to remain autonomous. Either through the most often occurring route of one nation's becoming victorious in a planetary war, or by the rarer influence of one man or one group bringing all peoples together (as happened on Vulcan), the majority of planets comprised by the Federation have one central form of government and one distinct culture.

Happily enough for the peace and stability of the galaxy, the majority of these planets used the freedom from constant strife to develop higher and peace-loving forms of civilization. But unhappily for the galaxy, others, such as the Klingons and the Romulans, did not.

Fans often write to ask, "Why were we never told the first names of most of the supporting characters . . . and what are they?"

As we saw relatively little of crewmembers "off duty," when first names would most likely come into use, these situations were always covered by the use of the last name only. Scotty was given a first name only when circumstances required that he give his full name and rank (such as when he was left in command of the ship), and Janice Rand had a full name so that as the captain's intended love interest (an idea quickly dropped) she would not have to respond to "Yeoman, darling" at a tender moment.

But what of Sulu, Uhura, and others? Fandom has generally accepted that Uhura's first name is Penda, which in Swahili means "love." A most appropriate name, to be sure, as she is not only loved by all of the crew, but her entire name, freely translated, means "She who loves freedom."

Sulu, on the other hand, has a more pedestrian appelation: Walter. How this name was chosen is somewhat a mystery, as many fans support the choice as being poor, and not reflective of Sulu's mixed Oriental ancestry; while others applaud it as being representative of a future when names need not carry ethnic overtones. So a decision is still up in the air, but I have chosen the "Walter" side of the issue, as George Takai himself stated that the name was a good choice.

Transporter Chief Kyle, being an Englishman, could have only one name: Winston. It is not only fitting in view of British history, but a nice salute to the actor who made so much of such a small part over the years, John Winston.

Another question which often pops up concerns the chain of command on the *Enterprise*. Many episodes showed Scotty filling in with full authority in the absence of Kirk and Spock, so the upper echelons are self-evident: Kirk, Spock, Scott, by rank and positions of authority. But the question of who is fourth-in-command is a touchy one. Some sources say Uhura, others Sulu. On the basis of past evidence, Sulu seems the most logical choice. He is (although it was never specifically stated) chief helmsman, and is in active training for command.

Uhura, on the other hand, holds an equal rank with Sulu, and she too is possibly in training for command (she wore a command gold uniform in early episodes). She holds the post of chief communications officer, as well as being the senior female crewperson aboard the ship—which isn't really saying much when you come right down to it!

So in the male-oriented world of Star Trek, Sulu would most probably be fourth-in-command, with Uhura fifth. However, there is a more compelling reason why Sulu would be fourth, and that is that he has obviously completed his primary starship training. As we have seen in "Where No Man Has Gone Before," Sulu served in different positions around the ship before settling into the demanding and important position of helmsman. Simple logic states that helmsman is a step up toward captain, while communications is pretty much of a dead end.

But we can't fault Uhura. Maybe she made the mistake of simply being too doggone good at her job. But she should eventually evolve into fourth-in-command, as Sulu would almost have to transfer to another ship to take his next step as a second officer. Maybe she will even get the chance to fire the phasers once in a while, instead of opening hailing frequencies.

Speaking of which, why aren't any of those come-and-go security chiefs considered in the chain of command? The most obvious reason is that they are not a part of the regular bridge crew, and therefore are not especially well versed in the day-to-day running of a starship, much less capable of taking over in an emergency.

But one would expect a security chief to be on the bridge, where he could keep an eye on developments, and, if nothing else, relieve Kirk of the necessity of having to call down to security every time something goes wrong.

The best explanation of why a security chief was never regularly on the bridge (and indeed, why there was never a regular security chief!) is that Kirk, having built up the best staff of executive officers in the fleet, was constantly frustrated by his failure to find a security officer that met those high standards. So none of them lasted very long, and none was allowed on the bridge.

It is a regrettable oversight that a strong security officer was not an integral part of Star Trek. If one had been included as part of the bridge crew, with a rank of lieutenant commander, he could have taken the sometimes needed part of the "hawk" that was given to others, none of whom looked comfortable in the role. Star Trek needed a hard-liner as counterpoint to Spock's coolness and McCoy's humanitarianism.

In closing, I would once again like to thank all of the readers who took the time and trouble to drive me crazy! But it is great fun, and I am very much looking forward to the next installment. Until then, I will leave you by quashing some of the rumors that have cropped up about the Star Trek movie: Scotty is not a drunk, Kirk is not married, McCoy is not a vet, and Spock does not die!

See, no mystery at all!

2.
COMMAND DECISION CRISIS: A STAR TREK FAN FICTION PARODY

by Walter Irwin

We've run several Star Trek parodies in Trek, *but one of the wildest is this spoof of bad Star Trek fan fiction called "Command Decision Crisis" (the title, appropriately enough, has nothing to do with the story). It is not only fun to read, but an excellent example of how* not *to write a Star Trek story.*

It was not a good day aboard the United Fedderbedding Planets Starship *Ennui*. Captain James T. Cute was mad. Good and mad.

"Why can't I find a Security Chief that is worth a Omnicronian *diskobeat*?" moaned Cute, rubbing his chin raw in consternation. "I have the finest crew in Starbeat, and I deserve to have them. I have worked long hours—"

"Eighty-six point two minutes, captain," interrupted Mr. Skunk from his science section.

Cute shot him a dirty look. "Well, maybe not *hours* exactly, but I have worked hard—"

"Ordering us about, he's worked," came a mutter from somewhere near Communications.

Cute chose to ignore it this time. "I repeat, I have worked hard and long—er, minutes—to make this the finest crew in Starbeat, and at the risk of repeating myself—"

"Again." This time the murmur was from Engineering.

"I repeat, I will not have it!" Cute shouted. "Now," he continued, trying to pull his tunic down over his stomach and failing (it was late in the season), "This ship will have a top-notch security chief or I will know the reason why!" Having made this pronouncement, Cute stood to his full height, teetered a moment on his high heels, and strode into the turbolift.

As the doors *swooshed* shut behind him, he heard another comment: "Maybe you are the reason why."

Dr. "Moans" Macaw was seated in his office hard at work cutting a new pair of soles for his boots with one of his favorite scalpels as Cute stormed in.

"Doctor," Cute blurted, "what about my security chief?"

Macaw looked at him in confusion. "Do we have a security chief in here today, Jimbo? I sweah, they die lahk flies, don't they?"

"No, no, no, no, no, no," cried Cute, shaking his boyish forelock with each emphatic "no." "I mean, how can you help me get a new security chief, one who will live up to the high standards of this crew I've put together, the finest in the fleet? I've worked long and hard . . ." Cute didn't know what to say after this, as no one had ever let him finish before.

Macaw gave him a slow smile, causing his eyes to crinkle appealingly at the edges. "Hang on a minute, Jim, while ah unstick mah eyes again." He pulled his lids up with a handy forceps (he had been using it to open a bottle of Smarmian brandy) and sighed. "Ah gotta quit smilin'. Couldn't get 'em open yesterday, and took out a fellah's appendix."

"That's good work with your eyes closed," said Cute, impressed.

"Yeah, too bad he was here fo' a hangnail. Now Jim, what's this huffin' and a puffin' about a security chief?"

"I just can't seem to find a chief that's any good," muttered Cute. "Doctor, could it be that it *is* my fault? Could it be that in my zeal to run everything on this ship I have undermined and emasculated every security chief we've ever had? Could it be I haven't been as fair and just as a starship captain should? Could it be . . . aw, nah. Starbeat Command is at fault, as usual."

"Jim, seein' as how I know every little nook an' cranny inside that head of yourn, I agree with you. Now, I'm a doctor, not a personnel executive, but what you need is somebody to be security chief that can take the heat. It's a tough job, and you need a tough man to handle it."

"Doctor, that makes sense."

Macaw sat up in surprise. "It does?"

"You bet," said Cute excitedly. "Let me call Skunk up here and we'll talk it over." Cute punched the intercom button, and after a few minutes on hold, asked his first officer to come to sick bay.

A few minutes later Commander Skunk sidled into the room. No matter how much they had been through together, Cute reflected, he was still always fascinated with Skunk. He was the issue of a Fulcan father and a human mother, and although he chose early in life to live as a logical and emotionless Fulcan, he sometimes demonstrated the human side of his nature by wearing loud-colored shirts, drinking beer from the can, and inviting hapless crewmembers over to watch endless boring home movies.

"Yes, captain?" Skunk asked in his flat, dull voice.

Macaw tossed him a whetstone from his medical bag. "Use this, you pointy-eared elf. We can't understand you."

Skunk stropped his tongue with several quick strokes. "Is this better, gentlemen?" As they nodded assent, he continued. "You requested my presence, sir?"

"Hold it a minute, Skunk," said Cute, snapping his fingers. "We can't get on with the story until we introduce Mr. Scotch." Once again he turned to the intercom, and called the ship's engineering officer to sick bay.

Commander Scotch burred his way into sick bay, helped himself to a couple of quarts of the doctor's brandy, wiped some grease off his hands with sterile bandages, danced a jig, and addressed Cute. "Commander Scotch rrrrreportin', sir."

Cute, miffed at having been upstaged by his executive officers, spoke sharply. "Gentlemen, the doctor and I have agreed that this ship needs a new security officer that is the meanest, toughest, hardest so-and-so in Starbeat, and I want you to find him for me. Skunk, get on the computer. Get me readouts of everyone in Starbeat who has been transferred for being too difficult—too hard to get along with. I want the man nobody else wants, and I intend to make him want to serve on this ship!"

"Captain," said Skunk slowly, "that was an impressive speech, and I am sure the only reason you wanted Mr. Scotch up here was so you would have more time to rehearse it"—Cute blushed, trapped in his ploy—"but without having to look at the computer records, I can tell you that we already have such a crewperson aboard this ship."

"Ship? This ship? Aboard this ship?" Cute long ago had discovered that repeating his officers' statements saved him memorizing an average of fourteen lines per episode. "Who is he?"

"It is not a 'he,' captain. The candidate I am proposing is a female."

"Skunk," exploded Macaw, "you must be out of yoah Fulcan mind. The *Ennui* can't have a woman security chief!"

"And why not, doctor?" Skunk answered coolly, relishing the opportunity to act superior by arguing with Macaw. "Studies on my planet have shown—"

Macaw snorted. "Weah dealing with Starbeat officers, not leprechauns."

Skunk was raising an eyebrow in preparation for a stinging reply when Cute reached over and pulled the eyebrow down.

"Save that for one of my last-minute tactical innovations, Mr. Skunk. And you," he said to Macaw, "keep quiet. Let Skunk explain his ridiculous statement and then we'll go on to something that makes sense. Proceed, Mr. Skunk."

"Captain, I object. We have just the person you described among our crew, and it is eminently logical that she—"

"Skunk, come off it," said Cute, shaking his head. "A woman can't be security chief. It is a man's job. Women aren't capable of it. I mean, a woman is round and soft, and . . . they don't even shave! How can someone who doesn't shave be security chief? Why, it would almost be obscene!"

"Aye," said Scotch, peering up from over the edge of the desk where he had slipped some time before. "I dinna ken ye, Skunk. A wee bit o' a lassie, mon, it wouldna do. . . ." He rambled off into a chorus of "How Are Things in Glocca Morra?" and slipped back under the desk.

"Gentlemen, I remind you of the United Fedderbedding Planets Charter, which guarantees full equality between the sexes in all areas of influence."

"Hey, Skunk," cajoled Cute with a wink, "you know all that stuff was only put in the Charter to keep the libbers quiet. And for sure it was never intended to let a woman be security chief."

"Captain," continued Skunk, "I might also remind you that Admiral Kojak has given you only three more months to get the *Ennui* back into shape, or he will 'have you flying a desk in the Neutral Zone.'"

"So?" asked Cute in annoyance. "And how did you know that, anyway? I didn't tell you."

"I learned it from your mind in our last adventure. You remember, 'Turnaround Intruder.'"

"Yes," answered Cute, recalling his distress at being trapped in a woman's body, and how Skunk had been the only one who knew the truth, thanks to the telepathic powers of his Fulcan mind melt. Cute could still feel Skunk's long sensitive fingers, probing and searching, then finally moving up to Cute's female face to begin the melt.

"I remember, Mr. Skunk. *Everything*." Skunk looked blandly at the ceiling. "But I did not include any conversation with Admiral Kojak in the information I gave you to prove my identity during the mind melt."

Skunk shrugged. "As long as I was in there, I decided to do a little shopping."

Cute reflected that he would have to take a little more care with Skunk in the future. "Be that as it may, Mr. Skunk, I still don't see what Admiral Kojak has to do with your recommending a woman to be my new security officer."

"The name of the crewperson I am proposing is Gloria Freidan Kojak."

Cute gulped. "You mean . . ."

"Exactly. The Admiral's daughter."

Cute turned to Macaw and gave him a withering look. "Moans, I'm ashamed of you! Of course a woman has an equal opportunity on this ship! I can only assume that you were having your fun with Mr. Skunk as usual. I'd hate to think my ship's physician was a male shopping list."

"Male *chauvinist*, captain," offered Skunk tiredly.

"Of course, chauvinist," amended Cute smoothly. He turned and led his first officer from the room. "Come on, Skunk. Let's go give our new security chief the good news."

As they left the room, Macaw gave a deep sigh and went back to repairing his boot. It was always so pleasant after Cute left, the doctor reflected . . . and so quiet, too. Now if only Scotchy would stop snoring . . .

Lieutenant Gloria Kojak was working out in the ship's gymnasium when the call came for her to report to briefing room A. Tossing the barbell she was hefting to a fellow crewman, she did three backflips out of the gym, relishing the man's scream as the weight carried him through the floor and subsequently decks 17, 16, and 15.

Lieutenant Kojak wondered why superman Cute wanted her in the briefing room. "Probably just now tomcatted his way down to the K's," she said to no one in particular as she pulled on her stockings and uniform skirt. Finishing dressing, she tossed her workout togs at the cleaning chute. The bundle missed the chute, but continued on through the wall, severing the artificial gravity controls for the gymnasium. "Missed again," cursed Kojak as she floated up to a bulkhead and propelled herself from the room.

Cute was vainly trying to find out what other items Skunk had found out during the mind melt when Lieutenant Kojak reported to the briefing room. As she came to a halt and introduced herself, Cute's mouth popped open in surprise, and a low moan escaped from his lips.

"I beg your pardon, sir?" asked Kojak.

Cute continued to stare at her without replying. Skunk answered for him. "The captain said nothing, lieutenant. That is his usual reaction to a beautiful woman."

It was true, Cute thought to himself as he sat entranced. The daughter of Admiral Kojak was a tiny, sublime creature who looked as if she would be more at home in a harem than aboard a starship. Perhaps, reflected Cute, this wouldn't be such a bad deal after all. A security chief has to work very closely with the captain. *Very* closely. The idea appealed to Cute immensely. He cleared his throat several times, and finally managed to speak.

"Lieutenant, we have some good news for you. Due to the unfortunate accident that befell Lieutenant Mooney yesterday..."

Skunk interrupted. "Yesterday was Commander Houston, sir. Lieutenant Mooney fell into the anti-matter chamber day before yesterday."

Cute smiled and shrugged. "Who can keep up? Anyway, lieutenant, because of the ... er, untimely ... er, vacancy—"

Gloria Kojak stoped him with a snort. "Do you mean you want me to be security chief? No thank you, captain. I'm too young to die. Security chiefs don't last a week on this ship."

Cute bridled. "Lieutenant, you forget yourself! You are at attention!" Kojak and Skunk exchanged puzzled glances, and Cute removed the bridle from his mouth. "I said you are at attention, lieutenant. It is not your place to question my orders, but for your information, many of our security chiefs have lasted much longer than a week. There was ... what was his name, Skunk?"

"Bonario. It was fourteen point six days before he was killed. But we spent thirteen days of that time in drydock around Starplate Seven."

"But it proves my point, nevertheless," said Cute triumphantly.

"Regardless of that, captain," sneered Kojak, "I thought only men were appointed security chief. This just looks like another way to get rid of me without having to make excuses to my father. In fact," she said bitterly, punching a hole in the bulkhead, "it is brilliant. How proud of me he would be if I died in battle. A glorious death for his problem child!"

"The fact that your father is an admiral in Starbeat has nothing to do with our decision to make you security chief—either way. You were chosen strictly on your qualifications. Mr. Skunk—and, ahem, myself, of course, feel that you will do an excellent job.

"In fact," he continued, "I will tell you frankly that some officers felt that your sex disqualified you from the position. As you will be working closely with these officers, I will mention no names."

At this he gave Kojak a surreptitious wink, and nodded his head in the direction of Skunk. Let this mankiller take her frustrations out on Skunk, Cute exulted to himself; that'll show him to go gadding about in my head.

Kojak considered the offer. It sounded genuine enough, although she didn't completely trust the captain. She knew his reputation with women, and that sooner or later he would be convinced that the Cute charm would unfreeze the icy demeanor she presented to him. But Gloria knew she could take care of that situation when it arose, and all in all, security chief was better than having her thirty-third transfer in eight months.

"All right, captain. I accept. But I have to warn you—"

Her warning to Cute was never completed, for at that moment the red alert klaxon sounded throughout the ship. Cute leaped to the intercom and ferociously thumbed the call button.

"Bridge!" he shouted. "What's going on?"

"Lieutenant Zulu, captain. Our shields just came on and sensors report a Rumbleon battle cruiser heading in our direction."

"Coming right up," snapped Cute. He turned to Skunk and Kojak. "Looks like you get quick duty, lieutenant. Let's go!"

As they arrived on the bridge, Skunk moved quickly to his station and gazed into his viewer. "Captain, it is indeed a Rumbleon ship. In fact, the latest model. Chopped and channeled, moon hubcaps, fender skirts, and a foxtail hanging from the antenna. They are obviously looking for a fight."

"They'll get one," promised Cute. "Sound battle stations, Mr. Zulu."

Lieutenant Zulu smiled the wicked grin he reserved for such occasions, and as he pressed the battle stations alarm with one hand, the other slipped down to his belt to check that the samurai sword slipped easily from its scabbard.

Ensign Checkup, on the other hand, was not quite as bloodthirsty. As battle stations sounded, he quietly leaned over and lost his lunch. It wasn't the physical danger that bothered him, but the fact that he tended to lose his accent in times of stress.

The new security chief was too busy to worry about the coming danger. She was attempting to perform her job at the same time she learned it, and as the entire security section had been killed over the last four months, she had no one to show her what to do. Things were complicated by the ensign on her right at Engineering who was trying to get her intercom number, and the yeoman on her left who was trying to ask her out for dinner after the battle.

"The Rumbleon ship is in visual range now, captain," stated Skunk.

"Very good. Lieutenant Yuhura, screens on."

The main viewing screen lit up and swiftly coalesced into a jumbled pattern of static. Skunk walked purposefully over to it and gave it a swift kick, and the Rumbleon ship appeared.

Everyone on the bridge gasped in surprise and shock. The Rumbleon ship was indeed frightening. It was several times larger than the *Ennui*, and obviously faster, better-weaponed, and with superior shielding. But what really scared the *Ennui* crew was the exterior of the ship itself. Painted a wicked candy-apple red, with scalloped flames along the sides, the eye was drawn irresistibly to the motto stenciled on the nose: "Born to Loot."

"All right," spoke Cute sharply into the silence. "So she's a hot mill. But the people inside are only Rumbleons, just like us—or at least just like Skunk—and I say we can shut them down."

Cute's words had a slightly cheering effect, but it was soon swept away as Yuhura announced a signal from the Rumbleon ship. The fearsome ship dissolved only to be replaced by the visage of a Rumbleon female. Again, a gasp went up on the bridge, and Checkup blurted, "Mr. Skunk, it's your girlfriend!"

"I thought we were rid of her," groused Cute. "Just what I needed today. A grudge fight." He raised his voice. "Greetings, commander. I am pleased to see you suffered no ill effects upon your return to your fleet."

The commander gave him a cold smile. "No thanks to you, Cute. Luckily I found that 'full confession' tape you planted on me before I arrived at our base."

"Just a little farewell gift," said Cute airily, ignoring a dirty look from Skunk.

"It was very thoughtful of you, captain. And as you can see, I intend to return the favor."

Cute smiled winningly. "Not necessary, commander. Glad to do it. Well, it was nice talking to you, but we really have to run. One of those diplomatic receptions at Starplate Eight. Boring, but necessary." Out of the side of his mouth, Cute whispered to Zulu, "Get ready to get us the heck out of here—this dame is trouble."

As Cute began to motion to the helmsman to warp them away, a squad of Rumbleon warriors suddenly materialized on the bridge. In one quick movement, they captured the helm and Navigation (rather easily, as Zulu had tripped over his sword and Checkup was once again retching), and had Engineering, Life Sciences, Communications, and the snack bar under phaser cover.

Cute leapt at the nearest Rumbleon warrior, who took a roundhouse swing at him. Neatly blocking the punch with the point of his chin, Cute managed to take the Rumbleon out of action as he collapsed on him.

Seeing two enormous Rumbleons advancing on him with leveled phasers, Skunk quickly used the Fulcan nerve pinch and knocked himself unconscious.

The only person left on the bridge in any position to fight was Lieutenant Kojak. She had already dismembered two Rumbleons and was in the process of tearing the ears off of another when the Rumbleon transporter once again came on and beamed them all onto the Rumbleon ship.

The Rumbleons materialized first, and after they stepped off the platform, the *Ennui* bridge crew was reformed. The Rumbleon transporter crew was having some fun, switching around heads, turning people inside out, and other pleasantries, when the commander arrived.

"Cut out the *lyfandqwpstoop*," she barked, and the crew was immediately materialized in their proper shapes, whereupon they were stunned into unconsciousness.

It was much later when Cute awoke to find himself and the others in a security cell on the Rumbleon ship. He had a terrific headache (not to mention a sore jaw) and it was not until he was looking around for someone to blame it all on that he noticed that Skunk was not in the cell with them.

He crawled over to Kojak, and as he shook her awake, she suddenly swung a vicious punch at his midsection. It was only through many years of prodigious practice and rigorous training that Cute was able to soften the blow by parrying it with his stomach.

Kojack came fully awake and leapt to his side. "I'm sorry, captain. The last thing I remember was fighting Rumbleons, and then all of a sudden there you were reaching for my . . ."

"It . . . it's all right," wheezed Cute. "You're just lucky it's . . . late in the season."

As she helped him to his feet, others of the crew began to awaken. Starbeat training took effect immediately, however, and aside from a bit of wailing and screaming, and Zulu calling Cute a few names, they remained calm and professional.

"Captain," said Yuhura, "I . . . I'm frightened." The dramatic effect of this statement was lessened by its being simultaneously said by the entire crew, who had all heard it many times before. Yuhura gave them a scathing look. "Well, what do you expect me to say? 'Feets don't fail me now'?"

"Take it easy," Cute ordered. "They didn't get Scotchy, and you can bet he's working on a way to get us out. All we have to do is play it cool."

Meanwhile, Skunk was in the quarters of the Rumbleon commander. She had changed from her uniform to a filmy negligee, and she had offered Skunk drinks and food.

"I fail to realize why I am not being incarcerated with the captain and the others. Surely I have earned your animosity to a greater degree than Captain Cute, yet he is in a detention cell and I am treated almost royally."

The commander smiled at him. "No, Skunk, you do not deserve a cell. Even though you have, shall we say, wronged me in the past, I can be quite forgiving."

Skunk stirred uneasily. "Commander . . ." he began.

"You know my private name, Skunk. Please use it." It was not a request, Skunk knew, as she leveled a phaser at him as she said it.

With a visible effort, Skunk said, "Trampolina."

"That's better."

"Trampolina, I must point out that my loyalties and aims have not changed since our last encounter. If you hope to ply me with kindness, I am obliged to point out that you are foredoomed to failure."

"No, Mr. Skunk," answered the commander. "I know you cannot be bought . . . by anything I have to offer. I just thought we'd make a little whoopee before I have you and your captain killed."

Skunk considered. He shrugged, picked up his drink, and offered her a toast. "Sounds logical to me."

Back in the detention cell, Cute was considering a method of escape. ". . . and I get a bar of soap, and carve it to look like a phaser. Then Zulu pretends to be sick and calls the guard over—"

"Let Checkup do it," sneered Zulu. "He won't have to pretend very hard."

"Jim, I can't allow it," spoke up Macaw. "This heah boy's too sick to pretend he's sick."

Cute swung around in astonishment. "Moans! How did you get in here?"

"Ah came onto the bridge just before the Rumbleons beamed aboard. The writer is supposed to go back an' put in a line or two tellin' about it, and the great fight I put up against those fellows, but he'll probably forget."

"Well, I'm glad you're here. We might need you."

Macaw grimaced. "Ah hope not. Ah cain't stand the sight of blood."

Yuhura pulled at Cute's sleeve. "Captain, about your escape plan . . ."

"Oh, yeah. As I was saying, Zulu will smuggle clothes out from the laundry, and when we have the tunnel finished, we'll use the clothes to make dummies that will fool the screws and give us a five- or six-hour head start."

Kojak gaped at him in astonishment. "You want to *tunnel* out of a *starship*?"

Cute gave her a cold stare. "I suppose you have a better idea?"

"How about this?" Kojak swiftly turned and punched a neat

hole in the bulkhead. She then reached out and switched off the force-field door.

As the prisoners crept out, Checkup whispered, "Where are the guards?"

Cute snickered, "They're all down at the end of the hall there watching that monitor. Come on, we'll take them by surprise."

They moved swiftly but silently along the corridor to striking range of the Rumbleons. When they were close enough, Cute shouted, "Now!" and immediately stumbled, tripping all of his companions. As they fell into a heap at the Rumbleons' feet, one of the guards was overcome by laughter and accidentally fired his weapon into the corridor wall. The beam struck a power lead and a bolt of electricity leapt across the hall and onto the metal armor the Rumbleons wore. All were electrocuted, leaving the *Ennui* crew to sort themselves out.

Cute staggered to his feet. "What happened?"

Kojak pointed at the shattered bulkhead. "His phaser went off, and the power fried them all."

"Oh," said Cute. "I see. Just as I planned it, of course. I hope no one was hurt in that fall, I couldn't warn you about it, of course, without revealing my plans to the Rumbleons."

Macaw massaged a shoulder. "Jimbo, do me a favor. Include me out o' any more plannin' you do, okay?" A chorus of assents from the rest of the crew followed this pronouncement.

Cute decided it was a good time to change the subject. "Let's see what they were so interested in." They all stared at the monitor screen which showed the interior of the commander's quarters.

"Well," said Cute after a few moments. "At least we know where Skunk is."

"Captain, I suggest we leave the vicinity. I haven't heard any alarms, but some kind of repair crew is sure to come along to fix that power lead."

"Good idea, security chief. I was just about to suggest that myself. Zulu, see if any of those communicators on those guards is still working. If so, we can call Scotchy and get out of here."

Zulu quickly looked over the guards' equipment and handed one of the communicators to Cute.

Cute flipped it open and adjusted the frequency. "*Ennui*, come in *Ennui*. Captain Cute calling. Come in *Ennui*."

The communicator crackled into life and Cute smiled at his companions. "Sub-Commander Troll here. Report."

"Oops," giggled Cute. "Wrong channel." He adjusted it again, and this time the welcome burr of Scotchy answered his call.

"Aye, 'tis a bonnie thing ye got through, captain. It took us a while to get the auxiliary bridge in operation, seein' as how we haven't used it since the first season."

"Good job, Scotchy. Beam us aboard."

In a matter of moments, they were aboard the *Ennui* once more, and Lieutenant Kite made his one and only appearance in this story by giving them a hearty welcome. Cute lost no time getting to the bridge, pausing only to take a shower, brush his teeth, have a drink, and get the intercom number of a cute new yeoman.

"Status report," he demanded of Scotch as he stumbled out of the turbolift.

"'Tis still a standoff, captain. One o' the other of us will gun his engine now and then, and we've been sending dirty limericks about Rumbleons out on hailin' frequencies, but nothin' serious."

Cute was satisfied with the actions of his engineering officer. A good man, thought Cute, and the limericks were a nice touch. Cute's usual pre-battle strategy was to insult his opponent's ancestors while Skunk supplied graphic illustration with his vast knowledge of ancient Fulcan obscene gestures.

That reminded Cute that his first officer was still aboard the Rumbleon ship.

"Scotchy, can we get Skunk off with the transporter?"

Scotchy considered, "Well, we did it once before, but ye'll remember Mr. Skunk had a communicator that time, and even then it was hard enough to sort him out from all those Rumbleons. It'd be a bonnie hard thing to do."

Cute gave Scotch a confident smile. "I'm sure if you turn your mind to it you can figure out a way." He let the smile fade. "You have ten minutes. I want to get back to Fedderbedding territory before dark."

"Captain," Scotch cried, "it canna be done in tha' short a time. Why I'd have to . . ." At this point Cute lost him, as Scotch had a tendency to speak in perfect, correct Latin without a trace of his normal Scots accent when discussing technical matters.

"Never mind, Mr. Scotch. You have nine minutes left."

Scotchy sighed in rueful assent, and with a last *"sic semper tyrannus,"* he left for the transporter room to get to work.

With a few moments' grace, Cute was left to consider the position his ship was in. They were caught in open space by a Rumbleon ship that was far superior to theirs in every way, his first officer was captive, and he had not once yet had an opportunity to take off his shirt. Not a very pretty picture. But he and his crew had pulled out of tougher scrapes, and they would this time. But how? How?

In the quarters of the Romulan commander, Mr. Skunk was at long last making his move.

"Knight to queen's level three."

As he moved the chess piece and captured her rook, Trampolina realized that this strange Fulcan had captured her heart as well. With a langurous movement of her hand, she tipped over her king in defeat.

"Never before have I met such a splendid mind! After our last encounter, I could not forget . . ." She let her words trail off, and began again in a softer, sexier tone. "You have bested me again. One more victory, and you will possess me as your chattel and lifelong slave, under the ancient Rumbleon rite of *bestthree outofour*. Or should I merely forfeit now, and save our time for better things?"

Before Skunk could answer, the door to the commander's quarters swept open and Sub-Commander Troll swept in accompanied by two guards armed with phasers.

The commander leapt up livid with fury. "Troll, I've told you a thousand times not to break in on my seductions! Explain yourself!"

"Commander," gulped Troll, "the prisoners have escaped, and our new overhead cam device is missing from the engine room."

The commander whirled on Skunk. "So, treachery once again. This time nothing will save you from my vengeance. I'll get you, Skunk . . . you, and your captain, and your ship, and your little dog, too!"

As Skunk stared at her in blank confusion, she motioned to the guards to hold him captive, and ran out of the room with Troll following after.

On the bridge of the *Ennui*, Cute was still in a quandary as to how to get his ship and crew home safely. He decided to ask his new security officer her opinion. He rose from his chair and walked over to her station.

"Lieutenant, my compliments on the way you handled your duties as security chief when we were aboard the Rumbleon ship."

"Thank you, captain." Gloria Kojak was suddenly flustered in the captain's presence. Perhaps it had something to do with the fact that they were totally alone, everyone else on the bridge having just stepped out to have coffee.

"Then we can be friends?" Cute asked with a charming smile.

"Did I miss something?" asked Kojak in return. "You compliment me, I thank you, and then all of a sudden you act like we are on the verge of young love."

Cute shrugged. "I suppose the writer figured that the readers have seen me in action so many times, he could skip all of the preliminaries and get right down to business."

"Yes," answered Kojak, rather breathlessly. "I'm beginning to realize that now, captain. We *can* be friends . . . perhaps more."

After they had kissed and exchanged vows of eternal faithfulness, and Cute had given her a brief history of his life (including the previous seventy-nine missions of the *Ennui*) and begun planning a family, Gloria suddenly pulled away from Cute's arms.

"How can you love me?" she wailed. "I can never be a complete woman."

Cute made a move to comfort her. "No, please don't touch me. You don't know the truth. And you will never know! I'll . . . I'll kill myself!"

With a last wild cry she turned and ran from the bridge. A sharp pain knifed through Cute's heart as he realized that he now had another problem on top of all his others: Where in the world was he going to find another security chief?

Skunk was seated at the desk of the Rumbleon commander in deep meditation, characterized by the typical Fulcan habit of loud snoring. The commander stormed back in, kicked Skunk's feet off her desk, and stood fuming over him as he picked himself up from the floor.

"Your accomplice has somehow managed to elude us this far, but I assure you he cannot escape with our cam device. You may as well confess your complicity in this espionage."

"I admit nothing," answered Skunk stonily, allowing a few pebbles to dribble to the floor as he continued. "We of the *Ennui* had no knowledge of your camshaft device, and even if we did, we wouldn't care, as Fedderbedding ships have Mazda engines that go hmmmm."

"Liar!" shouted the commander, whipping her whip across his face. "Little matter, however, as you will die this very moment. Guards!"

Skunk folded his hands behind his back. "I must remind you, commander, that under the sentence of death, I am allowed the Rumbleon Right of Statement."

"Oh, no," scoffed the commander. "You won't trick me with that one again. No Right of Statement."

Skunk stood his ground. "The Right is my right under your own laws and traditions."

"Spies have no rights to the Right. Isn't that right, Troll?"

Troll nodded assent. "Check."

Skunk gave him a look. "Copycat. At least, commander, if I am not to be allowed the Right of Statement, may I make a statement about not making a Right of Statement?"

"No statements about the Statement."

Skunk raised his eyebrow. "Surely you will not disallow me to state my belief that I have a right to make a statement about being denied my right to make a Right of Statement?"

"No!"

"Then may I state that—"

"Shut up!"

Skunk gave her a cold look. "Commander, I fail to understand why we cannot discuss this in a logical manner. Shouting is not necessary. I am merely endeavoring to point out—" A phaser was shoved into his left ear. "Then again—"

"Enough talk. Troll, take this creature down to the execution chamber."

As Troll took Skunk's arm, a high-pitched whining filled the room. The commander wailed, "Not again!" as Skunk (and Troll's left arm) swiftly dematerialized.

"Troll," said the commander in a soft voice, "get that patched up and then meet me on the bridge. We are going to destroy the *Ennui*." Troll gave her a lopsided salute and staggered from the room.

The commander stared for a long moment at the spot where Skunk had so recently stood. "Skunk," she whispered, "you never take me anywhere."

Cute leapt up in surprise and led the entire bridge crew in a cheer as Skunk stepped from the turbolift, followed by Scotch and Macaw.

"Skunk, how did you escape from the Rumbleon ship?"

"You may thank Mr. Scotch for my timely departure, captain."

Cute gave Scotchy a warm nod. "I knew you could do it, Mr. Scotch. But how?"

Scotch laughed. "It was a pretty problem indeed, until Dr. Macaw here reminded me of the one major physical difference between Fulcans and Rumbleons."

"Ah," said Skunk, understanding.

"Well, let me in on it," said Cute.

"It was simple, Jim." Macaw was enjoying the attention, even this late in the story. "Fulcan ears point back, Rumbleon ears point front."

Scotch continued for him. "Then it was but a wee matter o' programmin' in a Rumbleon configuration, and reversin' the ear phasing materialization sequence. One pull o' the levers and Mr. Skunk is back safe and sound."

"Well, it is all too technical for me," laughed Cute, "but congratulations, Mr. Scotch, and welcome back, Mr. Skunk."

"Thank you, captain. However, I do have some information to report. The Rumbleon commander seems to think that we stole their new camshaft device."

"Device? Camshaft device?" echoed Cute, stalling for time. Was there to be no end to his problems, no relief in sight?

"Skunk, if the Rumbleons are that concerned about this camshaft, then it must be pretty important to the operation of that ship, right?"

It cost Skunk a great deal, but he answered smoothly. "Check."

"And if it is that vital, gentlemen, then I intend to have it!" Cute glared at his officers as if challenging them to refute his statement. He was not disappointed.

"What?" "Are you crazy?" "Let's get out of here while the getting's good!" "Ach, me poor bairns!" "I vote we make peace." "Great Ceasar's ghost!"

Cute stood with his hands on hips staring at them. Then he gave an elaborate shrug, and grinned. "Gosh, it was just an idea."

He sat back down in his command chair. "Okay, let's get back to our own turf. Mr. Zulu, warp seven."

Zulu aimed a quick smile at Checkup and moved to engage the great starship's engines. But just as he was about to let in the clutch, a flashing light on his board caught his attention.

"Captain," he called, "someone is in the transporter room and has turned on the equipment!"

"Criminalinities!" Cute turned to Scotch. "Where is Lieutenant Kite? That's his station."

"Sorry, captain, but Kite has already made his appearance in this story. If I'da known this was gonna happen, I'da had him wait."

"Never mind," snapped Cute. "Yuhura, open a frequency to the transporter room. See who that is."

Macaw caught Cute's arm. "Jim, aren't you going to send some security men to the transporter room? That could be a Rumbleon!"

Cute looked at him in exasperation. "Doctor, how many security men have died aboard this ship in the last four months?"

"Eighty-three, but what's that—"

"And how many security men does the *Ennui* carry?"

"Eighty . . . three. Hmmm. I see your point."

Cute gave him a curt nod. "Exactly. We have no more security men . . . unless, of course, you would care to transfer to security, Moans?"

Macaw blanched. "Ah seem to have some things to do in mah office," he said hurriedly and ran into the turbolift. Cute was making clucking noises after him when Skunk halted him.

"Captain, you forget that the *Ennui* currently has a complement of eighty-*four* security officers. Ms. Kojak, to be explicit."

"That's right!" Cute exploded. "Where is she?"

His somewhat belated question was answered when Yuhura finally managed to reroute connections through Omaha and reach the transporter room. "Captain, it is Lieutenant Kojak using the transporter!"

Cute slammed his fist onto his intercom. It collapsed with a dull thud, and he had to nonchalantly move to Yuhura's station to talk to Gloria. But before he could say a word, her voice came over the intercom. "Please, Jim, save time and don't try to talk to me. It won't do any good. I heard all about the Rumbleon cam thing, and I'm going over there to try to get it. At least I can die a complete woman."

As she broke off communication, Cute turned his anguished face to Lieutenant Zulu. "Stop her. Use the manual override."

"I'm sorry, captain, but she's overridden the manual override."

Skunk reported, "Forty seconds until transporter operational."

Suddenly Lieutenant Yuhura called out, "Captain, a signal from the Rumbleon ship."

Cute slapped his hand to his head. "Now what do *they* want?"

An image of the Rumbleon commander appeared on the main viewing screen. "Captain Cute," she said in an embarrassed voice, "it seems that your people didn't steal our overhead cam after all. We have just learned that our cook has been using it to make donut holes."

Cute spun around. "Yuhura, pipe that into the transporter room!" Turning to the Rumbleon, he asked that she repeat her statement. After she did so, she asked, "May I speak to Mr. Skunk, please, captain?"

Skunk stepped forward into viewing range.

"Skunk, my apologies for accusing you of stealing our device. I am sorry."

Skunk answered, "It would be illogical for me to not accept your apology. Therefore, I accept."

The commander smiled. "Logical to the end. Very well, Skunk, captain, until next time."

The image faded. Cute said, "Skunk, you have the con," and made his way quickly down to the transporter room. There he found Gloria Kojak sitting on the edge of the transporter platform, loudly weeping.

Cute took her in his arms.

"It's all right now, darling. The Rumbleons are leaving. But why did you consider doing such a foolish thing?"

She turned her tearful face to his. "I told you that I couldn't let you know the truth about me."

Cute gave her a gentle sock on the jaw. "Silly, I don't care what it is, I love you, and that is all that really matters. Please, tell me about it."

With a tremendous effort, Gloria began through occasional sobs, hiccups, and nose blowings.

"You know that my father is Admiral Kojak, but what you don't know is that I am an only child. And when he learned that he would never have a son, he decided that I would be his son. He raised me like a boy. I never got to wear lipstick, or go to the prom, or have slumber parties. I spent all my time watching football games, telling dirty stories, and walking around in an old dirty undershirt. Daddy's little 'Skipper,' next in line for the Academy."

Cute kissed her hand in sympathy.

"But that's not the most terrible thing. I *liked* it! I thought it was wonderful, especially when I could beat up any of the other—I mean, any of the boys on the block."

"That's right," Cute recalled, "that enormous strength of yours. How did you get it?"

"Oh, I ate nothing but spinach until I was eighteen. Daddy says all sailors eat it. Anyway, I liked being a 'man' so much, it almost drove me crazy when I found out that women were discriminated against in Starbeat. So I became a feminist nutso troublemaker . . ." She trailed off. "Now you know the whole story, and you probably hate me."

Cute chuckled. "Darling, I've heard the same story a thousand times."

She looked up at him in surprise.

"It's true. You are not so different from most any other admiral's daughter. They all seem to have the same problem. Why, if famous men and high-ranking officers could have sons, half of my adventures would never happen."

"Then, you don't hate me?" Gloria asked, hope welling in her eyes. "You don't think I'm a freak, only half a woman?"

Cute took her in his arms once again. "You are more woman than any I have ever known, Gloria Friedan."

Breathless from his long, deep kiss, she finally managed to blurt out her last secret.

"Jim, my name isn't really Gloria Friedan Kojak. I changed it when I became a feminist."

"Oh, really?" Cute said. "What is your real name?"

She blushed. "It's Mary Sue."

Cute smiled. "I had a feeling that was it." And he kissed her once again as the *Ennui* flew on through ever-dark, ever-mysterious, and ever-changing space.

3.

THE STAR TREK MOVIE NOVEL AND COMICS ADAPTATIONS

by Van James

The breathless expectation of the Star Trek movie was matched only by the desire of fans to read Gene Roddenberry's first Star Trek novel, which was based on the movie screenplay. The large segment of Star Trek fans who are also comics fans also looked forward eagerly to Marvel Comics' illustrated version of the film. Van James is one of those fans, and in this article he tells why one adaptation of the movie worked, while the other failed.

Like any sane and rational person, I waited until I had seen the movie to read both Gene Roddenberry's novelization of *Star Trek: The Motion Picture* and Marvel Comic's illustrated adaptation of same.

The novel succeeds admirably and the comic fails miserably. You may very well ask why this is so, as both are based on the same story. But the reason, as we shall see, rests with the individuals involved with each of the adaptations.

In short, Gene Roddenberry knew what he was doing, and the people at Marvel Comics did not.

But first the novel. The style of writing in this book is so good one almost feels he is reading a fanzine. This is because the tale is so well crafted and written with so much love and respect for the characters; it matches the very best of fan fiction and makes the widely despised Bantam Star Trek novels pale by comparison.

But then who should have more love and knowledge of the Star Trek characters than the man who created them?

As one would expect, the major focus of the book is on Captain James T. Kirk. And this is as it should be. Fans have always suspected that there is much of one G. Roddenberry in our captain, and now those suspicions are confirmed. When Kirk speaks, you can almost envision Gene sitting over his typewriter, smiling and nodding in agreement.

The novel is notably different in one aspect from the movie, and that is humor. Very little of the typical "Star Trek humor" made it into the film, probably because of the need to advance the plot and because of the V'Ger situation. (It is hardly a laughing matter to be facing the destruction of an entire planet.) But in the novel, much of the humor is in Kirk's thoughts, and quite a bit more in the footnotes and asides which Kirk (as the ostensible "editor" of the book) offers throughout the story.

For instance, in his preface to the novel, Kirk laughingly states that his academy class was selected for their "somewhat more limited intellectual agility." And he later dismisses the rumors of a love affair with Spock by proclaiming that he would not be so stupid as to chose as a lover a person that came into sexual heat only every seven years.

Other examples of the use of humor in the book are the reactions of Chekov and Sulu to the arrival of Ilia, and the long and careful self-inspection that McCoy gives himself after being transported aboard the *Enterprise*.

But it is the background information about Kirk that Roddenberry gives us in the novel that is the most interesting and exciting thing we are offered in this prose version. We know the reasons why Kirk became dissatisfied with his admiralcy, and why he feels (with good reason) that Star Fleet has been using him. This look at the events in Kirk's life during the time between the ending of the series and the beginning of the movie makes his determination to retake command of the *Enterprise* much more believable and sympathetic. We also see—through Kirk's inner thoughts and fears—the pain he feels when he makes mistakes due to his unfamiliarity with the ship.

This same sort of detailed background also makes the scenes with Spock on Vulcan quite a bit more understandable. His abiding interest in the strange force he feels is clear to us in the novel. In the film, it never is.

We also know (by looking into Spock's thoughts) that it is very difficult for him to let go of the feelings he has for Kirk and the rest of his friends from the *Enterprise* crew; and we can understand the pain and need inside him that drove him to seek *Kolinahr* as a way to completeness as a being. And, unlike the movie, in which his aloofness can easily be mistaken for coldness, in the novel we see that Spock is feeling exactly the opposite—an overabundance of the emotions he believed he had mastered and discarded.

This kind of omniscient "information" makes the novel much more interesting from the characters' point of view. For instance, we can see in the thoughts of the male crewmembers the effect that Ilia has on them, and thus we can appreciate far more the hold she has on Decker's feelings. In the movie, Decker seems less of a man because of his love for Ilia—but in the novel he seems stronger because we can see the depth of that love, plus the attraction of her Deltan pheromones. Then we realize how hard it must have been for Decker to leave her years ago, and how he must master his emotions upon seeing her again.

This reviewer has never been overly impressed with Gene Roddenberry's writing skills, but in this book, he proves that he can do excellent work in prose.

The writing is generally crisp and clean. Vivid descriptions make for easy visualization of Roddenberry's scenes. This is obviously a talent Gene acquired in his years of scriptwriting, where no more than the necessary facts are required or wanted, but in the novel, we get it as a bonus. Too much of the Star Trek fiction (both the Bantam novels and the fanzines) is cluttered with unclear or highflown imagery. It is good to see straightforward storytelling for a change.

As one would expect, the dialogue in the novel is first-rate, easily surpassing that in the film. Even in the worst of the televised Star Trek episodes written by Roddenberry ("The Omega Glory," "Turnabout Intruder"), the dialogue was always believable and enjoyable. Now in prose, with the luxury of having description to complement dialogue, Roddenberry's characters speak both naturally and eloquently. The scene in Kirk's quarters when he questions Spock, and McCoy offers comments, is a brilliant example of this mixture.

It is a shame that Roddenberry has not chosen to pen a Star Trek novel every year or so. Not only would they be far superior to those we have had, but his skills would most likely have improved with each effort, and by this time the novels would really be worth looking forward to.

What the special-effects visuals attempted in the film was to impress the viewer with the startling immenseness of V'Ger. In many aspects, the film failed; but in the novel, Roddenberry gives a much stronger feeling of V'Ger's size by allowing us to look into the thoughts of the crew. We see their amazement, their fears, and their desire to succeed against the odds. The confrontation is much more suspenseful than in the film, thanks to such comments as "If a god should ever build a ship, it would be like this one" and "Had they annoyed it into angrily crushing them against its side?" Both quotes are from Kirk's thoughts, and we have other instances of similar thoughts and comments from him and other crew members. It builds a terrifying picture of V'Ger that special effects could never match.

The climax of the film is also much more exciting, enjoyable, and *understandable* in the novel. We are told in the novel rather early on that Decker had been raised by his mother, and due to her influence, he felt a kinship for the New Human movement, and shared that group's desire for unity of thought. So it makes much more sense from a character standpoint when Decker tells Kirk, "This is what *I* want," and offers himself as a sacrifice to achieve unity with V'Ger and Ilia.

This device also allows Roddenberry to restate one of his major themes of Star Trek: that as human life-styles become more complex and machine-assisted, man will become more individualistic in order to keep his humanity. That theme was largely forgotten as the series progressed, and has been almost completely ignored by fandom.

This theme is restated once again in the tag to the novel (which is not included in the movie).

In the film, after V'Ger is defeated, Kirk orders the *Enterprise* out for a "shakedown cruise," and the movie ends on that happy note of the crew reunited and all well with Earth and the Federation.

But the novel includes a few lines omitted from the movie, and from them we get a completely different feeling. Kirk ignores orders from Starfleet to report in for debriefing and orders the ship into space. This gives us a subtle feeling that Kirk may have had enough of the Federation and its restraints upon him, and we have a nagging thought that he just may never come back. It is an interesting thought, and a perfect capper for a story in which Kirk has found himself frustrated in almost every endeavor.

Roddenberry's inexperience with the novel form of writing does show up in several instances, however. The scenes featuring V'Ger's consciousness don't quite ring true, and only serve to destroy much of the mystery and suspense. Roddenberry also uses far too many italicized phrases, causing them to lose any value as important thoughts or exclamations over the course of the novel. The chapters are often too short, making the flow of the novel choppy in places. Twenty-eight chapters is too many for a book of only 252 pages in fairly large typeface.

But overall, the novel is a wonderful complement to the movie. The movie gives us the people, the scenes of the ship, and the special effects; while the novel gives us the background we need to fully understand and appreciate the story. Seeing the movie again after reading the novel is especially fun, and highly recommended.

It is also a pleasure to finally read a movie novelization that not only expands on and complements the film, but is well written to boot. So many movie novelizations have practically nothing to do with the film, or are just poorly written. (*Star Wars* was guilty of both of these.) We can be thankful that Gene decided to write the novel himself, and that he waited to write it until *after* the movie was at least in its final stages.

Speaking of which, one of the major faults of Marvel Comics' adaptation of *Star Trek: The Motion Picture* is that the writers and artists were forced to work from out-of-date and sketchy materials provided them by Paramount. That is why several scenes look and end differently than in the movie itself, and it may have also caused the several horrendous errors that showed up in the comic.

The most glaring error in the comics' adaptation is the inclusion of the captain in the spacewalk scene with Mr. Spock. This is especially bad as it includes a short sequence in which Kirk is covered by crystalline chunks, and Spock hesitates before going to the captain's rescue. Kirk then rewards this loyalty by chewing him out for leaving the ship. Very poorly written.

But the most glaring defect of the comic is the artwork. Penciled by Dave Cockrum and inked by Klaus Janson in a very pedestrian and sloppy fashion, the story is often so muddled that the reader cannot tell what is happening in individual panels. The art on the main characters is very bland, and supporting characters are indistinguishable from each other. In fact, some characters look different in every panel in which they appear!

The writing of the comic is also poorly done. Whenever dialogue from the film is expanded upon, it is usually done in clichés. And as slow as the pacing of the film was in places, it seems to whiz along compared with the comic. Much page space is wasted in large panels featuring the ship skimming through empty space, or extreme closeups of characters.

There is little point in discussing any more of the magazine's faults. This adaptation is simply a poor job. And after we fans had suffered through years of the awful Gold Key comics, we felt we deserved better from an established and powerful company such as Marvel. We didn't get it, and as the same creative team has been announced for the forthcoming regular Star Trek comic, it appears that we never will. If you haven't purchased this adaptation already, save your money.

And if you have bought it already, console yourself with the fact that Marvel screwed up and placed a $1.50 price tag on the book, instead of the $2 price that should have been there. That's fifty cents you didn't waste!

But now we get back to our original question: Why did the novelization of the movie work so well, but the comic fail? It all boils down to one thing: respect for the product.

Gene Roddenberry, whatever faults he may have, loves his creation and knows very well that millions of us out here love it too. Gene knew that we wanted more than the movie gave us, so he provided us with informative, interesting, and amusing background scenes and looks into the characters' thoughts.

The Marvel Comics' adaptation, however, followed the story of the movie too closely. This in itself would not necessarily have been bad if the artwork and writing had been well done. But with substandard production, the comic simply became a boring rehash of things we had already enjoyed in another medium.

So more comics featuring our heroes are on their way from Marvel—and chances are Gene Roddenberry will never write another novel. Too bad it's not the other way around.

4.

THE KLINGONS (?) IN *STAR TREK: THE MOTION PICTURE*

by Leslie Thompson

Having firmly established her credentials as the Number One Fan of the Klingons, Leslie Thompson is probably the most qualified to discuss the startling appearance of a "new" type of Klingon in the Star Trek movie. While she vents her frustration in a humorous way in this short article, Leslie also makes some telling points about the use and misuse of a stupendous budget in making the film.

Like many other Star Trek fans, I did my damnedest over the past six months or so not to discover any more of the plot elements of the Star Trek movie than I could possibly avoid. I wanted it all to be new and fresh to me, much as each new episode was back in the sixties. (Oh, do you remember those deliciously tantalizing plot synopses in each issue of *TV Guide*? And then having to wait ten or eleven days to even *see* the episode? Wow!) I couldn't help knowing that the original *Enterprise* crew was getting back together, that Earth was to be threatened by an "all-powerful" menace, and that a couple of new characters were to be introduced in the film—after all, I'm not a hermit. But any more than that . . . uh, uh. No way! I wanted to be surprised.

You readers can just imagine my delight when the very first scene of *Star Trek: The Motion Picture* featured not one, not two, but *three* beautifully detailed, superbly malevolent *Klingon battle cruisers*!

After cheering, whistling, and applauding (and gathering a

remarkable assortment of strange looks and pointed comments from the rest of the audience), I settled back in anticipation of my first good look at the bridge of a Klingon ship.

And in this I was not disappointed. The Klingons' bridge was suitably shabby. Rusty-looking machines of dubious function lined the greasy and slimy bulkheads, erotic mists crept up from God knows where, and all was surrounded by a sinister lack of lighting (most likely from the Klingon equivalent of the forty-watt bulb). As you would expect of the Klingons, the only equipment that seemed to be in first-class working order was the plush captain's chair and the various methods of destruction.

I was particularly impressed by the battle computer. Unlike the screen on the *Enterprise,* which constantly spewed out a stream of endless scientific information (much too detailed to be of any use in a time of crisis), the screen on the Klingon ship prominently featured targeting brackets, weapon ranges, and battle orders. Obviously, Klingon technology is designed to collect information *after* a battle, not before!

But all of this admiration is—I'm afraid—in retrospect, and mainly gathered from my second and third viewings of the film. For the first time around, I was too shocked to see anything but those . . . those . . . those whatever-the-heck-they-were *things* on a ship which should have been manned by my beloved Klingons!

My first impression was that the projectionist must have somehow gotten reels of film mixed up and put on part of *The Wizard of Oz,* because I would have sworn that I was seeing Munchkins on the screen. However, the sad truth soon dawned on me that these impostors were indeed supposed to be Klingons. So I clenched my teeth and said, "Okay. So let's see if you *act* like Klingons. Maybe Roddenberry got that much right."

And, not too surprisingly, they didn't. All three ships charged right into an unknown quantity, started firing, and were destroyed. No suspense, no lesson, no information for the viewer.

First, battle-loving though they may be, Klingons will *never* go charging in willy-nilly against an enemy they know nothing about. Klingons squirm about the edges, testing, evaluating, plotting—until they are able to destroy their foe, or can gain some new edge in weaponry or information by checking things out a little longer.

Add to this the fact that the commander of the three-ship wing would send in only *one* of his ships to do the investigating—and that one would certainly not be his own. Not when he has subordinates to do his dirty work for him.

And third, and most important, the Klingon ships logically would never have forced a confrontation with V'Ger. We can assume that their technology is nearly as advanced as the Federation's, so they should have been able to plot the course of V'Ger just as accurately as the Federation did. That course was directly to Earth.

True, that course may have taken V'Ger through part of the Klingon Empire, but unless V'Ger eliminated a few planets full of carbon-based units belonging to the Klingons along the way, typical Klingon style would have been to let V'Ger pass on through, and allow Earth and the Federation to discover any surprises the immense intruder had in store.

For the Klingon scenes in *Star Trek: The Motion Picture* to make any sense at all, we must assume that V'Ger inflicted some kind of serious damage on the Klingons. Otherwise, why would three ships be assigned to intercept and attempt to destroy it?

But that theory, while supplying the Klingons with a reason to confront V'Ger, has a serious flaw: If V'Ger *had* inflicted damage, then the Klingons would know of the incalculable power it commanded, and would have either tried something more subtle or else mounted an all-out attack with dozens of ships. Or even more in keeping with Klingon philosophy: Take the licking and smile, knowing more of the same would shortly be directed at the heart of the Federation.

Hmmmm . . . a mystery. But so is the radically changed appearance of the Klingons themselves.

Before I attempt to solve that one, I have a few comments to make on the "new" Klingons, and the (apparent) underlying reasons for the change.

Facetious comments about "Munchkins" aside, it is disturbing to see an entire race—an *established* race—so radically transformed. True, the spiny ridges on the skulls of the Klingons do give them much more of an "alien" look (and that, considering the few quick flashes of non-humans on the *Enterprise* and the *horrible* job done on Spock's ears—they ain't *elegant* any more, dang it!—was something sorely needed

KLINGONS (?) IN *STAR TREK: THE MOTION PICTURE* 41

in *STTMP*), but why not go all the way and give them tails and claws, and maybe an extra head while you're at it?

But it was obviously a money decision. A decision that was the exact opposite of those faced by the series. In those days, a lack of money was usually the problem. In the case of *Star Trek: The Motion Picture*, the problem was *too much* money.

When you have millions of dollars to spend, there is a great amount of pressure to spend it on something, lest it be taken away. And in the case of the Klingons, it was more expedient to make them completely over than to *not* spend the money and stay with the established image. It is now very easy for Roddenberry and staff to say, "Look at the care and effort we took on the movie. We could never do the Klingons right on television because we didn't have the time or money, but now we do. So this is the way the Klingons *really* look, and we were just fooling you before."

Change for the sake of change is not progress by any stretch of the imagination. The new look of the Klingons is an affront to Star Trek fans; especially since we are supposed to sit back and *accept* it, without any explanation of why it would be so, nor any real justification for it.

But there they are, ridges and all, thirty feet high and in living color, so once again it is up to the fans to correct a discrepancy in Star Trek. Lord knows there were enough unintentional ones in the series, but it is particularly irritating when the act is deliberate.

But the Star Trek universe is a very real one to all of us, and we cannot let such a serious matter go unexplained. Several fans have offered explanations for the change in the Klingons in the movie, including: self-inflicted mutation of the Klingon race in order to gain some mental or physical advantage; the Klingons seen in *STTMP* were only one of a variety of Klingon races (much as the Federation is made up of many differing species); these were the first *bald* Klingons we have seen, so how do we know the ridges have not always been there?; and the ridges were only some sort of intership communication devices worn in battle status (a development in Klingon technology since the aired episodes ended). My favorite, of course, is the explanation that the ridges are simply the Klingons' spines, pushed up over their skulls from constantly being kicked in the backsides by the Federation!

My opinion is a variation of the subspecies theory. The Klingons in *STTMP* are part of the original race which developed on Kling, but by some quirk of evolution, have a radically different appearance from the average Klingon.

It would make sense that these "different" Klingons would keep to themselves (as the average Klingon is not noted for his tolerance), and as a minority, they would be continually persecuted. The fact that they have survived and gained enough responsibility to man starships speaks well of their intelligence and battle prowess, for had they been lacking in either department, they would have long since been completely eradicated.

Spock once pointed out to his captain that "although warlike in the extreme, the Klingons are not berserkers." Perhaps in this one instance, Spock was incorrect. The Klingons we saw in *Star Trek: The Motion Picture* may very well *be* berserkers. This would follow, as I have established that they are even more warlike and vicious than the average Klingon, and would most likely not care for the plotting, backstabbing, and underhandedness of day-to-day life on Kling.

So, having failed to eliminate these berserkers, Klingon chieftains would have made an uneasy peace with them. After a time, the berserkers would become valuable shock troops in a battle with enemies, and it is likely that the success of Warlord Kling in gaining control of his planet depended in large part on his use of the berserkers.

The tradition would continue to the time of Star Trek. Left pretty much alone, and given ships which could roam the galaxy at will, the berserkers are usually the first to come into contact with new races and civilizations. And when they do, they fight. If they are successful, another glorious legend is added to Klingon history. If they are defeated, the Klingonese hierarchy is forewarned, and will proceed much more cautiously in that area of space thereafter.

So by establishing that the Klingons seen in *STTMP* were indeed Klingons (although of a small minority we have never seen before), we find the solution to the mystery of why the Klingons acted atypically when confronting V'Ger: They were *berserkers*, and staying true to form, attacked the unknown rather than exploring it.

Now that a subspecies of Klingon has appeared, it is interesting to speculate if there are any others. Perhaps so. Mara in "Day of the Dove," for example, could be one of a subspecies of Klingon "amazons," which would help account for her obvious mental and physical capabilities, and explain the amount of respect she commanded from the chauvinistic Klingon males.

So while the unexpected and dramatic appearance of the "new" Klingons in *Star Trek: The Motion Picture* caused much consternation in fandom, it has also enabled us to have that much more fun expanding the Star Trek universe. And that's what we are all about, isn't it?

5.
WALTER KOENIG: AN INTERVIEW

Having had a great response to our earlier interviews with Walter Koenig, we were most anxious to get his views on Star Trek: The Motion Picture. *Walter's comments are always pithy and refreshing, reflecting the skill he showed as a writer in his diary of the making of the movie. This interview was conducted at Houstoncon in June 1979, by Walter Irwin, G.B. Love, and John Murphy.*

TREK: Walter, there's been all sorts of rumors going around about the forthcoming Star Trek movie. Why don't we get the major one out of the way right now? Does Spock die?

KOENIG: Nobody dies. . . . Well, none of the running characters die. . . . None of the characters that were on television suffers any kind of debilitating trauma that leaves them comatose . . . or worse. (*He laughs.*) How's that for talking around the issue?

TREK: Pretty good. Now that thousands of fans can breathe again, why don't you tell us what you've been doing lately?

KOENIG: Thank you for asking. Now I can get in my plug. (*Laughter from all.*) I wrote a journal on the making of the Star Trek movie, covering mainly what was happening backstage, and Pocket Books is going to publish it. And they are very enthusiastic about it.

Unfortunately, the publication date is somewhat up in the air, due to reasons that I don't think I should get into out of tact and diplomacy. So it could be released anywhere from December (*1979*) to February (*1980*).

I'd love to see it released in December, because that is when the movie is to be released, as you know. (*Here Walter takes on a "pitchman's" voice.*) It would make a marvelous Christmas present... (*laughter*)... and all those other very crass, commercial reasons.

But everyone that has read it seems quite convinced that it is very entertaining and edifying, and that it would be fun reading for anyone that has seen the movie or is about to see the movie. In it, I relate the kind of situations that are meaningful occurrences on the set... what happened in this particular scene, how everybody broke up, or how it was done, that sort of thing. When you see the picture, you will know what went on behind the scenes from what I've talked about in the book.

I submitted it to two or three publishers and had a very happy reaction from all of them, but it seemed to be the shortest distance between two points—and the most beneficial to me—to go to Pocket Books. But while my book was making the rounds, I was pleased with the interest my writing had received from publishers, and so I have finished synopsizing a novel I had been working on.

I had sort of put it aside and didn't know if I would ever get back to it, but with this renewed interest, I have gone on with it. It is a story about the supernatural. My agent now has forty-five completed pages—about eleven thousand words—and the rest in synopsis. He loved the forty-five pages, but hasn't read the synopsis yet, which of course could change his whole opinion. (*Laughs.*) But I am going to press on with that and try to get a book sale. Maybe even a hardcover version....

Other than teaching at UCLA and at a film school in Los Angeles, that's pretty much what I've been doing lately. Acting, of course, has been pretty dismal—with the exception of the Star Trek movie, I haven't had much opportunity in that area.

TREK: At the time of this interview, the first color publicity photos have just been released of the *Enterprise* crew in their new uniforms, and they have gotten a lot of negative fan reactions. How did you feel about them?

KOENIG: My feeling is that most people react negatively just because the uniforms are different, and somehow it's unsettling to their whole concept of what Star Trek has been, and that they sense the new uniforms represent wholesale changes that have occurred in story, characters, plotting, the ship, etc. I think it is more of an emotional response than an aesthetic one.

I think the uniforms are neat. They fit very well, and I think they evolve well from current military concepts and look like something that will be worn in the future. And they're functional. You can move well in them, and it's easy to work in them.

I think they're very handsome. I would perhaps have liked to see them choose a color other than beige... the steel blue is a very pretty color... and naturally, I don't have a steel blue, I have a beige. (*Laughs.*)

TREK: I like the two-tone uniforms that Shatner wears.

KOENIG: Bill's uniforms look good, and he also has several other combinations you'll see in the movie.

TREK: Do you think that the uniforms will "move" better on the screen than they look in still photographs?

KOENIG: Maybe, I don't know. I just feel that people are ... (*He shakes his head.*) Even several of the actors were kind of crying the blues when we first put them on. It's more of a tempest in a teapot than anything. Look, if you were to really analyze the uniforms on the television series, they looked like pajamas.... They were comfortable and colorful.

TREK: And designed for a color television set where everything is four inches high.

KOENIG: Right, reds and blues. I think there are some marvelous things about the way the movie's put on film, things you cannot depict on a television screen... the way the lighting has been done, for instance.

And this really does relate to the uniforms, and I'll make my point in a second....

You get the sense that you are not in an audience, but an eyewitness, looking through a keyhole at a real ship. Very realistic. It's subdued, there are areas of shade, areas of light, the way it would be on a ship. Yet all this lighting is very controlled, so when you have to have somebody highlighted or want to bring up someone in the background, it can be done.

You have the sense you are really on board the *Enterprise*, and not simply on a merry-go-round. Very often on the television show, what with our uniforms and sets and other props, they went for an obvious aesthetic reward . . . you know, bright colors, shine, glitter, that sort of thing.

So back to the uniforms. With the subdued lighting, and the sense of the weight of a shot, you get the feeling that you really are on a starship going somewhere; and the more subdued uniforms—with their concept of a military guard—are a large part of that feeling.

TREK: So the uniforms are merely one part of an effort to give a feeling of reality to the movie. How about the sets? We've heard they are stupendous. Do they also promote that feeling of reality?

KOENIG: Some of the sets are sensational. The engine room is spectacular, and I go into some length describing it in my book. It's a forced perspective, somewhat in the way the original was, but much more interesting. You get the sense that it goes back hundreds and hundreds of feet, with the appearance of combustible gases passing through transparent and translucent pieces of machinery. It's very dynamic! It's three stories high, and even has elevators that function, going up and down.

There is a lot of lighting, as well. Floor lighting, wall lighting, ceiling lighting . . . not only in engineering, but everywhere on the ship. Much more than we ever had on the series.

Even the corridors are exciting. They've used sheets of aluminum to cover the walls, and you get a sense of something really functional . . . that you are not just in Disneyland, but in an operating starship.

TREK: You never could tell where the lights were on television.

KOENIG: Right, but now there's built-in lighting. I don't have any idea of what the electrical bill might have cost, but I know it must have been tremendous. They really spared nothing in the art area. For example, the recreation hall set is practically the size of an entire soundstage, big enough to show 320 crewmembers converging at the same time, and we only used the set for two or three days at most. It was that kind of care that was taken to ensure that the picture will be as good as it can be. Really, *nothing* was spared.

TREK: Apparently not, because the first team of effects people were released after having spent millions of dollars, and a completely different crew was handed the assignment. Have you seen any of the special-effects work yet?

KOENIG: I haven't seen any of the effects work yet, but I was pleased with what was written about the effects in the script, and I can only hope that they are coming together. I have been assured by people that have seen dailies and rushes of the effects that the work is coming along nicely.

Doug Trumbull and John Dykstra are both working hard doing opticals, miniatures, interiors, etc. I've had reports that the miniatures are looking very good, and that the effects work that is now coming in sight is very much in keeping with the original concepts.

The way the effects sequences read on the scripted page was exciting, and if it can be translated from the written word to celluloid, we'll have a superior product, I think. It isn't going to be simply bigger and better than *Star Wars* or *Close Encounters*. . . . If they follow through with the visual concepts that were outlined in the shooting script, you will have something that will enter a whole new realm, a different kind of dimension, much more surrealistic, much more in keeping with the spirit of *2001* than *Star Wars*.

I don't think it was ever the intention or the objective of the Star Trek people—at least not Gene or his co-writers at Paramount—to try to make a film with "bigger" or "better" models than *Star Wars* or other films. They wanted something more than to simply capitalize on others' success in that same area.

TREK: You seem to be pleased with the script overall, but were you happy with your part?

KOENIG: I'll preface my comments by admitting that they might be self-serving to a certain degree. . . . The main characters were very well illuminated, very well depicted, and very consistent with what you saw on the television series.

The rest of us, with the possible exception of Jimmy Doohan, suffered a bit, as we did in many episodes. This is due to the fact that there isn't really time to delve into each person's character, and still advance the story line. It was, after all, a herculean project—eleven speaking characters—and it's not really possible to feature all of them, not in two hours.

I must say that I really didn't anticipate anything else. I may have had daydreams and fantasies that they would do something different, but I didn't expect that there would be more to the part than there was. So I wasn't particularly disappointed.

So, on that basis, it wasn't an artistically rewarding experience, but it *was* a very happy and pleasant experience. I enjoyed the four months I spent working on the picture; but I think George and Nichelle would agree that we really weren't fully dimensionalized characters. There have been television episodes where we had more to do, just as there have been those where we had less to do.

But if a viewer is looking for Nichelle's sexiness or the way she related to Kirk, or looking for George's swordplay and flamboyance, or whatever, he's not going to find it.

That doesn't mean you might not find it in a subsequent effort—and that anticipates one of your questions. . . .

Yes, there has been talk of a sequel, but nothing official; and the talk I've heard has been from persons fairly low in the studio hierarchy, so I'm talking just from rumor. But perhaps in a future project, we will have more to do.

TREK: Didn't your contract for the film have an option for a sequel or sequels?

KOENIG: In fact, we all signed a contract that optioned our services when we were going to do the new television series, but there is no way to convert those options into another feature project, as they were not picked up. That doesn't mean anything, as we were all available for the picture, and I guess they feel we will all be available if they want us again for a subsequent motion picture.

TREK: Just how active was Gene Roddenberry in the day-to-day activity on the set?

KOENIG: He wasn't on the set every day, but he was in his office every day, writing and controlling things the way a producer should. We saw him a few minutes every two or three days. Whenever there was a story conference, or something had to be changed, or altered, or analyzed, or discussed, he would come by. But he was at the studio. It wasn't like the third year of the series when he walked away from the show. He was very much an integral part of everything that was happening.

TREK: We have heard that much of the control of the project had been taken away from Gene by the studio because of the rising budget.

KOENIG: There are *so* many rumors! You know, the word "rumor" has got to be synonymous with—or defined by— the word "virulent," because I never heard a good rumor.

All rumors seem to be bad, and I think they're the product of people who have a chip on their shoulder and they want to downplay a project or to find fault. . . . I heard at one time that DeForest had died, and that he wasn't in the picture at all! (*Laughter.*)

This is the insane kind of thing that people are saying. You can discount ninety-nine and one-half percent of everything you hear, especially if it sounds inconsistent with what should be happening. Gene Roddenberry was the creator of the series, he was the creator of the screenplay in conjunction with Harold Livingstone, and he was very much involved in the production of the film.

TREK: Aside from the effects work, have you seen any of the film?

KOENIG: I've seen several of the dailies, and they look very good, very exciting. I don't think you can deny that the universal appeal of the film will have to be based on the opticals, but I think the Star Trek audience will be very happy and satisfied with the story. It is developed and identifiable as a Star Trek story. What's going to give it the mass appeal needed to get back that thirty million and more spent to make it are the special effects, but if they do indeed fulfill the promise of the written word, this picture will be an exceptional financial success, as well as an artistic success.

WALTER KOENIG: AN INTERVIEW

TREK: But you have actually seen very little of the finished product, then?

KOENIG: I guess I could have gone over there and looked at the dailies more, but I've been busy with other things. I'm sure that we will get a chance to see the finished film before it is released. But that may be as little as ten days before it is released, as they tell me that the deadline they're working on is so tight that they may not have the picture ready more than a couple of weeks before it is scheduled to go into theaters.

TREK: How do you feel about the experience now that it is done? Are you just waiting, like the rest of us, to see how the final product turns out?

KOENIG: When the Star Trek series was over—if I can philosophize for a moment—I was pretty easily able to put that behind me, and say, "Well, that was a part of my life and I enjoyed it, and it was fun and I enjoyed the celebrity and the affection of an audience, and the recognition and all those things." It was over and I went about my life, and for two or three years I ignored the minor ripples that went on from time to time about Star Trek.

With the advent of the conventions, I got involved again to a certain degree, but I always held myself back because I felt—and I've expressed this before—that we were kind of lauding a ghost, that it was something that had already expired, and I didn't want to become one of those actors whose whole life centered around something that he had done in the past. I don't like to feel that's all I have going for me, a character I once played, and that that would be the extent of my contribution to art and the industry.

I always had a very self-conscious feeling even when attending the conventions, although there were practical considerations why I did. But as we got back to the point where Star Trek became a viable product again, and they were planning to make a motion picture, my enthusiasm returned with less restraint. I figured, "Well, now we are talking about a current or soon to be current project, and the character I play is no longer simply a ghost image, but something that will be yet on celluloid, new and fresh."

So what I'm leading up to is that I really find myself

identifying again with Star Trek, feeling very close to it, and very warmly disposed toward it. I would love nothing better than for the movie to be an outstanding success. I'm rooting for Star Trek, both for emotional and practical reasons; and you might take that into consideration when you listen to what I say, because it may be a subjective analysis of what's transpired. I would like to think that I still have my feet on the ground regarding the motion picture, but certainly if I could will it to be terrific, I would do so.

TREK: Your view of "putting the show behind you" is interesting, and one we have heard from other Star Trek actors. For instance, Bill Shatner has gone on to do many other things, from movies to selling margarine, but he could have more or less played Kirk, for the rest of his life. So it is evident that his enthusiasm has also been revived.

KOENIG: He does indeed enjoy playing Kirk, and it's interesting you should say that, because he of all people has had a very fruitful career since Star Trek. He certainly doesn't need Star Trek from a career point of view. He does have a tremendous enthusiasm for playing Kirk, and like the rest of us, he had a good time.

TREK: We've heard that there were many, many changes in the script while shooting was going on, literally day to day. Is this true?

KOENIG: We had an enormous number of changes in the third act. It was so difficult because some of it was totally rewritten by the time we got to it, and it was being rewritten daily! When we were shooting that third act, we were getting changes not daily, but three times a day! We were getting eight-a.m. changes, one-p.m. changes, and four-thirty-p.m. changes . . . sometimes six-p.m. changes! Mostly it became just a matter of slight shadings and nuances in dialogue.

Also, by the time we got to the third act, Len and Bill had script approval, so not only were Gene and Harold and Robert Wise making changes and suggestions for changes, Len and Bill were involved at that juncture. So when you have that many people talking about the script, commas and periods would come under discussion, and that's what we were faced with.

So we did indeed have a great number of script changes,

particularly in the third act. But I think, ultimately, it came together quite well. . . . Despite the odds, having "too many cooks," everyone seemed to blend quite well, and the result of all that interaction was a far better product than we could have thought possible. Committees usually don't work, but in this case . . .

You see, Bill and Len are both very bright, very incisive, and very perceptive about their own characters and story structure. So it wasn't two actors being self-serving, it was two actors really trying to be constructive and make the film better.

I was not privy to all these story conferences, but on occasion they had the entire cast sit down and we went through the script. Again, that's all in the third part of my book, when I discuss what went on in those kinds of meetings.

TREK: Robert Wise is almost a legend. How was it to work with him? Was he a leader? A tyrant? Or understanding?

KOENIG: He certainly isn't the tyrant. At the same time, there is no question that he is in control. He is a gentle man, as well as being a gentleman. He is very quiet, there's no tension on the set when he's there, and he is extremely patient. He was a film editor, so what he does is pretty much edit on film, cutting the picture as he makes it, so there's very little left over for the editor to do. It's pretty much a matter of the editor putting together what we printed, and that's eighty percent of what we shot. He sees it all in his head.

Because of this ability, he was able to improvise and change scenes around whenever things weren't functioning properly. He had the confidence and ego strength to be structured on the one hand and be able to improvise on the other, and to know that the improvisation would work, that he could fashion it into the completed product.

Personally, we were never close, but it was always a professional, respectful relationship, and I can't ask any more than that. It makes for a professional product.

We had so many problems that if Robert Wise had been less able to meet the challenges, it would have reflected in the way that the rest of us did our jobs. But because he dealt with things with such equanimity, not getting hysterical or upset, the rest of us were able to function that much better.

TREK: Our time is running out, but before we go, could you give us a few excerpts from your book?

KOENIG: I'm afraid it would suffer a bit in translation. I write better than I talk. I can tell you that *Chekov's Enterprise* deals on a day-to-day basis with the four months I spent on the movie. What took place, the kind of things that happened, gags that we played backstage . . .

I also go into some of the technical aspects of what we did—the use of the blue screen and matting processes, why some scenes were shot in twenty-four frames or forty-eight frames, and so on—so I think the book gives a sense of how we were responding during the filming of the picture.

It's a human, very personal account. . . . It's not a "tell all" book, I'm not capable of writing that sort of thing. At the same time, I think I have been very honest in my depiction of the people that I worked with, and how we all related to each other and the problems that we confronted in the filming. As I say, it's all from a very personal point of view, and I think it's entertaining.

TREK: Thank you, Walter. Any last words?

KOENIG: Everybody go see the movie, and read the book.

6.

PARALLELS IN *STAR TREK: THE MOTION PICTURE* VS. THE SERIES

by Lynn Adams

Many fans have commented on some of the striking similarities of the Star Trek movie to plot elements in several of the televised Star Trek episodes. In this article, Lynn Adams discusses these parallels, and even points out a few that may not have occurred to some fans.

When you have the most-popular and longest-enduring science fiction series in the history of television to draw on, it's difficult not to incorporate in any new project some of the ideas and characteristics that initially reaped such overwhelming success.

The forces that be—namely, Harold Livingstone in his screenplay, Alan Dean Foster in his story, Gene Roddenberry as producer, and Robert Wise as director—have done just that in preparing the return of Star Trek in the much ballyhooed *Star Trek: The Motion Picture*.

In short, if you happened to miss a dozen or so of the Star Trek episodes (which is a feat in itself, considering the constant showings in syndicated reruns) then *STTMP* will, at least to some degree, allude to those missed episodes. But you can't really blame the Star Trek movie creators. After all, three of the episodes bearing some resemblance to *STTMP* were nominees for the coveted Hugo Award, the honor representing the finest in science fiction.

Moreover, though the strongest link with the series does not surface until the waning stages of *STTMP*, the plot of the film is directly related to the machine-gone-awry plot of "The Changeling." Personally, "The Changeling" was one of my favorite Star Trek episodes, but it would seem that Roddenberry and Co. could have conceived another plot to express their overriding concern that machines are taking over and the consequences of such mechanical dominance.

Let's compare *STTMP* to "The Changeling":

In "The Changeling," Nomad attacks the *Enterprise*. But before the starship can be destroyed by Nomad's volatile blasts, Captain Kirk is able to communicate with it.

The high-powered machine is beamed aboard the ship for closer scrutiny. It is at this point that we discover Nomad to be a deep-space probe launched from Earth shortly after the turn of the century. After being severely damaged, Nomad "united" with an alien craft that had also suffered damage. But the self-repairs and merging of two sets of programmed instructions have caused the newly powerful Nomad to seek out and destroy all imperfect life forms—Nomad's definition of "imperfect" being any life form different from Nomad.

Nomad is feverishly searching for its creator (one Jackson Roykirk) and is determined to reach its "point of origin"—Earth—where it will, understandably, find nothing but imperfections in the humans and be forced to destroy all life on the planet.

Thanks to its damaged memory tapes, Nomad accepts Captain Kirk as its "creator," and this mistake allows Kirk to cause Nomad to destroy itself by logically pointing out that Nomad has made a mistake and is therefore imperfect.

See how similar this portion of the plot of *Star Trek: The Motion Picture* sounds to the plot of "The Changeling":

The entity, called V'Ger (pronounced Veejur), if headed for Earth to rid that planet of its "carbon-based infestations"—humans to the layperson—and is on an undying search for its "creator."

Upon initial encounter with the *Enterprise*, V'Ger attempts to destroy the starship. But at the last possible moment, Spock manages to communicate with the entity and halt the attack. (By the way, both Nomad's and V'Ger's communication systems were a binary-based format.)

V'Ger, which in reality is the twentieth-century probe Voyager 6 sent into the far reaches of space by NASA on an information-seeking mission, instructs the *Enterprise* crew that its mission is to make a "union" with the "creator" on Earth.

While on its original mission, which we assume from the vague date of launch is shortly before Nomad's lift-off early in the twenty-first century, Voyager 6 is pulled into a black hole and sent to the far side of the universe, where it arrives severely damaged, and crashes on a planet ruled by immensely powerful "living" machines.

The machines were able to decipher from Voyager 6's programming that it was to collect and compile all information available and report back to its "creator" or "point of origin." To this end, the machines "reconstruct" Voyager 6 in a powerful form like their own, and send it on its menacing route back to Earth. But because the machines that repaired Voyager 6 (now V'Ger after a few letters on its nameplate were erased in the interstellar damage) are independent unto themselves, all human life is considered an infestation of any other machine and must be destroyed.

And like the M-5 computer of Dr. Daystrom in "The Ultimate Computer," V'Ger is anything but hesitant about disposing of its enemies—the carbon-based infestations—and even goes out of its way to accomplish this task. Just ask the Klingons.

Star Trek: The Motion Picture opens much like the "Balance of Terror" episode began, with news from a deep-space outpost of some horrible attack. In *STTMP*, it's V'Ger destroying all three Klingon cruisers. In the series, it's a Romulan vessel making rubble out of a Federation outpost. And, coincidentally, the commander of the alien starships in both instances is Mark Lenard, who also portrayed Spock's father in "Journey to Babel."

And like the Vulcan crew of the *Intrepid* in "The Immunity Syndrome," the Klingon crews are unable to deal with or even comprehend their destruction at the hands of the enormous, "unstoppable" entity that is wreaking havoc throughout the universe.

As *STTMP* progresses, we discover Spock to be in a deep soul-searching ritual on his native planet of Vulcan. He is heeding the tremendous pull of oneness and responsibility to his planet, reminiscent of the factors presented in "Amok Time." (In *STTMP*, however, Spock is pursuing "total logic," rather than the "total sex" of "Amok Time" 's *pon farr*.) And, as in the series, Spock is in the presence of Vulcan's hierarchy.

Again, as in the series, Spock returns to his "home" aboard the *Enterprise* amid some surprising and heart-rending chain of events on Vulcan. By the way, "Amok Time" was one of those Hugo Award nominees, along with "Mirror, Mirror" and "The Doomsday Machine."

At this point, let's focus on the novel's similarities (the movie failed to delve into this subject) to the "Mirror, Mirror" episode.

In the series, Kirk-2 has a "Captain's Woman"—for you laypersons, that's a mistress. In the book, Vice Admiral Lori Ciana fills this role in Kirk's initial year as an admiral after returning from his historic five-year mission in deep space.

In the novel and the movie, we find ever-youthful Ensign Chekov in a new role at the weapons-defense station on the *Enterprise*. He is also security chief, and you will remember that Chekov-2 was chief of security aboard the *Enterprise* in "Mirror, Mirror."

As the *Enterprise* undergoes rushed preparations for departure from drydock and is beaming aboard personnel, the transporter malfunctions. Enter "The Enemy Within" episode events. While there were no deaths in the series version, the transporter malfunction was a drastic one and resulted in particularly unpleasant circumstances.

Ilia, the scantily dressed navigator from Delta Four, could fill the role of the Dohlman in "Ellan of Troyius," were it not for her shaven head and civilized bearing. But like the super love potion of the Dohlman's tears that rendered men helplessly in her power and starving for love, Ilia possesses the sexually arousing pheromones characteristic of all women on her planet (another subject more graphically described in the novel adaptation).

And, although not quite as drastically as in "The Enemy Within," Captain Kirk exhibits opposing personalities in *STTMP*, as diagnosed by Dr. McCoy. In the series, Kirk was split into separate bodies—one good and one evil. While in *STTMP*, Kirk first exhibits traits of an obsession to regain (and keep) command of the *Enterprise* regardless of the consequences to his crew or Starfleet. (Similar to the episode "Obsession," is it not?) Then, after McCoy points out these uncaptainlike shortcomings to Kirk, Jim undergoes a rebirth into the loyal, caring, duty-bound, anything-for-Starfleet captain we remember from the series.

In pursuit of V'Ger, the *Enterprise* comes into direct contact with the entity into which Ilia is "kidnapped." Enter events from "What Are Little Girls Made Of?" and "I,

PARALLELS IN THE FILM VS. THE SERIES 59

Mudd." Like the perfect, humanlike androids of Dr. Roger Korby in the former and Harry Mudd in the latter, V'Ger returns Ilia to the *Enterprise* as an alien replica of the Deltan sexpot, complete with those sensuous pheromones.

Like the androids in the two aforementioned episodes, the Ilia replica has a basic purpose programmed into it, but is still capable of some sensuality and independent thought that eventually results in her demise.

When V'Ger pulls the *Enterprise* into its huge hull, we envision shades of "The Tholian Web," in which the ship is trapped without an escape, but, of course, finds one in the end.

With V'Ger on the perimeter of Earth's atmosphere and positioning its plasma-energy bombs to destroy the populace, Kirk and Scott (per Roddenberry's book version) revert to the tactics used in "By Any Other Name." Kirk instructs Scotty to self-destruct the *Enterprise* at a specific time if necessary to destroy V'Ger.

Then, at one point on the bridge when Spock opts for research and a better understanding of V'Ger rather than destruction of the mammoth terror, we find Decker exhibiting the same doubts about Spock's loyalty that Lieutenant Stiles exhibited in "Balance of Terror." Of course, Spock is loyal to the core, and both Decker and Stiles later have their distrust replaced by admiration and respect for the science officer.

Throughout the ordeal within V'Ger, Spock, Kirk, and McCoy refer to the entity as "a child." And V'Ger eventually shows a volatile and destructive temper, as did its predecessors in the series, Trelane in "The Squire of Gothos" and "Charlie."

Then, just as he exhibited his knack for logic and his willingness to take a gamble in "The Changeling" and "The Ultimate Computer," Kirk manages to bluff V'Ger and gain more time for Earth.

Finally, following the example of his father in "The Doomsday Machine," Will Decker sacrifices himself for Earth and the *Enterprise* in order to halt V'Ger. You'll remember that Commodore Matt Decker's efforts, unlike his son's were unsuccessful, but provided the clue Kirk needed to defeat the Berserker. It would appear that the Decker officers have wishes for martyrdom and undying heroism. Incidentally, both Will and his father were not in command of the vessel from which they departed to perform their heroics, although both were of command rank.

After Decker's sacrifice, V'Ger dissolves itself into nothingness. Although not quite as dramatic as Nomad's death, the result is the same.

And, if you really want to nitpick, you could even compare *Star Trek: The Motion Picture* to "The Menagerie." In the film, Decker is the exec; in "Menagerie," the exec is number one. In both instances, Spock is science officer, and replaces both as second-in-command.

So you can see that *STTMP* owes a great deal to many of the concepts and events presented in the televised Star Trek episodes. Whether this was intentional, and future Star Trek movies will follow the same pattern, only Gene Roddenberry can say for sure.

7.
A SAMPLING of "TREK ROUNDTABLE"

If there is one common denominator in Star Trek fandom, it is (as the ads in the magazines used to say) "a restless urge to write." Some fans write fiction or articles such as the ones featured in this collection, but almost every Star Trekker writes letters. They write to each other, to television networks, to movie studios, to publishers, and to Trek. We are proud that our "Trek Roundtable" has become one of the most popular and highly respected forums for fans to discuss the ever-changing ideas and ideals of Star Trek fandom.

Karen Ellis, Halifax, N.S., Canada

By way of introduction, I've been reading science fiction avidly for years, but I'm a dedicated nonviewer of television—when you consider what Hollywood usually does with SF, can you altogether blame me? As a result, I completely missed Star Trek until last spring, when I finally read the Blish adaptations. I made the mistake of going through all of them in a lump, and the impact was overwhelming. The following month is very vague in my memory, and I don't expect I'll ever recover completely....

In this corner of North America, Star Trek is available only on cable television (which I don't have), on one station, one hour a week. The fact that I am up and halfway across the city well before ten A.M. every Sunday morning in sun, rain, sleet, snow, or whatever just to watch Star Trek has my friends shaking their heads in disbelief. But by now I've seen most of the first-season shows and one *grim* third-season episode. And, being book-oriented, I've read everything relevant I can get my hands on.

Which leads me (finally!) to the point which is bothering me: Why do so many fans assume that *pon farr* is normally fatal unless the drive is fulfilled? (Obviously, it has such lovely dramatic possibilities, but . . .)

Granted, I have not yet seen "Amok Time," but in neither the Fotonovel nor the Blish adaptation can I find any general statement to that effect, while there is considerable evidence to the contrary.

Okay, it was potentially fatal to Spock at that time, but you *cannot* infer an absolute rule from one isolated example. It is neither scientific thinking nor logical thinking.

Consider: Spock is not the only Vulcan in Starfleet. The *Intrepid* was crewed entirely by Vulcans, and there are undoubtedly others. If every Vulcan male must get home (or whatever) every seven years or die, then Starfleet is going to be aware of it.

Yet Spock says to McCoy (quoting the Fotonovel), "It's obvious you've surmised my problem, doctor. My compliments on your insight." In other words, McCoy has made an educated *guess*. However, Starfleet is not going to expect Vulcan officers to go through their long and expensive training, serve whatever portion of their seven years remains, then die quietly on duty. Starfleet regulations are going to recognize this aspect of Vulcan biology and provide ample leave for male Vulcans to cope with *pon farr* in a manner appropriate to their culture. And no sane Vulcan, faced with the alternative of going on leave or dying, is going to choose to remain on duty. That would be a form of suicide, and suicide is irrational.

There is the question of how much forewarning the individual has. After the first couple of times he would have a good idea of when to expect a recurrence, and in any case, such dramatic biological changes do not take place overnight. Given the self-control we know Vulcans have, by the time *pon farr* becomes intense enough to be evident to humans, it has been building up for some time.

Also, if the period of onset is relatively brief, those Starfleet regulations are going to provide for emergency leave. They are certainly not going to sacrifice the life of one of their best officers for a reason as trivial as a starship's attendance at a presidential inauguration ceremony—especially with two other starships attending.

There are also some complicated evolutionary arguments which I'll avoid except for the conclusions: The root of a seven-year cycle to mate or die is genetic, and such genes are self-defeating. Either they will quickly be weeded out of the gene pool, or the species is on a rapid downhill road to extinction. I would hate to think the Vulcans are in such a position!

Moving from generalities to the specific case in question, we do not know Spock's age, but at the time of "Journey to Babel," he has been in Starfleet eighteen years. While the longer Vulcan life span may mean they mature more slowly (and this does not necessarily follow), it still could be that "Amok Time" was not Spock's first *pon farr*. It is very likely that, one way or another, he has survived it in the past. And the fact remains that he survived it again, in spite of T'Pring's refusal to go through with the marriage. Granted that the cure was extremely drastic, but it *was* an alternative cure.

So I conclude that *pon farr* is normally not fatal, which raises the question of why it was potentially fatal for Spock in "Amok Time."

Several factors could have contributed. Suppression of the drive for one or more cycles could increase the intensity of successive cycles until a crucial limit is reached, and the only alternative becomes death. Spock's hybrid metabolism undoubtedly complicates his physiology. The human half of his genetic heritage could have upset what must be a very delicate balance.

And the influence of the unfulfilled bond with T'Pring, coupled with the close proximity of the *Enterprise* to Vulcan at the critical time, very probably irritated the situation. The route of the *Enterprise* is variable, and if Spock did not know in advance that his ship would be so close to Vulcan at that time, this could explain why he did not realize until too late that he had to go home or die.

A few miscellaneous comments:

I enjoyed the article on time travel with the *Enterprise*, and the rebuttal, but I have one question. Time travel in "The Naked Time" would appear to be one-way only. As Spock says, "We have three days to live over." In other words, if you go back x years, you are x years older when you return to your starting point. And since a person x years older is not altogether identical to his younger self, he may well be able to occupy two places at one time.

Time travel by the atavachron is essentially one-way, and travel through the Guardian appears to depend on departing through the Guardian and avoiding any changes in the past while there.

The only reliable two-way method seems to be the "slingshot" effect—if so drastic a maneuver can be considered reliable. I'm sure there are other implications of the one-way limitation, but I'll let them rest for now. I'd just like to see that limitation taken into consideration (or explained away) in a time-travel article.

New Voyages 2: I'll reserve judgment until I finish reading it all (I ration my Star Trek reading carefully now, otherwise it would be a case of short feasts and long famines), but I want to register a dissident opinion. I much enjoyed "Surprise." Granted, it's light comedy, and my well-developed nit-picking instincts took exception to several details, but comedy has its place in Star Trek.

And I have very mixed feelings about "The Procrustean Petard." I'm in complete sympathy with the ideas they were trying to convey (and one could argue that Kirk had it coming to him!), but I didn't think that present-day gender-role problems translated well into Star Trek time. Also, as a biologist who has specialized in cellular biology and cytogenetics, the idea of Spock's already complicated chromosomes being further put out of balance by an extra "Y" leaves me cold.

I'm enjoying *Trek* much, especially articles like "A Brief Look at Kirk's Career" and "The Romulan-Klingon Alliance," which assemble a mass of isolated details into a whole greater than the sum of its parts. And the "Roundtable." It's a relief to know there are others out there who share my dementia.

And one vote, for what it is worth. Confine the contents of *Trek* to Star Trek. With the possible exception of comparison articles, I'm totally disinterested in reading about other shows (I don't watch TV, remember?)—although I did think Scott Hoyer's comments on *Star Wars (The Best of Trek #2)* were extremely well put.

Dorothy Bradley, Palo Alto, Ca.

As a subscriber to *Trek* for several years, I'd like to finally get around to writing you. I am going to discuss (or more correctly, give my opinions on) three topics:

1. In recent issues, I've noticed the controversy over whether *Trek* should print material other than Star Trek. I would prefer non-Star Trek material kept to a minimum for this reason: There are a number of other very good periodicals which are devoted to general science fiction and fantasy, whereas *Trek* is the only one I know of that is primarily Star Trek. If people want general SF, then they can purchase the other periodicals as well as *Trek*.

2. I was greatly disappointed in *New Voyages*. First of all, I felt the works chosen were not representative of the material available. Secondly, I did not feel the editorial judgment was very good. I (and many other local fans) felt that the original version of "Mind Sifter" as published in *Showcase #1* was much better than the edited version that appeared in *New Voyages #1*.

3. I enjoyed Houston's "Rise of the Federation" (*The Best of Trek #2*). I thought it was generally well thought out except for one point. In the last section (date: 2038), he states that the Western Allies were the ones who sent the sleeper ship containing Kahn into space. I believe this to be incorrect.

In the episode "Space Seed," Spock tells Kirk that Kahn and several other "supermen" disappeared at the end of the Eugenics Wars and no trace of them was ever found. Is Houston proposing a "Watergate" coverup? Otherwise, why would the "official history tapes" in the computer show them as having just disappeared?

Furthermore, given the state of mind of the powers after such a war, I do not think that the peoples would allow the leaders of the "supermen" to just be sent away. I would be much more inclined to believe that these vanquished leaders would have been brought to trial much as the Nazis were tried at Nuremberg after World War II. . . . It is much more logical that Kahn et al. accepted the fact that they lost the war on Terra and used the sleeper ship as a last-ditch effort to avoid capture.

Gloria-Ann Rovelstad, Elgin, Ill.

I really enjoyed *Trek* No. 13. The McCoy picture on the front was great.

It was interesting to hear Joyce Smith's reaction to "Another View of the Psychology of Mr. Spock's Popularity" (*The Best of Trek #2*).

Kendra Hunter's article "Characterization Rape" (*BOT #2*) was an excellent and definitive summary of fan fiction past and present.

I appreciate Beverley Wood's well-written article "I Love Spock" (*BOT #2*), especially the last few paragraphs. It certainly is possible to feel love for a fictional character or group of people, even without having any interest in the actual actors. I am very fond of the Star Trek characters, but not their actors, although I realize that a good part of their own personalities carry over into their portrayals of said characters.

Love has many forms, and need not be restricted to actual people or pets. And for those who haven't found many worthy humans to love, it's fine to be able to love someone who has such high ideals and good character. It's a start. There's an old saying, "Better to have loved and lost than never to have loved at all." I don't think one loses anything by loving, it enriches one's personality for being able to reach out, even in a small way.

That's what all the hundreds (thousands, by now) of fan fiction stories are about, and the hundreds of fanzines that just break even—if that—in publishing them. There are thousands of writers and artists inspired to participate actively in Star Trek fandom—all for the love of Star Trek and its beautiful crew!

And they have gained, improved through it. Although I'm an artist, I never drew people until I became a Star Trek fan. I never tried to write fiction before that either, and though those efforts were all Star Trek oriented, they may be useful later.

So I very much agree with Beverley's article. I also love Spock, and Star Trek. May they live long and prosper!

Patricia Napolitano, Hillside, Ill.

It seems each time I pick up your magazine I have to write a letter.

First to Mr. Bates. I gathered from his rambling column that his "88 Character Universe" is going to be a regular feature concerned with Star Trek authors. I agree with Mr. Bates that the writers are not as appreciated as the more visible contributors to Star Trek, such as the actors and producer, and I welcome a column about them.

However, in defending his "Serpent's Tooth" from Mr. Norton's criticism, I feel that Mr. Bates is confusing textual analysis with background research. He seems to be saying that Norton's criticism cannot be analysis because Norton did not have information on how much Filmation paid for scripts, about studio censorship, etc.

I think this is an unfair demand upon Norton and the rest of us "critics." Mr. Bates must be aware that most fans do not work for Filmation or Paramount and are not privy to inside information on the making of any show. Also, many fans are so callous and perverse that they judge a script by what comes across on the screen, and not by the circumstances that surrounded its creation. We fans are heartless tyrants. We want beautiful results without making allowances for the author's being underpaid, or having a headache the day the script was due, or being a nice guy—or even for being censored. If a television executive mauls a script, that explains the damage, but does not repair it, and most fans are no more accepting of a flawed script than a flawed set or performance.

I have to admit that information on the creation of a show is not only very interesting, but does help in the appreciation of a show. That's why fans buy *The Making of Star Trek* and *The World of Star Trek*, etc. I am sure that *Trek* readers will be fascinated by and grateful for any insight that Mr. Bates can give us. But for most fans the ultimate test of a script is on the screen or page. If a script entertains us, or moves us, or teaches us something, we applaud. If it offends us, we boo. If it bores us, we yawn. We do not give an "E" for effort.

As to "Serpent's Tooth"—I saw that show about three years ago and do not have a script at hand, so I cannot give a detailed criticism of the script.

But I can recall being disappointed in yet *another* show in which the *Enterprise* encounters a figure from Earth history. After all, our gallant crew had already met, in one form or another, Apollo, Abe Lincoln, Genghis Kahn, Wyatt Earp, Leonardo da Vinci, Jack the Ripper, Satan, and others.

Now some of these "historical" episodes were pretty good, but constant repetition of this unlikely theme has strained my credulity to the breaking point. It seems an awfully big galaxy to have Kirk and company constantly tripping over their own ancestors. This may not be analysis, but I most enjoy those episodes that were the most credible and "real"; and it is my unscientific opinion that while you are likely to meet many strange things in outer space, Abraham Lincoln will not be one of them.

As to Mr. Bates' "Patient Parasites"—Bates has the basic characterizations and the Star Trek "flavor" down pretty well, but I find it hard to get excited about that plot. I find it very unlikely that the people who have created Finder have not developed or obtained the secret of warp drive when they have sent to a distant star a machine capable of transforming matter into energy, destroying a starship, transporting minds across light-years, and more.

I also wonder what Finder is finding on a planet described as "uninhabited . . . desert and desolation." When Kirk asks Finder if it understands his measurement of time, it replies, "I have access to repositories that contain your concepts." Does that mean that Finder already knew Federation concepts which would include the secret of warp drive? And where would it get these "repositories"? Is it referring to the trapped crewmen? Why, when Finder trapped the crewmen in the force bubble, did it conveniently omit Spock and Sulu? Seems that the plot is just a shaky device to set up Kirk to "outlogic" a machine—just like in "The Ultimate Computer" and "The Changeling."

Most of the animated shows had interesting features. They tried to introduce new technology, and two new alien regulars (neither of whom were ever developed much as characters), but I felt it did not really continue Star Trek. For one thing, too many of the shows were mechanical, dull rehashes.

The only shows that really had a life of their own were "Slaver Weapon" and "Yesteryear." "Yesteryear" was another Spock-shows-his-human-side story, but I feel that these two episodes alone from the animated series really expanded our knowledge of the Star Trek universe.

Carolyn Atkinson, San Diego, Ca.

I have just finished reading a copy of *Trek*, and there is this small voice inside of me urging me to subscribe. The last time I listened to this voice, I ended up volunteering to lead a panel discussion on blood disorders which nearly caused my premature demise. However, that is all in the past (and totally beside the point, anyway), and I am going to listen to the voice once more.

I come from a family of Star Trek fans; however, I didn't find this out until about four years ago when I myself became hooked. Little had I guessed that my father felt kinship with

Scotty, or that my mother was in love with Kirk, or that both of them were fans of the original series. I am indebted to my younger brother for introducing me to the show.

Once I joined the Saturday-night rerun ritual, I realized what a beautiful, inspirational show Star Trek really is. From that moment, I was hooked and discovered the truth about my parents. I delved further into the concepts of life in the Federation that are the basis of Star Trek: equality of all peoples, understanding of the beauty, mystery, and fragility of all life, and the miracle of existence. And that's only for starters.

I began to view my fellow man with more compassion; a view that will aid me in my future nursing career. I even toyed with the idea of writing a theme paper for one of my college courses on the phenomenon of Star Trek, and projecting its effect on the future of mankind. (Unfortunately, my professor wasn't of the same mind as I, and I ended up writing a mundane paper on the topic of women in music.)

My friends take my loyalty to Star Trek as just another manifestation of my slightly crazy personality, compounded by bad family influence. Indeed, I used to wonder if we were the only ones with the burning interest. We realize now that we are not alone; still, it seems to be a big joke to my friends that I shut myself up with my tape recorder every Sunday evening to tape my weekly episode. It is a good thing that in my four years of college I have had understanding roommates who don't mind getting kicked out of the room while I do my taping.

I am nineteen and a third-year nursing student at Rush University in Chicago. I drive a shuttlecraft (so christened by my friends), and I enjoy playing the piano, writing (as evidenced by this overlengthy letter), helping people in my capacity as a nursing student (and someday, nurse), making homemade pizza, and, of course, watching Star Trek and involving myself in related activities. I am also a self-proclaimed trivia expert. My greatest dream is to attend a real convention. The only one I have ever attended was a poor excuse for one in Waterloo, Iowa, in 1977. Jimmy Doohan and Jesco von Puttkamer were there, but that's about all that could be said for it.

I apologize for the length of this letter. I enjoy writing, and felt that I had to explain myself a bit. Also, once I start, I find it hard to stop. I'll close now by saying that I look forward to getting *Trek* very eagerly.

Ginny Thorn, Davis, Ill.

My first inclination after reading *Trek* No. 13 was to write a check to renew my subscription. But on reflection, I decided to include a letter of appreciation for this superb issue. Even Russell Bates' caustic comments were interesting! I will look forward to reading his future columns.

"A New Year's Revolution" by Mary Jo Lawrence (*The Best of Trek #2*) was dear to my heart. I too am a "johnny-come-lately" and have experienced almost the same "six stages" she mentions in her article. However, I don't have a good friend and confidant to share my feelings and treks to the bookstores. I envy her for that. The dog-eared copies of Blish and Foster at the library convinced me to buy my own. And, despite gentle teasing from my husband and son, I continue to watch Star Trek reruns, haunt bookstores, and scan catalogs for new Star Trek publications. I hope to read more about Mary Jo's adventures in her search for "trekstacy."

As I happily wandered through *Trek* No. 13 (reading slowly to make it last longer), I finally arrived at *the* article: "I Love Spock." Beverley Wood, it was fantastic!

The urge to shout "Amen!" now and then during the reading of the article was almost too much to suppress. All of Vulcan would have been astonished, I'm sure, to observe a human with such wonderfully controlled emotions. I read Ms. Wood's revelation twice to make sure I hadn't missed anything, and will probably read it again many times.

To a fan almost completely isolated from Trek fandom and its activities, this article was welcome evidence that someone else feels as I do about Spock. Of course, Kirk and McCoy are definitely top-drawer, too, but Spock is dream material of the first quality. And as a mature fan, such material is best kept to one's self. Please keep on writing, Ms. Wood. Eventually even T'Pring may get the message.

I'd like to make several comments about the movie. I agree with Herb Nelson about the uniforms. I think all of us instinctively want our ideas about Star Trek to remain the same in every respect. However, passage of time does change places and appearances, and fashion is a most fleeting standard. Let's hope the "improvements" made for the movie will not be too startling. My greatest apprehension is the theme song and background music. It was so well done in the series that no-

A SAMPLING OF "TREK ROUNDTABLE" 71

ticeable changes may destroy the "mood" of Star Trek as we know it.

Nevertheless, if Paramount, Mr. Roddenberry, Mr. Wise, and the cast can put that wonderful crew and the *Enterprise* back into orbit again, we should have an enjoyable evening at the movies by the end of the year.

I did not ignore the other articles in *Trek* No. 13—they were also very good. My interest in *Trek* has been a slow kindling of excitement and anticipation. If you can continue to offer issues as fascinating as No. 13, you'll have a devoted subscriber from this point in the galaxy for some time to come!

Larry Nemecek, Ada, Okla.

I have followed your fine, one-of-a-kind publication since issue No. 8. I have been intending to write this letter since *The Best of Trek* (#1) came out—for a variety of reasons—and since I have just finished *Trek* No. 13, I cannot put it off any longer.

Before I begin, let me state that one of my main beliefs about Star Trek is that it affects no two people in exactly the same way. Also, a corollary of that statement—no two people ever have the exact same opinion about any aspect of Star Trek fandom.

Therefore, when I bring up another author, viewpoint, or magazine, it is not to knock your great periodical, but to present another side to a question (or debate) that your growing readership may not be familiar with or have access to. Again, many of the things I have and want to say have been building up and are just now finally spilling out onto paper, so here goes.

To begin with, I do not share what appears to be most of Trekdom's infatuation with fiction, either fan or pro. Because it was the continuity from show to show regarding the technology, history, and other background aspects that intrigued me about Star Trek from the beginning, my library started with the Whitfield and Gerrold background paperbacks. It expanded into the tech manual, Concordance, Medical Reference, all the various sets of blueprints, and other reference works largely available only by mail. The only fiction I own is the "New Voyages" stories, a few of the new Bantam novels, and some of the Fotonovels.

This is not to say that I have no feeling for the characters and relationships as evolved on the show. What I do object to (and disregard most fan fiction for) is the near total fascination with Spock or Kirk, or any combination thereof. This point hit me when I went shopping for my first Star Trek poster many moons ago, at a time when I had no "favorite character." The only poster nationally mass-marketed—and therefore the most readily available at that time—was a giant collage of stills, featuring the starship and several shots of the captain and first officer—but nobody else, not even a group shot!

So, because of my "take up for the underdog" streak, I immediately took up the banner for the other characters—especially Scotty and McCoy.

As time went on, I developed earnest support and sympathy for the doctor—besides his oft-quoted wit and humanitarianism, I just love his earthy sarcasm. Just when Kirk and Spock would be all wound up in their idealism and "the wonder of it all," here would come McCoy to pop the bubble and bring everything back to earth. And when you talk about relationships, how about the always hinted, but rarely seen, Scott-McCoy duo? Now there's one no one has even begun to touch (although there was a great scene in "Turnabout Intruder" between the two), let alone the other four minor characters. But enough of that topic for preaching.

I would like to offer an alternative view to Mark Golding's now three-part series about warp drive and other technical matters. The way I see it, he points up the inconsistencies in the show regarding physics and speed/distance factors—of which there are many—but then goes on to explain it by means of his time and warp-field drive, and more important, his "Gateway" warp tunnels.

Now this is something out of the old *Clue* game—"secret passage to Conservatory, one move"—or some such. As far as is known, warps probably do occur naturally—at least black holes—but I don't think the Star Trek people meant for them to be so natural that they were the main means of propulsion.

To me, he is saying in essence that the *Enterprise* and similar warp vessels travel by way of *naturally occurring* rather than *ship generated and controlled* subspace "pocket" or "bubble" warps.

The latter is a theory I have always embraced, especially since everything that was ever done on Star Trek navi-

A SAMPLING OF "TREK ROUNDTABLE" 73

gationally and engineering-wise seemed to leave no other conclusion. I know of the discrepancies that have been pointed out between the basic warp drive factor formula and the speed/distance factors demonstrated on the show; but another fan researcher, Geoffrey Mandell, has handled this by postulating a "Cochrane's Constant," which is figured into the basic formula and takes care of these discrepancies. This whole aspect of Star Trek background is thoroughly explained by Mandell in several articles and books, including the old *Poster* books and his own *Starfleet Handbook* series.

Golding's main pitfall, to me, is that in his rush to resolve real science with Star Trek "facts"—a philosophy I believe every true Star Trek researcher must abide by—he does not allow for three-hundred years of social and cultural advancement. In other words, he explains the Star Trek world in terms of 1979 physics, rather than in those of 2279—not taking into account unforeseeable developments over that span of time. Imagine describing our everyday technology to someone from 1679—in their terms!

Golding also says that interstellar governments can't take up solid volumes of space. . . . I say *au contraire*. Here he goes against my other Trek researcher's credo: That all Star Trek nonfiction writers, since they are performing a service that the rest of fandom wants (but does not always understand the complexities of), should strive to resolve their work with each other and with older research efforts, above all, the original Star Trek facts as laid down by the Great Bird and associates.

By "older efforts," I mean national mass-market references such as the works cited above, and as many other worthwhile limited printing jobs as possible. I have always worked diligently on this point in my writings on Star Trek astrography and place/name nomenclature systems (the results of which, including a series of star charts, a star system catalog with pertinent data, and a nomenclature article, will be published in Mandell's next volume).

But this is not to say that I regard all published fan reference books as perfect, and that just because something is in print means it is infallible. Franz Joseph Schnaubelt had several horrendous screwups in the technical manual, and they have caused a lot of anguish and debate in fan circles.

So you see, what all this means is that now not only do we have to solve the original Star Trek "mysteries" (as Ms.

Thompson has done in your magazine), but also resolve the mysteries and glaring inconsistencies among the nationally published Trek researchers. In trying to fill in the gaps of knowledge about Star Trek, they often make things worse—and just harder to resolve.

What's going to be interesting is how all fan fiction and nonfiction writers are going to resolve twelve years of creations and postulations with whatever facts are presented in the new movie. Remember, folks, nowhere in aired Trek is it mentioned that Vulcan's sun is 40 Eridani—and in the movie, even a sacred fan fact like that may be contradicted. Oh well . . .

As you can see, I do not hold with any of Mr. Golding's opinions regarding these aspects—of course, that is just the type of difference of thought that makes any discussion (or any "Trek Roundtable") so interesting.

There is one aspect of his article in *Trek* No. 13 that I find fascinating and mind-boggling: the section on the Preserver's seeding of human and Vulcan races around on habitable planets. In fact, Mark, why didn't you let this stand as a whole article and expand on it? It's going to take a few rereadings to fathom all your implications, but my only comment for now is: What about all of the other Federation races?

There is another fallacy in much of fan writing—to only dwell on well-developed concepts as seen aired, but to do little with the more seldom-discussed aspects of the show.

I mean, all this Vulcan background is okay, but they *aren't* the only "fascinating" race in the galaxy. For instance, what about the Andorian-Orion races? Or the Kzinti-Caitian-Vedalan strain? Or the Aurelian-Skorr race? Or any other race mentioned only briefly in the live or animated episodes? Especially, what about one of the most neglected of species—and in fact one of the UFP founders—the Tellerites? Come on, fandom, doesn't anyone find anything worth exploring or fleshing out about our friends from 61 Cygni V?

As far as the time-travel debates go, my main thinking is, "If it's on film, it's got to be explained rather than discounted." Besides, if you really want a scientifically inaccurate episode, how about "Alternative Factor"? The writer did not understand the nature of antimatter, for he apparently believes that only a hunk of matter and its exact physical double in antimatter can set off the gigantic annihilation—the two Laz-

A SAMPLING OF "TREK ROUNDTABLE" 75

aruses (Lazeri?)—whereas, in reality, *any* antimatter coming into direct contact with *any* matter (as with Kirk in the other dimension or the AM Lazarus in ours) *will* cause the blow. Someone correct me if I'm wrong, but this basic point completely blows the whole dramatic plotline of the episode—and I've never seen or heard anything discussed about this.

All these "Psychology of Lt. Smith's Popularity" articles are fine, but as I said, everything about Star Trek hits everyone differently. Still, it is interesting to see people trying to explain just why they feel the way they do about the characters.

And now, a glaring fault in the Eugenics Wars article that no one else seems to have noticed yet, incredibly enough. According to the episode "Space Seed" (as well as the Concordance), the wars were fought into the 1990s. Why then does this time line continue into the 2030s and not even stop there? To me, this is an obvious goof on Mr. Houston's part, and he should be severely lashed with a tricorder strap.

Finally, your two best articles were the McCoy article and the Romulan/Klingon Alliance article (or update memo). Superb! It represents the best in what I consider to be fresh Star Trek background creating.

Let me wrap up this letter by reiterating some points:

First, to all you readers. In case you didn't know, there is lots more to the Star Trek world than the Blish and Foster novelizations! Most of the best of the new Star Trek background genesis is available only by mail, especially since the "poster" books folded. If you're interested, send off for catalogs from *Trek* and other zines—you won't be sorry, and you'll be amazed at the diversity available in all areas.

Second, don't get the idea that this has been a session of "Gripes 101." I just wanted to get all my comments in—only I've been saving mine for quite a while. You are the only Trekzine of your kind, and besides that, you are of consistently high quality and classy, both in format and execution. I will always buy *Trek* to see what others are coming up with and formulating and debating. With all of the junk that is sure to be thrown at the public in December, we need a good nonfiction forum like yours.

Mary Phelan, Webster Groves, Mo.

Just received my introductory issue of *Trek* (No. 13), and found it quite enjoyable. The articles were interesting and imaginative.

I must, however, take to task a point raised by Kendra Hunter in her article "Characterization Rape."

I believe she has read too much into the Kirk/Spock relationship. It is emotional, intellectual, and complimentary, but it is not in the least homosexual. Why must a deep and abiding friendship between persons of the same sex instantly raise questions of homosexuality?

The idea of Kirk giving in to bisexuality to save Spock's life from the ravages of *pon farr* may be somewhat possible but highly improbable. Spock would not permit it, and the social mores of his race would forbid it—in all events, Spock himself is too staunch and too much of a Victorian to allow it to happen.

It would be much more realistic to suppose that if Spock were in the grip of *pon farr* and too far from Vulcan, he would seek out one of the female crewmembers to help him in his hour of need. Nurse Chapel would probably be the number-one candidate, with Uhura or Rand as alternate choices.

For the moment, let us assume that it *has* happened. Kirk enters a homosexual relationship to save Spock from death. Would Spock allow Kirk to be destroyed by any guilt over it? He would probably release him from any remorse by taking the memory from him, or at least the "worst" of it.

But then what of Spock? If Kirk could be consumed with guilt, wouldn't it also follow that Spock could also be torn with regret? He is not, after all, as liberal and as casual about sex as is Kirk.

I could continue in this vein for some length. It is an interesting line of speculation, but there is a possibility of becoming redundant on the subject.

Overall, I found *Trek* to be a very professional magazine. This is somewhat rare in a fanzine, as most have good intentions, but are poorly done.

John Williamson, P.O. Box 1000 10-W, Chattahoochee, Fla. 32324

I have just finished reading *The Best of Trek*, and was thoroughly delighted with the excerpts from your magazine.

I am currently in the state hospital at Chattahoochee. I am twenty-four and single, and have been hospitalized since 1975.

I have been aware that there are magazines devoted to Star Trek. I count myself as an "original" fan, as in 1966 when I was but eleven, Star Trek turned me on to the vast field of science fiction, and I have been an avid SF reader since seeing my first episode of Star Trek ("The Corbomite Maneuver") over thirteen years ago.

As I said, I had been aware of magazines devoted to Star Trek. Unfortunately, I was completely unaware of your work. I happened to be in the hospital library to pick up some novels the librarian had graciously ordered for me (I must admit, the dear woman has been a lifesaver to me these past four years, ordering books to feed my almost insatiable reading appetite!) when I noticed your book sitting neglected on the shelf.

The cover threw me at first, until I thought of copyright, etc., but I eagerly looked through it, and of course checked it out.

The writing in your magazine is *vastly* superior to any I've seen. So much so, I decided to write. (A great effort, as I suffer from a muscular disorder which makes it difficult for me to write.)

I am very much interested in the current events. I know the picture is being made and will be out soon. I won't be able to see it (I missed *Star Wars* and *Close Encounters*, too), but I look forward to the books.

I would be very grateful if you or any of your readers could help me or any of the other patients here out. If you know anyone who would be interested in corresponding, I would also be grateful. Though I am confined, I try very hard to keep up with current events.

Thank you for your letter, John. We appreciate the effort it took to write us, and a complimentary subscription to Trek is on its way to you. We would also like to encourage our readers to send their extra copies of Star Trek books and magazines not only to your hospital, but to any others they may know of. In this small way, we can all help to repay Star Trek for all the pleasure it has given us by sharing that pleasure with those less fortunate.

8.
A LETTER FROM JUDITH WOLPER

Every once in a while, we get a letter addressed to our "Trek Roundtable" that is long and involved enough to almost stand as a separate article. Usually, we are forced to cut out all but the most exceptional of comments from such letters (one of the hardest duties of an editor!), but occasionally, the opinions and ideas expressed in such a letter simply cannot be discarded. The following letter from Trek *subscriber Judith Wolper is a perfect example of this, and we think you will enjoy reading her comments just as much as we did.*

I have just finished *The Best of Trek #2*, and I would like to share my views on the articles as well as Star Trek in general. First, I would like to say that my experience with Star Trek is similar to Mary Jo Lawrence's ("A New Year's Revolution"). I did watch Star Trek when it was first on, but I was not old enough to really grasp it. Later, I occasionally watched the reruns if there was nothing better on.

About two years ago, a book club that my father belonged to offered *The Star Trek Reader I* and *II* by James Blish, and for the heck of it, I ordered No. II. The book then sat around my house for a few weeks, but finally I started to read it. At first I only read the stories of the episodes I remembered, but then I started reading the others. After that, I couldn't wait to see the episodes themselves. Once I started watching the show, something fascinating happened: I discovered Mr. Spock. For years I had heard that Mr. Spock was desired by thousands of women and that he was endowed with immense sex appeal. But I could never understand what was so great about him.

Captain Kirk, maybe, but that skinny, pointy-eared Vulcan? Then, out of the blue, it hit me, and I have been a moderate but confirmed Trekker ever since.

As to the articles, I was very impressed by Joyce Tullock's analysis of Dr. McCoy (" 'Just' a Simple Country Doctor?"). It showed that Dr. McCoy is not only an important ingredient of Star Trek, but also a very complex character. One of my criticisms of *Star Trek: The Motion Picture* (which I will discuss later) is that Dr. McCoy was far too superficial. All he did was lose his temper and make jokes. I, personally, have never analyzed McCoy as deeply as Joyce Tullock, but I have always appreciated the depth of his character, especially in his relationship with Spock. Certainly, McCoy teased Spock, sometimes lightheartedly and sometimes in anger, but there was more to their relationship than that. When McCoy said, "Good luck, Spock" in "The Immunity Syndrome" after the doors of the hangar deck had closed; his sincere apology to Spock in "The Tholian Web" after they had heard the captain's last orders; his concern for Spock in "Amok Time"—those are the type of incidents that lent realism and depth to that relationship, yet none of that came out in the movie.

Patrick R. Wilson's article "The Romulan/Klingon Alliance" was very interesting, but I was especially impressed by the last two paragraphs, which state: "We, members of the Federation, who share what we believe to be our more 'civilized' attitudes, must not forget the bitter lessons of our collective history: that unshared idealism is dangerous, and that the Romulans and Klingons have their own perception of the universe and their—and our—place in it.

"Thus, until war and conquest once again prove themselves the grand illusion they always were—to *all* powers—we of the Starfleet must remain on call. We must be prepared to resist the threat of the Romulan/Klingon Alliance, and the key to successful resistance is proper preparation."

Those remarks apply perfectly to the United States' relationship with Russia. I have always felt that even though our people and our government believe in democracy and world peace, we have no guarantee that the Russians feel that way. The United States is a civilized nation and I think it is safe to say that our attempts at peace are honorable, but if our enemies are uncivilized and do not keep their promises, then there can be no peace. If our enemies play dirty, then we have to play dirty. The crew of the *Enterprise* struck a perfect balance between idealism and realism. Whenever the *Enterprise* was attacked, Captain Kirk would always explain that their mission was peaceful. Then, if the alien attacked again, the *Enterprise* fought back. However, after battle, Kirk proposed peace. Kirk upheld the ideals of the Federation by never attacking anyone, but he was realistic enough to fight back when he had to. It's a shame we can't achieve that balance in our country. If we try to make peace, especially with the Russians, everyone thinks we're weak. If the government starts spending too much on defense, we're branded warmongers. At any rate, Patrick Wilson presented the case for a strong defense better than any politician.

Pamela Rose made some valid points in her article "Women in the Federation," but many people seem to forget that although Star Trek was set in the twenty-third century, it was aimed at a 1960s audience—and supervised by censors out of the 1900s.

The 1960s were a time when everyone—blacks, young people, women— was trying to find a place in society. Women's lib was not even organized until after Star Trek was canceled. The television audience at that time, which consisted of not only urban liberals, but of rural, traditional conservatives as well, was simply not ready for total equality between the sexes. Even now, there are women who don't want to be liberated. The Mormons still believe that a woman should be subordinate to her husband, and Marabel Morgan has sold thousands of copies of her two books, *The Total Woman* and *Total Joy*, which encourage women to be their husband's "slaves."

Therefore, it is unfair to blame Star Trek for simply reflecting the values of the times in which it was written. Television can help to legitimize new ideas, but it cannot impose them upon an unreceptive public. However, *Star Trek: The Motion Picture* corrected most of the inequalities of the series. Nurse Chapel became Dr. Chapel, Janice Rand was made transporter chief, and the new navagator was a woman, Ilia—an alien woman, at that. And after she was kidnapped, her replacement at the station was also female. The movie, like the series, reflected the values of its time. And the female crewmen all wore pants, too!

Richard Van Treuren's article "On Ship-to-Surface Transportation" made me realize that in the field of science fiction, there are those who are interested in the science part and those who are interested in the fiction part. While Mr. Van Treuren labels the episode "The Enemy Within" "ridiculous," I think that it is one of the best episodes of the series. (I am sure that Mr. Van Treuren's complaints about the transporter are valid, but I do not even understand how Star Trek gets inside my television, let alone whether something like the transporter is possible.) What I liked about "The Enemy Within" was that the subject matter was intellectual yet the message came across clearly.

In one of my college English classes, I had to read a short story, "The Jolly Corner" by Henry James, that was one of the most boring, tedious, vague stories I have ever read. However, I managed to figure out what it was all about.

"The Enemy Within" dealt with the same subject, i.e. the alter ego, the dark side of a person's nature, but it did it in a clear and entertaining way. The stories were especially similar in that James' character, Brydon, encounters his alter ego and is disgusted by it. He tells his girlfriend, Alice, that it "wasn't him." Kirk tells Dr. McCoy that he wished he didn't have to take the "impostor" back inside himself. Alice tells Brydon that she saw his alter ego in a dream and that she wasn't disgusted by him; she accepted him. McCoy tells his captain that the impostor is part of Kirk and makes him the person that he and Spock know; McCoy and Spock accept the impostor.

The episode was also an excellent character study of Captain Kirk. In subsequent episodes, I could really see the wolf side of him. He would often make arbitrary decisions; he would even argue with Spock and Dr. McCoy, his two best friends. He could use people if he had to, and he could be very tough. Also, in this episode, Mr. Spock was able to make an interesting statement about the duality of his own nature.

The implausibility of the transporter malfunction did not mar my enjoyment of "The Enemy Within." I think the malfunction was as good an excuse as any to trigger an interesting and thought-provoking story. It is my belief that Star Trek's main purpose was to be entertainment, not a weekly documentary on scientific technology. Star Trek's portrayal of futuristic technology might have been inconsistent, but its portrayal of people was right on target. It is the characters and situations in any kind of fiction that really move the audience, not the accuracy of the background.

As a Spock lover myself, I really enjoyed Beverley Wood's article "I Love Spock." However, there are a few points that I disagree with. She describes Christine Chapel as "beautiful, misunderstood, trying-to-make-the-best-of-a-bad-situation Christine," and says that she isn't given enough credit for her strength of character. I have never had any sympathy for Christine. I think that she acts like a moony adolescent instead of a mature, intelligent woman. If she knows that she can never have a relationship with Spock, she should have enough self-respect to find herself a man who can love her, instead of playing the martyr. I am not that familiar with fan fiction, but I know that female authors use all kinds of devices to "get" Spock, including the ever-popular *pon farr*. However, none of them use the only thing that Spock can't resist: logic.

I recently wrote a story that is going to be published in *Saurian Brandy Digest* in which I too (through my character) get Spock. My character, Lieutenant Vicky Kendall, falls in love with Spock, but instead of moping around hoping he'll notice her, she takes a direct stand in which she is prepared to win Spock or lose him. She doesn't lose him, but if she did, she'd say the hell with Spock and find someone who would appreciate her. As it is, she shows Spock why it is logical for him to love her. She points out that in spite of his claims that he has no emotions, he does love Captain Kirk, and she keeps at Spock until he admits it. She also makes him realize that it is illogical for him to deny his human half, especially since he lives among humans. Vicky loves Spock, but she doesn't make a fool of herself over him.

Mrs. Wood also offers her views on *pon farr* (an irresistible subject), and I would like to offer mine. First, even though in "The Cloud Minders" Spock said, "The seven-year [mating] cycle is biologically inherent in all Vulcans," I do not believe it is biological. In "All Our Yesterdays," Dr. McCoy said that the pre-logic Vulcans almost destroyed themselves with their own passions, and that is the generally accepted view of Vulcan history. Therefore, I can't believe that the Vulcans could have been passionate while only having had sex once every seven years. Warlike barbarians usually love as hard as they fight. On the other hand, the Vulcans could certainly repress their sex drive just as they suppressed their other emotions. However, the passion of pre-logic times would eventually build up and need to be released. The Vulcans, with their powerful minds, could program this release to come at a specific time.

Mrs. Wood suggests that Vulcan females are fertile at all times, thus ensuring conception during *pon farr*. This is also to keep the population within the limits necessitated by a somewhat hostile environment. My feeling is that Vulcan females are *not* fertile at all times. If a Vulcan woman becomes fertile during each *pon farr*, that would mean that every Vulcan family would end up with the same number of children. More important, it would leave Vulcan with a bigger population problem than Gideon. I don't know when a Vulcan male goes through his first *pon farr*, but let's suppose it is in his sixties. (Pamela Rose suggests that Sarek was that age when Spock was born.) Since Vulcans live to be 250 or so, that would mean that each Vulcan family would have twenty-seven children. However, if Vulcan females are not fertile at all times, several seven-year cycles would be necessary to ensure the continuation of the species.

As for Vulcan's hostile environment, any people as technologically advanced as the Vulcans could certainly have tamed their environment by the twenty-third century. The United States was a hostile environment when the Pilgrims came, but it isn't anymore. Therefore, many births in case some babies die would not be necessary.

I do agree that T'Pring was nuts, but being a Vulcan, she really wouldn't have known what to do with Spock anyway.

In "Characterization Rape," Kendra Hunter attacks another of my favorite episodes, "The *Galileo* Seven." She says that the crew of the *Galileo* is forced out of synch as the writers continually demand insubordination from them. "Regardless of how the crew feel about Mr. Spock or his ability to command, these people are militarily trained and as such would not vocalize mutinous opinions." The crew of the *Enterprise* may be militarily trained, but they are not tin soldiers. On top of that, they are human beings with feelings. The annals of the *Enterprise* are filled with instances of insubordination. In "The *Galileo* Seven," while Spock's crew was challenging him, Captain Kirk was doing his utmost to avoid obeying Mr. Ferris. In "A Taste of Armageddon," Scotty directly disobeyed Ambassador Fox, and in "The Trouble with Tribbles," Captain Kirk was not only insubordinate, but downright rude to Nilz Baris. Dr. McCoy has never behaved in a military fashion, and he has questioned Kirk's decisions as often as he has Spock's. Therefore, I do not think the crew of the *Galileo* was forced out of synch.

I also think the circumstances on Taurus II contributed to the crew's insubordination. They were all alone on a hostile planet, fighting for survival, and were vividly exposed to the possibility of death. Since Mr. Spock was their leader, they looked to him not only for answers, but for hope. And when neither were forthcoming, they naturally became frustrated and therefore arrogant.

From a dramatic point of view, the insubordination was essential, since without conflict, you have no story.

I agree it was a little odd that Mr. Spock had never commanded a mission before the *Galileo*, but I think the good points of this episode more than make up for this error. What impressed me most was that the crew made such a point of giving their dead comrades a proper burial (even risking their lives to do so), and yet they were chomping at the bit to attack the creatures with phasers blazing. That is so typical of humans. We are told that we shouldn't speak ill of the dead, and funerals are often spectacular affairs. Yet we often do not show half that consideration to the living. We do not even know what death is, let alone whether the dead can eavesdrop on the living, yet we illogically feel they deserve more respect than living people, who can appreciate it.

The crew's eagerness to attack the creatures was also typical. Gaetano's statement "But if we hit them hard, they'll think twice about attacking" is the kind of thing you could hear anywhere from a locker room to the Pentagon. As the writers of the episode logically pointed out, humans can be heartless and aggressive toward living people (or creatures) but are fanatic in their concern for the dead.

I found Walter Irwin's article "Jim's Little Black Book" extremely interesting. One of the reasons I became interested in Star Trek was that Captain Kirk was so different from Steve McGarrett of *Hawaii Five-O*, a show I had a love-hate relationship with. Steve McGarrett was supposed to be a red-blooded American male, yet he had less than one love affair a year. Mr. Spock's record was better than that! Furthermore, when McGarrett did get involved with a woman, he always held back emotionally. All he did with women was ask them questions. In the last few years, Samantha Eggar, Jean Simmons, Carol Lynley, and Lucianna Paluzzi crossed his path, yet his attitude was "Don't bother me, lady." After ten years of that, it was quite refreshing to see a man who knows what to do with a woman. What I admire about the captain is that he falls in love quickly and completely (in most cases), and when it's over he regrets it. Even though he has used women, it still shows that Kirk is as much a lover as a fighter.

Mr. Irwin also discusses "The City on the Edge of Forever," a highly popular episode and one that I, too, used to like. However, there are two flaws in this episode that completely destroy its credibility. Mr. Irwin says that Edith Keeler is the woman Kirk is "literally ready to sacrifice a universe for." Kendra Hunter says in "Characterization Rape," "When Kirk watches Edith die—and he must let her die—all of Trekdom cries." The fact is, Edith's death in 1930 would have no bearing on Kirk's relationship with her. Once he returned to the twenty-third century, she would be dead, whether she died in 1930 or 1980. It was essentially the same situation that Spock had with Zarabeth in "All Our Yesterdays." When Spock left Zarabeth, she was alive, yet the end of their relationship was just as final as was Kirk's with Edith.

Then there is the question: What would Kirk do with Edith if she hadn't died? I think that this problem confronted the writer of "The Paradise Syndrome" as well. I thought it was very convenient when the pregnant Miramanee died from being hit with a rock. Dr. McCoy has saved a Horta, restored Spock's brain, and found cures for many strange diseases, but he couldn't save Miramanee. The fact is, Kirk could not stay with Edith or Miramanee, nor could they accompany him on the *Enterprise*. Therefore, they both had to be eliminated. However, if Captain Kirk really loved Edith enough to sacrifice not the universe, but his career for her, all he would have to do is go through the Guardian of Forever to a time prior to Edith's death. I don't understand how a person returns from the Guardian, but if it were possible, Kirk could simply leave through the Guardian right before Edith died and start all over again. As Mr. Spock says, "There are always alternatives."

Another error in "City" is the premise that Edith Keeler's peace movement could have prevented the United States' entry into World War II. That is totally illogical. The period between the wars was indeed a time of isolationism in this country, and while the government supported England and helped them by giving discounts on supplies, there was a great reluctance to enter the war militarily. However, Pearl Harbor could be interpreted only as an act of war. After the U.S. declared war on Japan, Germany declared war *on us*. Therefore, we were in the war against Germany whether we liked it or not. Edith Keeler couldn't have changed the situation because she had no influence over Japan and Germany.

I also question the validity of Edith's peace movement. This goes back to what Patrick R. Wilson said. England and France wanted peace in Europe, and therefore tried to appease Hitler, but that did nothing to further the cause of peace. It is fine to be idealistic, but not when one evil man is trying to achieve world domination. There is a big difference between wanting peace and surrendering. I wonder how Edith would have felt about millions of Jews being tortured and killed in concentration camps, not to mention the millions who died in the actual fighting. I also cannot believe that large numbers of Americans would join a pacifist movement in light of the atrocities being committed in Europe.

As Captain Kirk said in "The Return of the Archons," "Freedom is never a gift. It has to be earned." I think Americans realize that, and realize that there are some things worth fighting for. If Edith Keeler could look at the world situation in the late 1930s and early 1940s and still blindly advocate peace, then not only was she unlike Captain Kirk, she was not worthy of him.

I agree with Mr. Irwin that Captain Kirk will probably never marry, but I think that is the best thing for him and the women in his life. In a recent television movie, *Seizure*, Leonard Nimoy played a brain surgeon, and while he was very happy with his life, his wife was dissatisfied. She was very nice and sophisticated, but it was obvious that she was jealous of her husband's career. He was satisfied with a part-time marriage, but she wanted more. Captain Kirk is also married to his work, but he has never promised a woman more than he can deliver. When he's in love with a woman, she's the most important thing in his life, but when it's time to go back to work, the affair is over. At least that way, Captain Kirk gets some sex and a relief from his loneliness while the woman isn't trapped into a continually frustrating relationship.

In "Characterization Rape," Kendra Hunter discusses a

theme which some authors have adopted, that of a homosexual relationship between Kirk and Spock. It is my opinion that although these two men obviously love each other, there is no reason why their relationship should become sexual.

In the mainstream of our society, there is only one relationship in which sex is acceptable, and that is the relationship between a man and a woman.

However, there are many types of love. Parents love their children, a child can love a toy, people love their pets, sisters and brothers love each other, people love their friends, and people can even love God. These days, it is even possible to have friends of the opposite sex. All of these relationships can be deeply satisfying, but they are not normally sexual.

Captain Kirk and Mr. Spock are like brothers, and although we know that Kirk loved his brother, Sam, it is unlikely he had sex with him. As far as sex goes, it is not always a beautiful, spiritual experience anyway. Prostitutes perform with complete strangers for money, women are brutally raped, even many husbands and wives have sexual problems. Obviously, then, sex and love can exist independent of each other.

The relationship between Kirk and Spock is that of a beautiful friendship, and there is no need for writers to go beyond that, because there *is* nothing beyond that. There are certain characteristics which define friendship and others that define romantic love. While sex is considered a desirable and necessary ingredient in a romantic relationship, it is not a requirement of friendship. Friendship is by nature simply nonsexual.

Furthermore, neither Spock nor Kirk were socialized with the idea of homosexuality. Captain Kirk is definitely a ladies' man, while Spock can hardly bring himself to admit that he has emotions. Though the two men love each other, I do not think that either one of them would be comfortable with the idea of a homosexual relationship. I am not saying that homosexuality is wrong, but just as it seems "natural" to those that are homosexual, it seems "unnatural" to those that are not. I think that Captain Kirk is simply accustomed to having sex with women, and would feel uncomfortable having sex with a man. Spock, under normal circumstances, would probably feel strange having sex with *anybody*—it is hard enough for him to even talk about it.

I have always found the Kirk/Spock relationship very beautiful, especially because it shows that two people—even men—can love each other. One of the goals of the feminist movement is to prove that we are all people, not simply men and women, and we can appreciate each other in ways other than sexually. I would like to think that Kirk and Spock have not had and would not have a homosexual relationship. I think that it would mar the purity of their friendship, and I do not think it would make them any closer than they already are.

Regarding *Star Trek: The Motion Picture*, I found it extremely disappointing, and considering that the film cost $42 million to make, I find the situation tragic. I think all that money went to everyone's head. I have read that while Gene Roddenberry was making the series, he was always complaining that the studio wouldn't give him enough money to do what he wanted; the budget was a big problem. I have always considered this a blessing. Because the producers of the show did not have the money (or the time or technology) for spectacular special effects, they were forced to compensate with well-written stories and well-developed characters. In that way, Star Trek was not simply visually impressive science fiction, it was moving, intelligent drama.

This was not true of *Star Trek: The Motion Picture*. The special effects were impressive, but the story wasn't. The basic plot: "Gigantic creature headed toward Earth. Starship *Enterprise* has three days to save the world." That sounds like one of those fifties sci-fi movies where Godzilla eats Tokyo. The time limit, instead of creating suspense, inhibited the plot. Everyone was so preoccupied and so worried about the "thing" that there was no room for subplots. Even Decker's relationship with Ilia was connected with the pursuit of V'Ger.

In the series, the *Enterprise* crew was frequently confronted by time limits, but there was never that urgency found in the movie. For example, in "The Naked Time," the *Enterprise* had six minutes before it crashed into a planet. However, in that time, Captain Kirk made a personally revealing speech, Spock admitted his friendship for Kirk, Spock and Scotty figured out a formula for mixing matter and antimatter "cold," and everybody on the bridge got a close-up. In the series, the emphasis was on each minute in a time-limit situation, whereas in the movie, everyone was concerned about the future.

The story itself was very vague. V'Ger, as an adversary,

was simply too big to comprehend. In a way, it was like Nomad in "The Changeling," but Nomad was small enough to deal with on a one-to-one basis. Furthermore, the message in "The Changeling" was fairly clear. In the movie, the message was far from clear, and I have no idea why Will Decker wanted to be a martyr. The very idea of a human joining with an immense "living machine" is incomprehensible. What kind of life form would come out of that? It's like mating an amoeba with an elephant. Furthermore, we never did see what happened to V'Ger. Just because Decker and Ilia joined with V'Ger doesn't necessarily mean that V'Ger was rendered harmless.

Another problem with the story was that it lacked the depth of character found in the series. Captain Kirk, Mr. Spock, and Dr. McCoy were recognizable in the movie, but they were shallow reflections of their former selves. Kirk was strong yet fallible, Spock was coolly logical with a little emotion showing through, and McCoy was irascible and funny. But that was it. Captain Kirk was competing with Decker in the beginning, but that problem seemed to resolve itself. Mr. Spock was unusually reticent when he first came aboard, but his subsequent "thawing" was not very dramatic, and was due more to V'Ger than to his relationships with his friends.

The series episode "The Tholian Web" revealed much more of the relationship between Kirk, Spock, and McCoy than the $42 million movie did—and it was a third-season episode!

In it, not only did Dr. McCoy reveal his temper, he also revealed his humanity and his ability to admit he could be wrong. Spock showed his concern for Kirk by risking the ship and its crew, and he demonstrated courtesy and understanding for the illogical humans serving under him. Captain Kirk, in his last orders, showed his understanding of Spock and McCoy and of their precarious relationship. By taking Kirk's advice, Spock and McCoy showed their great respect for him.

"The Tholian Web" was not full of special effects, and the plot was fairly simple; but unlike the movie, it reinforced and restated the beautiful relationship among the three. Somewhere along the line, the people making *Star Trek: The Motion Picture* forgot that it was that relationship that made Star Trek special.

Even the direction reflected this lack of interest in the characters. I have always felt that the series was beautifully directed. There were always revealing close-ups and tight shots, especially during moments of tension. The feelings of the characters were literally written on their faces, and the camera captured them. The lighting was also very good, especially soft lighting on a person's face to emphasize the eyes. The movie, however, was quite lacking in close-ups—except for those of Persis Khambatta, and even in hers, she didn't have any dialogue. All she did was look longingly at Decker.

I especially disliked the new design of the *Enterprise* and the costumes. The colors were boring in both cases. The bridge of the new *Enterprise* was all silver and white, unlike the old bridge, which had touches of color. The old uniforms may not have been perfect, but at least they were colorful. On a small screen, the new uniforms would have been bad, but on a large movie screen, they looked even worse. Some of the crew blended in with the walls.

I was also disappointed with the view of the planet Vulcan. Vulcan supposedly has a highly advanced technology, yet all we ever get to see of it is barren desert. I, for one, would like to see the cities.

I enjoyed your collection from your magazine, and am looking forward to seeing more of it.

9.
BRIDGING THE GAP: THE PROMETHEAN STAR TREK

by Joyce Tullock

We are only sorry that this article by Joyce Tullock is appearing in Trek *just as the manuscript for* The Best of Trek *#3 is going to the printer, because we would have loved to include some of the letters the article is sure to elicit. You may agree or disagree with Joyce's opinions, but you will not be able to ignore them. As Joyce said in her letter accompanying the article, "Gentlemen, this is a can of worms. I'm offering you some." And we proudly offer it to you.*

. . . looking for God, we made the journey back to Ourselves . . .

During an interview on Tom Snyder's *Tomorrow* program, De Forest Kelley is reported to have remarked that if a Star Trek movie were ever made, it would have to present a big idea—something like man meeting Christ in space and discovering that He is really Lucifer.

Snyder quickly dismissed the idea. He doubted that the viewing public would be up to accepting such a story line. Although I've only read a written account of the interview, I can easily imagine the hint of a devilish glimmer in Kelley's eyes.

Recalling the incident in the light of the movie, I began to think things over. Something at the bottom of that seemingly outlandish statement rang true. And a question that had been nagging me for some time began to take new shape—and answers appeared. A pattern observed in so many of the aired episodes came more sharply into focus . . .

It's embarrassing that it took so long to catch on. Because one thing is sure: Gene Roddenberry and the Star Trek writers do not overlook the topic of religion in either the series or the movie. It is a very real, almost constant theme. After all, how can you discuss man and his place in the past, present, or future without giving some serious attention to his relationship to religion? Man's relationship with God . . . gods . . . Supreme Being . . . or in Star Trek's case, more precisely, with man's desire to find a way to "bridge the gap" between the known and the unknown.

Anthropologists tell us that man's need for religion and the existence of some sort of religion in every civilization directly involves man's desire to explain the unexplained and to satisfy his fears about the mysteries of the universe—to "bridge the gap."

That's a big part of what Star Trek is all about, isn't it?

Take inventory: Man versus the Universe, God versus Evil, Logic versus Emotion. We have presented in Star Trek episodes a whole universe of "strange new worlds" to be explored on many levels; the inner worlds of our heroes as well as the varying ideas and philosophies they encounter along their journey.

Religion is one of the "worlds" that Star Trek explores with a notable degree of depth. But it was as ticklish a subject in the sixties as it is today. And so it was generally treated as a subtle sideline, or as a sociological or even a technical matter. Very seldom did Star Trek deal in black and white, and while the writers wisely chose to remain objective about man's relationship to religion, certain themes do pop up. Something is definitely being said about religion and its influence on the future of man.

No conclusions were offered in the episodes—only hints or suggestions. That's the beauty of it . . . the question is too big for pat answers and too important to be ignored. And Star Trek handled it well by dividing the questions into two general categories: man's longing for "Paradise"; or man's need for some kind of god or supreme intelligence to guide and shelter him.

After all, the men and women of Star Trek's time are still a little lonely, still looking for a Way, or they wouldn't be out there in the first place. So the *Enterprise* is doing her part, trying to find the answers to give comfort and security to the established world. Exploring, searching, challenging the darkness. The man of Star Trek's time hasn't given up on God . . . he's just started looking in other places. And he wants to find a few of the answers on his own.

Kirk, Spock, and McCoy do learn a few things, too. They get stuck in "Paradise" more than once . . . and discover what a hell it can be.

In "The Return of the Archons," we get a good, heavy dose of what is to be Star Trek's general comment on both Paradise and godhood.

Under the control of the computer/god "Landru," the people of Beta III live in perfect harmony and bliss. Their society, however, has stagnated. The human capacities to think independently, to create, dream, and imagine, are forbidden. Only a select, dissenting few are able to resist the computer which makes people "part of the body."

Like so many leaders, Landru meant well, but failed. The computer/god he left behind for his people had great knowledge, but lacked human wisdom and compassion. It could not conceive of the need for human individuality. The most essential human need, the striving for spiritual growth, is ironically overlooked in the scientist's well-meaning attempt to build a physical Utopia.

And look what Utopia does to Spock and McCoy in "This Side of Paradise." Discovering that the colonists on Omnicron Ceti III haven't accomplished one thing in three years, the *Enterprise* crew soon finds out that the influence of mysterious, harmony-bringing spores has caused the problem. Like Landru, the spores also "mean well." They provide excellent health and emotional harmony. There is no laboring, no suffering. But there is also no progress, no growth.

When Bones and Spock are affected by the spores, and temporarily lose what might be called the "negative side" of their true natures, we got a good lesson in the value of contrariness.

The fiery, sharp-witted McCoy loses his animatedness, becoming lazy and, even worse, complacent. He's a McCoy we don't mind watching for a little while, but deep down we know that if he were to stay that way for long, he'd bore us.

Mr. Spock's icy reserve breaks down under the influence of the spores, and he ends up in the arms of Leila Kalomi— happy, smiling, and in love. It's kind of fun. We're amused.

But Spock is not Spock anymore. Without the loftiness, without that mysterious charismatic isolation, Spock becomes just another one of the guys.

As does Bones. Both men lose their individuality to the extent that their personalities are almost interchangeable. A very frightening prospect indeed. And although it's all in fun, and we can enjoy the change of pace, I like to think that somewhere in the back of our minds an observation is being made, and a tiny voice is whispering, "Bones is dead. Spock is dead. I miss them."

Thank goodness Kirk loves the *Enterprise* more than heaven itself, and that love helps him to overcome the effect of the spores. Then, with what is a little less than godlike wisdom, he finds a way to stir his crew to anger, nullifying the effect of the spores and bringing everyone back to their complete, intelligent selves. And everyone learns that bliss without productivity is only another form of death.

"The Apple" takes us to Paradise once more, and again we see the same overriding theme: Blind obedience plus numbing comfort leads to stagnation.

The civilization on Gamma Trianguli VI, run by another computer/god named Vaal, is sociologically dead. It's not all that clear whether or not Vaal "means well," but he does depend on the people of Gamma Trianguli VI for his existence via daily "feedings." So now we have a god who depends on his worshipers just as much as they depend on him. It's a theme we'll see again. God, in this episode, isn't the hotshot he thinks he is. So what does that say about man?

It is a point that McCoy and Spock argue. McCoy insists that all peoples have an inherent right to develop naturally. And in this case, he sees a people that have become slaves to their god. They exist to serve Vaal, with no intellectual growth, no human initiative, and, interestingly enough, no sex. Of course, Vaal has a beautiful excuse for forbidding sex. You see, no one dies on Gamma Trianguli VI—at least not for a long, long time—so if no one dies, no new people need to be born. Bones said it best—"There goes Paradise!"

(There is also a hint of sexual repression in "The Return of the Archons." The "Festival" seems to be a day reserved for the release of the people's baser desires and tensions. So the machine/gods would appear to link sexual expression with disobedience.)

Spock, on the other hand, applies logic and the tenets of

the Prime Directive to the matter of Vaal and his followers. He questions whether if the society is working, the Federation has the right to intervene.

There's the clincher. Two points of view. McCoy sees a stagnant society; Spock sees an efficient one. Necessity, however, forces a solution. For Vaal is draining the power of the *Enterprise*, and the situation becomes one of "either us or them" for Kirk and his crew. The god is destroyed, and either fortunately or unfortunately for the people of Gamma Trianguli VI, they are now free to learn to grow.

As selfish as some gods are, all of them are not prudes. Look at Apollo in "Who Mourns for Adonais?" Now, as gods go, Apollo is the most "human" of the lot. In fact, he is rather likable in his own innocent, male chauvinist way.

Apollo would have made a pretty darn good god, if it weren't for one fatal flaw—he couldn't handle loneliness. Not only did he fall in love with the beautiful Lieutenant Palamas, but he wanted to keep Kirk and the entire crew as worshiping pets. He'd care for them, feed them, see that they would never want . . . if only they would worship him in return. He needed them.

Kirk tried to be kind about it. He explained to Apollo that man had been down that road before. He'd discovered its shortcomings, and learned from them. The crew of the *Enterprise* and the people of Star Trek's time couldn't exist on Apollo's terms. Maybe once, thousands of years ago, but no more. The human creature of Star Trek's universe is on the move, growing, reaching for a new, greater existence than Apollo had once given him. Man now needs more than a god to love—he needs challenge.

Apollo didn't take it too well.

Kirk, using the technology of the *Enterprise*, somewhat regretfully put Apollo in his place by destroying his hidden power source. And so the god found man's power equal to his own. You can't be worshiped by an equal, and Apollo, too long a god, was unwilling to exist as man's peer. He "spread himself upon the wind" and returned to the cosmos.

Somehow, it seems that the writers of "Who Mourns for Adonais?" are making a very real statement about their hopes for mankind and about man's relationship to religion. And let's be honest—that statement is not just for Star Trek's world, but our own. After all, science fiction is only a clever means of discussing the present world. The Kirk who destroyed Apollo is not a godless man, he is just a grown-up one. Or maybe we should say, a growing one.

But if gods are dying in Star Trek, they are also being born. The universe is a busy place, with infinite levels of development occurring at the same time. "Bread and Circuses" leads us to a world which has experienced a rather peculiar case of parallel development with Earth. It is a world where the Roman Empire never crumbled, giving us a weird view of automobiles, television, gladiators, and religious martyrdom all existing simultaneously. But a Christian faith is just beginning to take root.

Whether or not that world is all that different from ours today, or whether the eventual growth of the worship of "The Son" will improve conditions in that brutal society, is, in fact, an open question. The "Son" worshipers are certainly benevolent and morally superior to the decadent Romanlike establishment, so the implication is that the planet's civilization is bound to improve. Let's hope it will.

The *Enterprise* leaves it a growing, changing civilization, in accordance with the Prime Directive. But there seems to be something rather naive in the attitude of the crew as they leave the planet. It's as though none of them have ever heard of the Crusades, the Dark Ages, or the witch trials.

But it's easy enough to see why. It is the kind of flaw necessitated by the sensitivity of the subject and the policy of the studio executives. Law Number One: Don't Knock Religion. Don't even question. Not *any* religion.

But someone sneaks a little something in on the side when none of us is looking for it. No one is offended; it's clever, a joke. Or maybe it's just that the sardonic Dr. McCoy can get away with things with the viewers, just as he does with his captain. And the sting is gone, because it occurs at the beginning of the episode, and we only see the humor of it later.

No sooner have the three beamed down to the planet's surface when Bones says, "Just once I'd like to beam down, spread my arms, and say, 'Behold, I am the Archangel Gabriel.'"

We know what you mean, Bones. We know what you mean. And in spite of Spock's impatience with your remark, he does too. And if Spock *really* does fail to see the humor in McCoy's remark, it is doubtful that the poignancy escapes him. The famous McCoy wit is a two-edged sword—anyone who takes it as less just isn't listening.

And the doctor's statement, however innocently made, might well be a premonition of what is to come.

But before we talk about the old "man as creator" motif, about man's flirtation with godhood, perhaps we should discuss something else which is of equal importance in the Star Trek universe. An essential quality of a developing race is the ability to sacrifice; to give whatever is necessary, be it out of logic, love, or the need for the preservation of the race. If nothing else, Kirk, Spock, and McCoy have proved time and time again that they care for one another and are willing to sacrifice themselves for one another. And if Spock insists upon explaining his behavior as *logical*, let him. That's fine. It's what that logic leads to that's important. It leads to a higher form of intelligent existence.

Which brings us to that curiosity, "The Empath." Does this episode ever get its share of criticism! I'm almost afraid to mention it. "Sadistic," they say. (Now if you want sadism, go to "Plato's Stepchildren." That's sadism!) "Irrational, illogical," they cry. Well, my goodness, you can't be rational and sadistic at the same time. Or can you? Those superintelligent Vians, Thann and Lal, evidently thought they could. Or, rather, they saw no immorality in using insignificant, lower animals (man, of course) in their "worthy" experiment. It is all a matter of viewpoint. Ask any laboratory rat.

But let's not sidetrack the issue. "The Empath" is not about cruelty, it's about the exact opposite. "The Empath" is Star Trek's passion play. It's the final word about our heroes' worth. The entire question is settled; each of the three is willing to forfeit his life for the others. But the show is beautifully, sensitively performed, so that a story which might have been sticky with *Little House* sentimentality becomes a quiet, thoughtful statement about the relationship between the three. And it shows what man can be at his best.

As for old Bones, well, it figures that he would get the worst of things—he usually does. (He seems to have been Star Trek's resident Tonto—or Job.) But in this case, it is right. Kirk, no doubt, would have tried to convince the Vians to take him in place of either of his officers. Spock, more than willing, had already deduced that he, himself, was the only "logical" choice. The only problem was, neither of them took into account Bones' devilishness. And perhaps that is what makes the whole thing work.

McCoy doesn't worry about protocol, propriety, or

heroics—he just does what comes natural. The doctor could see that Kirk and Spock had immediately dismissed the idea that *he* might be the Vians' "guinea pig." And one gets the feeling that McCoy is feeling a little insulted, and a little guilty, as he whips out his trusty hypospray and settles the question with a doctor's prerogative: Put the bigshots out of action for a while, and the Vians have to settle for potluck!

And with one longing backward glance, Bones becomes a special kind of hero. Like it or not, by virtue of his own actions, he enters the category of human self-sacrifice.

But in a passion play, you have to have a Resurrection.

The real significance of this Star Trek passion play is that it does not truly parallel the Crucifixion. That is, if we keep in mind the continuing theme we've seen in other episodes—the idea that man is an imperfect, but promising, growing being—then we have to appreciate the fact that the good doctor is not an idealistic saint.

We are heading in another direction. And that's why McCoy is probably the wisest choice for the role of "sacrificial lamb"; he's the least "perfect" of the three. He is unfettered by the "purity" of Spock or the still somewhat starry-eyed idealism of Kirk.

Face it, the man Kirk "takes down from the cross" is an earthy, loving, often cynical human being. We know that he's run the gamut of life's experiences, from parenthood to divorce, disillusionment to embitterment, and finally to new, but cautious, friendships.

If McCoy feels that he has accomplished something in "saving" Kirk, Spock, and Gem, it's because he's saved them for what they are—as opposed to *from* what they are. Bones doesn't care one whit about their "sins" or faults, he is concerned only with the promise they show. Maybe he isn't so sure about himself one way or the other, but he knows that his friends are worth sparing. He is a kind of a teacher and savior—but so are they all. In "The Empath," man learns about and finds salvation in his own worth. And McCoy, by virtue of his own humanity, becomes chief participant in that drama.

If Kirk, Spock, and McCoy teach the Vians anything, they teach them that the "inferior being," man, is in fact a most promising creature indeed. The godlike Thann and Lal have been on an ego trip, wrapped up in their own mental superiority; man is "unimportant and underdeveloped."

When Kirk, with passionate defiance, puts them in their place by pointing out their moral stagnation, we are reminded, fleetingly, of the hapless and scorned Apollo. There is the implication that the Vians will shortly cease to exist as a race. They have simply been outclassed—shamed. They had power over life and death, but lacked an understanding of life's true value. They knew that life was to be preserved, but had forgotten why. They were living, unfeeling robots, as much "computer gods" as Vaal and Landru. Like Apollo, they lacked insight, failing to examine man in any but the most superficial of ways. So their sheepish "resurrection" of the dying McCoy was anticlimactic—they were dwarfed before him.

That underlying theme of "human drama" and the progress of man is leading to a touchy question: In Star Trek, is man vying with God? Is that sinful, blundering little creature trying to take front seat?

Let's put it this way: The mankind of Star Trek is tired of standing, hands in pockets, toes kicking the dirt. With Promethean resolve, man has decided to take his chances with the universe and go for broke. He can't help himself, he's evolving. And as Kirk would remind us, although man has a lot to lose, "The chances for reward are infinite."

There is a not-so-subtle suggestion in Star Trek that Captain Kirk is a kind of Prometheus. He is the "defiant one" of the *Enterprise,* greedy to learn from the universe and "go where no man has gone before." He has spirit, he's eager to snatch a coal from that Ethereal Fire and bring it back to man . . . where it can do some good.

Spock's pointed ears aside, Kirk is the figure closest to Milton's Satan in Star Trek—ambitious, lusty, bored with orthodoxy. He thrives on command, has to keep on the move. He is pure, human energy. And although Spock and McCoy become happy "lotus eaters" in "This Side of Paradise," Kirk, even under the influence of the spores, is defiant. He can't leave his *Enterprise* and her promise of adventure. Contentment doesn't interest him; he wants glory and challenge. Time after time, he rejects the retreat of Paradise as a form of "death in life." The spores can't hold him, the amnesia from which he suffers in "The Paradise Syndrome" is unable to keep him happy in that Indian paradise world (he suffers from strange, recurring dreams about his ship and crew), and one suspects that Kirk would be among those rare few who are immune to the brainwashing powers of the computer/god Landru in "The Return of the Archons."

The captain is a powerhouse, a challenger, and very nearly a god among men. He is the spirit of progress, so it's hardly surprising that the writers of "The Changeling" chose Kirk to represent "the creator."

But let's not go off the deep end. Kirk is no god. He's human to an entertaining fault, and at times he even lacks the wisdom of restraint. That's why it's handy to have Spock there, with his cool, mathematical reserve. And at other times, Kirk is in need of the wisdom of introspection and self-knowledge, so Bones, with his human warmth and insight, fills in those gaps. Spock is the experience of scientific wisdom, Bones is the experience of emotional insight, and Kirk is the clever handyman who balances those qualities and uses them together as a fine tool. If he is a creator, that's the kind of creativity he practices—he takes what is already known and molds it into something new, beautiful, and valuable. The "conflict of opposites" doesn't bother our captain. He appreciates differences and delights in the challenges of the two friendships. More precisely, he is the "master" of the Kirk/Spock/McCoy triad, the unifying force.

And the captain represents a special kind of human strength, for in spite of his genuine humanness, he is responsible for holding the world of the *Enterprise* together. He unites man, machine, ambition, and good will . . . and sets it all on the course of progress. He is the stern, loving father. His self-confidence makes us all feel secure.

But not too secure, thank goodness. After all, the main point of Kirk and his *Enterprise* is the quest for *adventure*. Taking chances with "strange new worlds" and exploring the unknown. Even the security aboard the *Enterprise* is temporary. Threats come from everywhere—as often from within as from without. And just when our heroes think everything is okay, the "unexpected" pops up. Sometimes it's due to an alien force. Sometimes it's due to human wickedness or confusion. And other times, it's just plain hard luck.

And speaking of hard luck! One chance in fifty thousand . . . and look who comes down with Xenopolycythemia . . . that's right, Bones. In "For the World Is Hollow and I Have Touched the Sky," our heroes are confronted with a seemingly insurmountable problem: McCoy is dying of an incurable disease. Sounds like a cheap audience-getter, doesn't it? Well, maybe it is, but more significantly, it serves to catapult the viewer into what is probably the most obviously rebellious of the "religious" episodes. And for all of its third-season shortcomings, "For the World Is Hollow" deserves close inspection.

A condensation is taking place. It's like a collection of all the religious themes that have come before it—man versus the "computer/god," man versus "Paradise," man versus "blind obedience," and most important, man's duty to himself versus his guilt-ridden bondage to the wise, loving, and vengeful god of his fathers. "For the World Is Hollow" takes a volatile topic and nonchalantly brushes it past millions of viewers as a heart-rending life-and-death struggle and a bittersweet love story. Take what you like from it. But if we care to—or dare to—look, we can see some things that could have brought a God-fearing, Sunday-churchgoing nation to arms.

In this story, the people of the asteroid ship Yonada are faced with a moral and practical problem; they must give up blind obedience to their "Oracle" or die as a race. These people, aboard a "seed" ship designed by their Fabrini ancestors to create the illusion of a real world, are (due to mechanical failure) on a collision course with a heavily populated Federation Planet. The ancestors meant well in all they did. Thinking to provide everything for their future children, they even included a computer/god called "The Oracle of the People" to guide them in all matters—and to keep them innocent of the truth. And of course, all the inhabitants are fitted with the "Instrument of Obedience," a potentially painful little gadget inserted just above the temple which effectively discourages rebellious or questioning thought. A literal employment of the fear "God will hear you and get you for that."

And so it is that a god who was intended to be a guide and a guardian of life becomes a tyrant, holding nothing for his people but the promise of a certain, hellfire death.

So much for gods made by man.

And that's where Bones comes in. In "For the World Is Hollow," Bones is even more human than usual—he's a tired, frightened man on the verge of giving up. He's looking for a place to hide, for life and shelter, with only the prospect of death ahead. And looking back on a life that, for all its accomplishments, now seems wasted in loneliness, McCoy elects to join the people of Yonada. He accepts the Instrument of Obedience, and embraces in marriage the loving, sheltering, and very beautiful Natira. He wants to live while he still can, and his behavior very closely parallels the dying man's hope for a life after death.

Now I don't blame Bones, and I doubt that anyone else does either. Except maybe Kirk. The captain is disappointed in his old friend. You see, the captain, with that same old defiant spirit, simply refuses to give Bones up for dead. Not yet. And although he believes the diagnosis, he also believes in the ability of man. The possibility of a cure is very slim, but to Kirk it is also very real—a cure *could* be found. And Kirk wants his friend to be in a place where he can be helped, not soothed. Kirk phrases it differently, but his attitude is essentially the same as Mr. Spock's—McCoy's behavior is "illogical."

Well, of course it is! That's the whole point of "For the World Is Hollow"—the very human McCoy is confronted with a problem and the solution is beyond his understanding. He seems to be physically and emotionally weakened by the disease (which for McCoy is nothing less than that old bugaboo, the "unknown"), and if Natira and her Yonada can't provide real answers for him, at least they can "bridge the gap" by offering him comfort and their own version of life and happiness in the time remaining to him. They don't explain or satisfy, they merely offer an illusion saying, "Why worry? Accept things as they are, and be comforted that we love you."

Of course, there's one catch: Bones has to give himself over, body and soul, to the will of the Oracle.

Bones agrees, and the rest is history. His experience is one which has been lived through time and time and time again on our own planet. Throughout history, when confronted with the unknown, many people chose acceptance of a "way" which promised to deal with that unknown. The "way" is not always religion; sometimes it is a Hitler. But eventually, out of both love and necessity, there is a rebellion. Sometimes a thoughtful rebellion, but rebellion nonetheless.

Braving the punishment of the Instrument of Obedience, McCoy tells Kirk how to get past the Oracle and get to the ship's control room. With that information, Kirk and Spock are able to correct the fault, change the direction of Yonada, and send it back on the course its makers intended.

BRIDGING THE GAP: THE PROMETHEAN STAR TREK 103

Once the computer/god Oracle is out of the way, the vast store of practical knowledge of the ancient Fabrini is uncovered. So by destroying the Oracle, Kirk, Spock, and McCoy are able to provide the world with a massive amount of new information, including a cure for McCoy's disease.

But even before McCoy is aware of the cure, he has come to terms with the "unknown." Through Kirk's example of intelligent defiance and Spock's rational positiveness, McCoy is able to observe his own mistake, and he experiences a kind of catharsis. Casting fear aside, he decides to leave Yonada, and spend the rest of his life in finding answers. It is the only way for him, he decides. And so he is back on the road of human progress.

Thanks, Jim. Thanks Spock. What would we do without you?

The fact is, without that excellent combination of humanity, spirit, and logic exemplified by our heroes, the human race wouldn't have gotten very far at all. We'd still be planting by the light of the full moon.

Star Trek is the prophetic story of the progress of man. And looking through the seventy-nine episodes and *Star Trek: The Motion Picture*, we can see where it's all leading. The previous episodes work like a multicolored glass, showing flecks and pieces of themes which vary and yet magically unite. If we want, we can look through them to see the movie as a greater complexity.

Once the shock of the movie is over and we relax with it, things start to fall into place. The movie and the aired episodes become a unit, a whole; each independent, and yet somehow interconnected. And the delicate thread of connection weaves an almost mathematical web of religious themes; themes brought to mind by words like "creator," "understand," "explain," "obey," "cleanse," "impurities," and by the general motif of "coming home to the comfort of God," to the "creator," to "Paradise," to be "one with God."

The movie's alien, V'Ger, is NASA's Voyager 6, a space probe sent out from our own century to "learn all that is learnable," and return that information to man. Like so many of our dreams, it gets lost for a while, then returns when we least expect it. So V'Ger, man's desire "to know," has gone off without man and, too long separated from his guidance, it returns to Earth a technologically evolved but confused entity. Its mathematical mind is superior to ours only by the numbers—it can record the precision of a daisy, but not the beauty of it. V'Ger represents our desire to save ourselves from the Darkness. Learn the unlearnable, and bring it back. And on that day of Revelation, what does it do? It returns with a question. The joke's on us, for V'Ger is asking that same old question that Man has been asking for centuries: God? Where are you?

So there is V'Ger: our desire to know. Our Christ. Our Satan. Us.

And the three-sided equation is worked out for us again, Spock's logic, McCoy's emotion, Kirk's spirit—they all work together to see us through. The stumbling saviors. They go looking for a god out in space, and find themselves staring, open-mouthed, at their own reflection.

Spock's science, McCoy's insight, and Kirk's determination allow the *Enterprise* to survive its biggest adventure. A new world has been explored, and a new life form is born of logic, emotion, and human will. The "threat" of V'Ger is, once again, one of misunderstanding and fear. We've been looking for form, denying essence. We've failed to appreciate our own beauty.

So poor child V'Ger, with its mountains of information, still requires more. Infinitely more. It wants to "understand" about the creator. It wants to "be one with the creator." It wants to "bridge the gap." And for all we know, it does. But this time, it is young Will Decker who makes the sacrifice, and the evolution of man continues.

Well, now. Could it be? Remember Milton? Is V'Ger a kind of Christ/Satan? The personification of man's ambition? Of his longing to know God? Has man met Christ in space and found himself face to face with Lucifer?

I can't dismiss the thought. V'Ger could be man's old desire to learn, to come full flower—a personification of man's defiant will to grow. If it is, then man's sins have come back to him, and he discovers that they are not sins at all. They are his logic, his emotion, his spirit. V'Ger is no alien, he is man discovering himself, seeking out his own value.

And in *STTMP*, man, more than ever before, puts away traditional ideas of divinity and appreciates his own worth. In the person of Decker, man joins with his own handiwork, emerging with it to become something/someone new. Man the Greater. He isn't God, and doesn't want to be. That would be no fun. How could he continue trying to "bridge the gap"?

So *STTMP* is a natural outgrowth of the series. There are changes. Our characters continue to grow. Spock learns about his human value, and even admits it for a change! Kirk learns about his own weaknesses, and becomes stronger for it. He's a more complex character by the end of the picture, and we like him even better than before. McCoy's stature among the three has increased noticeably. Of the three, he is the only one who returns to the *Enterprise* simply because he is needed. He is a more confident figure now, more at ease with himself.

But they are all still growing, still reaching for that mysterious something called *truth*. Let's hope they never completely grasp it. For without the reaching, the striving, they would cease to be. Remember all those times we nearly lost them in Paradise? Where there is no questioning, there is no real human life.

In Star Trek, the old concept of Paradise is an illusion. It is a kind of death. But *STTMP* hints of a new kind of Paradise. Very likely, it is this new Paradise to which Mr. Spock is referring in "The Way to Eden," when he encourages the hippie pilgrims to continue their search.

The new Paradise of Star Trek is not so much a physical place as it is a condition of the human mind and spirit. It is a state of being which is discovered gradually. It is a positive born of contraries. It is something special the individual becomes. We get a feeling of hope for that paradise as we watch V'Ger/Decker/Ilia unite in logic, spirit, and emotion, and transform into something/someone new—the finest form of growth.

And like the McCoy of the novel, I find myself transfixed by that sparkling, flickering glimpse of a new dimension. Names flash through my mind—Dante, Galileo, Newton, Leonardo, Aristotle, Milton, Blake, Einstein . . . all kinds of people—flawed but creative, challengers, givers. Men and women, defiers of a thousand Oracles, using all of their logic, emotion, and spirit to reach for the forbidden answers. Discoverers of themselves, of the obvious.

And then I think about the names yet unborn.

After all, it's a wide, wide gap . . . and the human race is young.

10.
SULU'S PROFILE

by Colleen Arima

Our readers love the "background" articles we do about the Star Trek characters, and constantly clamor for more. We are trying to get around to everyone, so it is especially gratifying and surprising when the mail brings just the sort of article we had been hoping for. In this article, Colleen Arima gives us the fascinating details of the ebullient Walter Sulu's life. How about you Scotty, Uhura, and Chekov fans? We would like to run profiles on them as well. So start writing.

Walter Sulu, the only child of Kenji and Sumiko, was born and raised in the Pacific Northwestern United States.

Growing up in this area, with its rugged mountains, icy streams, swiftly flowing rivers and sparkling blue lakes, lush green rain forests, it was inevitable that Walt become an avid outdoorsman.

Kenji often took his son along when he went hiking and skiing; but the favorite pastime of both was to go deep into the Cascade Mountains on fishing expeditions. The calm and scenic atmosphere provided an excellent release of tension, and Walt and his father both relished the serenity provided by lazy fishing. They enjoyed being together and were very close.

This early closeness led young Walter to take an avid interest in Kenji's work as a physicist. The quiet, contemplative Northwest had become sort of a scientific sanctum for the theorists in aerospace physics, and Kenji gravitated to the area from Hawaii after marrying the petite Sumiko (whose work as a computer programmer allowed her to continue her career as well).

In this atmosphere, Walt's curiosity was continually stimulated. The boy's questions were intelligent beyond his years, thought-provoking and demanding diligent consideration.

His inquisitiveness soon focused on the heavens. At the age of ten, Walt had gone far beyond his father's own literature and sought out more on his own. He then proudly announced his intention to one day serve in Starfleet.

His parents considered it the dream of an impressionable child, a passing desire to be forgotten by age eleven. Dream it was for Walt, but it soon matured into a goal, a goal he would labor for and make sacrifices to achieve.

In an effort to teach Walt of his heritage and the rich culture of his ancestors, Kenji and Sumiko took the boy on many trips to Hawaii and the Far East. Walter particularly enjoyed Japan.

He learned his native language, the customs and history of the Japanese people, and was enthralled by the samurai, as he was a direct descendant of these noble warriors. Kenji had often spoken of the concepts of *Bushido*, the samurai's code of ethics, and now that Walt expressed an interest in learning them, Kenji agreed to teach him in detail when Walt was older.

Aside from suffering the usual teenage growing pains, young Sulu matured secure in his relationships with family and friends. Starfleet was always foremost in his mind, however, and he feverently applied himself to his studies.

When Walt's dedication to his ambition finally led him to fatigue himself so badly that it alarmed his parents, Kenji stepped in. He convinced Walt that life was precious and should be lived to its fullest each day. Walt abhorred the thought of being sidetracked from his plans, but bowed to his father's insistence that he involve himself in the activities of the body as well.

Grudgingly, he complied by joining one of his school's basketball teams. Despite his small size, he was fast, agile, and had a good shooting eye, and quickly won a place on the squad.

To his surprise, Walt found that he enjoyed competitive sports, and although he worked twice as hard as anyone else on the team, his small stature ultimately proved to be his undoing. Walt *knew* that he could run circles around the taller players and score almost at will if only he had been a bit taller. He was frustrated and angry—but he also learned a valuable lesson in recognizing and accepting his own limitations.

Still fired with the competitive spirit, Walt turned to a sport where his speed and agility would more than compensate for his size—fencing. His emergence as a top-class fencer in a very short while pleased him, and from the experience he emerged a young man who knew the value of being able to use his strengths to compensate for his weaknesses. Kenji realized that his son was growing up, and that he was now ready to learn the code of *Bushido*.

He was also ready by this time to leave for Starfleet Academy. His years of extensive study and perseverance had finally made his dream come true. His parents were very proud of him, but knew they would miss him terribly. Kenji had done some traveling of his own before settling down, and he knew how alluring the galaxy could be. It called to the curious, the brave, and the adventurous; and like a siren, it couldn't be ignored.

Knowing that Walter faced the grueling four years of Starfleet Academy life, and then the beauty and dangers of space, Kenji offered his son the gift of *Bushido*. The principles that had shaped thousands of lives—passed from father to son for countless generations—would help Walt to succeed in his life and chosen career.

As Kenji explained to his son, *Bushido* was an unwritten code of ethics observed by the warrior nobleman—or samurai—of feudal Japan. Like the rules of chivalry in medieval Europe, *Bushido* was based upon such virtues as rectitude, endurance, frugality, courage, politeness, veracity, and, especially, loyalty to one's ruler or country.

Only through the exercise of these virtues could a warrior maintain his honor, and one who forfeited his honor was compelled to commit suicide by hara-kiri. The samurai lived by the strict code of *Bushido*, their extraordinary pride and devotion being unequaled by contemporary cultures or social standards. When feudalism was abolished by the middle of the nineteenth century, the code was abandoned, but the principles behind it continued to have a deep effect on Japanese culture.

After much thought, Walter decided that he would accept *Bushido* as a guideline in his life. He would emulate the code's virtues, and accept and labor at any endeavor presented him. The code of *Bushido* was idealistic, but Walter realized that it was an asset to anyone prepared to abide by its laws. Thus fortified, Walt bid farewell to his parents and went off to the Academy.

Sulu formed an instant friendship with his Academy roommate Kevin Riley, a native of Dublin. They shared many interests beyond those of green and scared Academy plebes, and formed a comradeship that would endure for years.

The Irishman, lacking Sulu's dedication, showed glimmers of promise, but was often distracted from his studies—usually by one or another of his amazing assortment of young ladies. To have so many successes, he had many more rejections, and he increased his efforts in that area, instead of in his studies.

Sulu decently helped to bail his friend out of trouble time after time with last-minute tutoring, but the reasons for Riley's difficulties were not lost on him. Sulu decided that he could not afford any relationship that could interfere with his career. He also did not want to hurt anyone—and not wanting to be hurt himself, he kept his female relationships casual.

By doing so, Sulu became one of the very few Academy graduates to complete the four-year curriculum without ever "going steady"; and as a surprise benefit of this policy, he found himself with more feminine companionship than he would have had otherwise. It seemed that there were also many dedicated female Academy students, and they were more than willing to enter into affairs with Walter on the same "no commitment" basis he insisted on.

Sulu was very happy with such an arrangement. He was still very young, and all of his time and energy were directed toward his career. He could afford to settle down once his future was secure. Until then, he could wait.

Sulu was enchanted by his exposure at the Academy to the sciences of biology, alien botany and biology, xenobiology, and biophysics and physiology. The naturalist in him, formed by the love of the outdoors in his youth, responded to the boundless areas for research and challenge. He seriously considered changing his major to the sciences, but eventually decided to remain in command. But he did not forget his love for botany, and it became a lifelong hobby.

About the same time, Sulu started his second hobby when he was given an ancient revolver as a birthday gift. Although the cylinder was so rusty it refused to budge, Sulu treasured the gun, and began to study weapons that fired lead projectiles utilizing gunpowder. Spending many hours restoring the gun to good condition, Sulu was chagrined to discover that ammunition for the weapon was practically nonexistent.

That didn't deter him for long, for after some research, and a few hours in the chem lab and the metal shop, Sulu proudly slipped his handmade bullets into the pistol and fired. The loud explosion startled him, but it excited him as well. It was then Sulu decided to start collecting and restoring old guns.

Afterward, Sulu spent much of his spare time polishing his prized possession and cultivating the many alien greens that sometimes threatened to overflow the cadets' modest quarters. Riley bemoaned the fact that he was living with a mad Oriental who played with potentially lethal toys and raised vegetation of questionable origin. He even charged one particular plant with being carnivorous—a complaint Walt enjoyed perpetuating.

It was this sort of banter that made them such close friends, and provided Sulu with the kinship of the brother he had never had.

Also at this time, Sulu developed a glowing affection for Commodore Timothy Emmett, an instructor and the former commander of the Starship *Hood*. Emmett's long and distinguished career reflected the type of officer Sulu hoped to be. He was strong and decisive, yet fair and compassionate, and he was noted for his ability to effectively communicate with aliens.

He was a staunch believer in the theory of Starfleet officer as diplomat (one of his greatest accomplishments was preventing a war in the Cilylle System by peacefully bringing the opposing factions together), and he encouraged his students to approach problems with thorough thought and preparation.

Emmett was well aware that Starfleet's future was in the classroom, and he was determined to do all he could to help prepare his students to assume their responsibilities.

Sulu respected Emmett not only for his accomplishments but as a teacher who took a special interest in each of his students, instilling the confidence so badly needed by the young cadets. Emmett was a fount of knowledge, offering his experiences, anecdotes, and the kind of wisdom that couldn't

Admiral Kirk
(Mary Lowe)

Spock's Ensign
(Martin Cannon)

Spock
(Martin Cannon)

Idle Hands
(Martin Cannon)

One of Those Days
(Martin Cannon)

War Machines
(Ralph Fowler)

Spock On Vulcan
(Ron Wilbur)

The Triumvirate
(Mary Lowe)

be found in a textbook. An exuberant individual, he inspired his students with the desire to do their best.

As finals approached, Sulu and Riley started cramming. They studied into the early-morning hours, and even quizzed each other at mealtime between bites of food. Classmates laughingly called them the "Brothers Grim," but at graduation, their perseverance paid off. Sulu placed near the top of his class, and even the happy-go-lucky Riley finished in the top third. Without much delay, they were ordered aboard Starfleet vessels, a prerequisite to Command School.

The Brothers Grim had a hard time finding the appropriate words at parting. They decided not to say goodbye, as they both agreed the separation was only temporary, and their paths were bound to cross again. Riley then left for his post on the destroyer *Hannibal*, and Sulu reported to his new assignment on the scout ship *Paul Revere*.

The commander of the *Revere*, Captain Trenton Forbes, was a solemn, unsmiling man with a reputation for being harsh on midshipmen. Sulu was naturally nervous, having heard all of the gloomy stories about Forbes, but the code of *Bushido* demanded loyalty to his superiors, and his own natural optimism enabled him to have a "wait-and-see" attitude.

The first several weeks were particularly rough as Forbes, a strict disciplinarian, established rigid standards for all his recruits. If it was at all possible, Sulu reflected, the routine onboard the *Revere* was even more rigorous than the Academy's. But after a while, Sulu felt he was finally getting into the groove, and the challenge of his work began to interest and excite him. This helped him to become more comfortable on the bridge and less aware of Forbes' scrutiny—which probably wasn't nearly as intense as Sulu imagined it to be.

Although busy at the helm, and still undergoing a period of adjustment, Sulu found that he enjoyed the company of his co-worker Lynn Mihara, the *Revere*'s navigator. She was a lithe and lovely young woman from Kyoto, one of Japan's largest metropolitan areas, and she and Sulu found that they had much in common—similar career goals, heritage, and a basic agreement on the concepts of life. They frequently deliberated over the ideals of *Bushido*, and how it applied to them as individuals.

Because their schedules coincided, they found time to be together during most of their off-duty hours. Soon, Sulu realized they were growing toward the very type of relationship he had vowed to avoid. He tried to caution himself against any involvement, but found his feelings too strong to ignore or contain. It was much easier to yield to desire than to grapple with practicality.

Conversation soon became unnecessary for the exchange of sentiments, Lynn arousing in Walt a response he hadn't thought possible. For the first time in his young life, he experienced the ardor, zeal, passion, and ecstasy of love. He had stumbled through puppy love before, but never had he felt the ultimate joy of completely giving his total self.

Each day he lived just to be with Lynn, to share with her his feelings, frustrations, hopes, and desires. In return, she tended to be honest, caring, and sensitive—her commitment was also complete. Like Walt, she did not want to be hurt, but couldn't resist her impulses and yearnings.

Reflecting on the wondrous turn of events, Sulu found himself in a confused daze. He wanted to spend the rest of his life with Lynn, but feared having to make an emotionally difficult decision. He put off the decision until the point where, if the relationship was to survive, painful questions had to be dealt with.

He still sought a career in Starfleet Command, but would relinquish that choice in favor of a future with Lynn. Dual careers and marriage was not impossible, but the time demanded of each individual would definitely interfere with any attempts to build a life together.

To Sulu's disappointment, the harder he sought an answer, the more elusive a solution became. The only fact he was certain of was that a future together would require sacrifices from both. He failed to comprehend just what or to what extent the sacrifices would reach.

After a week of wrestling with the problem, Sulu finally confided in Lynn, only to discover that she had been struggling with the same dilemma. He wasn't too surprised, as they thought alike in many areas—especially when it came to each other. By combining their ideas and opinions, they managed to come to a mutual agreement. They would bide their time, hoping to avoid any mistakes a premature decision could cause, and live each day while waiting to see what tomorrow would bring. It was not really a decision at all, but they were happy and desperately wanted to remain so.

Sulu was satisfied with the decision, as it allowed him to

continue keeping company with Lynn, while also pursuing his career. He was aware that his personal life could affect his performance on the bridge, and was relieved that his anguish was over, as he was determined to avoid any lack of professionalism in his work. The captain knew about the situation—as he knew everything about his crewmembers—but both Sulu and Mihara showed potential as good officer material, and Forbes refused to interfere in a crewman's private life unless absolutely necessary.

The *Revere* made numerous visits to alien worlds where Sulu learned firsthand the art of diplomacy. He recalled the teachings of his Academy mentor Timothy Emmett, who had said that a diplomat could sometimes be more effective than the most powerful weapon, and, at times, more deadly. Sulu also ascertained Starfleet's role as peacemaker, as well as peace-keeper. He saw when intervention was imperative—and when it was forbidden. The difference was not lost on him.

About two months before Sulu was due to report to Command School, Lynn fell ill with a rare disease. The prognosis was fatal, but Sulu refused to accept it, and feverishly continued to make plans for their future. It was not until Lynn died in his arms that Walt realized the truth—and part of him also died.

Confused and bitter, nothing seemed of any importance to him. He somehow managed to perform his helm duties, but all of his free time he spent alone. Command School, his future, his career—all were forgotten as he struggled to find some logic or rationality to Lynn's death.

Forbes, having grown to like Sulu, and concerned with the apparent destruction of a promising career, made a rare excursion down to the crew's quarters to speak to Walter.

He pointed out that Lynn had loved Walt's ambition and resolve, and to give up would disappoint and cheat her memory. By showing Sulu this aspect of the situation, Forbes allowed the youth to gain a perspective he needed badly. Dealing with his sorrow was still difficult, but Walt immersed himself in his work, salvaging the time he had lost, and determined to do his best as a gesture of respect for the woman he had loved.

Forbes was gratified to see that his advice had helped, and realizing that Sulu would appreciate work to occupy his time, Forbes gave him a major role in the ship's next assignment.

Supply ships to a remote geologic outpost were being attacked by a mysterious invader, and the *Revere* was assigned to escort the next convoy. Forbes entrusted Sulu with the responsibility of determining when and where the invaders would strike, and Sulu relished the opportunity.

Trying to look at the situation from the raiders' point of view, Walt realized that such attacks could only be intended to drive the geologists from an apparently worthless planet. Why was something that would have to wait, as Sulu had discovered an alien ship trailing the cargo vessels just where he had thought it would show up.

In short order, Forbes ordered a Red Alert, and the *Revere* was engaging the enemy in battle. Sulu's skillful handling of the helm became even more expert in the heat of his first battle, and under the direction of the battle-wise Forbes, the alien ship was soon disabled. By overriding interference, they got a look at the alien bridge, and Walt was amazed by his first look at Klingons. It didn't last long, as they very quickly self-destructed the ship.

Now that Walt realized that Klingons were involved, he presented his speculations to Forbes, and was allowed to beam down to the planet to investigate further.

Discovering that one of the geologists was a Klingon agent, Sulu had him arrested and then sought to find out why the Klingons had gone to so much trouble to force the Federation to abandon the planet.

With the aid of a few instruments, Sulu found a deserted shaft littered with rich deposits of dilithium crystals. The agent, discovering the lode, had told the rest of the party the shaft was worthless. But he had immediately contacted his commander, and the attacks on the cargo ships started soon thereafter.

Forbes rewarded Sulu with a very favorable report to speed him on his way to Command School. Sulu was doubly grateful, for without Forbes' aid, he would most likely not even be attending Command, much less arriving there with a commendation. It was with deep regret that Walt left the *Revere*, with all of the good and bad memories he had gained aboard her.

Although he resumed fencing at Command School in a concerted effort to fill his spare time, Walt soon found that he had little idle time—which was a blessing in disguise. For Walt was driven by pain—working until he dropped into bed exhausted. He widened his range of interests, developing an impressive aptitude in astronomy, chemistry, electronics, and math. He also honed his skills in the martial arts. But he chose a few friends with great caution, never daring to give too much of himself. He was relieved to discover that his peers respected his wishes.

By the time graduation rolled around, Sulu was molded into a reliable young ensign whose record earned him a berth on the destroyer *Hua C'hing*, his first assignment as a Starfleet officer.

Sulu realized his good fortune when he learned his commanding officer was to be James T. Kirk, a man with an impressive past and a promising future. He would also be serving with the renowned engineer Montgomery Scott, whose textbooks Sulu had studied at the Academy; and Kirk's best friend, Gary Mitchell, would be executive officer and chief navigator, working the chair next to Sulu's helm.

Walt acquired a great deal of self-assurance under Kirk's tutelage, learning to approach his duties with confident aggressiveness. He was determined to be much more than the average helmsman, and at times found himself trying too hard. Kirk assessed the problem quickly, and perhaps drawing from personal experience, advised Sulu to relax, to take things as they came, one step at a time.

Kirk's patience and perceptiveness gained his ensign's respect, loyalty, and trust. With his help, Walt gradually settled into the bridge family, and his fears and apprehensions were finally laid to rest.

Sulu saw his second action with Kirk as the *Hua C'hing* engaged the Kzinti; and in the Arualian System, Sulu had his first taste of violent, all-out battle against the Klingons. As a result of this confrontation, Sulu received an Award of Valor and a commendation from his captain. Of the two, Walt was prouder of the commendation.

An even greater source of pride was his promotion to lieutenant, a rank well deserved, and, according to Kirk, long overdue.

Sulu was now secure with himself. He was finally able to think about Lynn without pain, and began to once again reach out to others and form friendships. He was fast becoming a seasoned space veteran, capable of making decisions and reaching conclusions based on experience as well as reasoning.

Displaying leadership tendencies, Walt was at times entrusted by Kirk with temporary command of the ship; and at these times, he gained much respect from his peers.

When Kirk was given command of the *Enterprise* after four years on the *Hua C'hing*, he opted to take along some of his crew: Mitchell, Scott, and Sulu. He also combed the fleet for the finest officers he could gather, including Lee Kelso, Uhura and—to the surprise and joy of Sulu—Kevin Riley. They were to join the Vulcan Spock, who had served under Chris Pike on the *Enterprise,* and had signed on for another tour.

To the *Enterprise,* Walter Sulu brought his loyalty to Starfleet and Captain Kirk, his high standards, his idealism, and his revived romanticism. His skill and courage would merit him many more awards, but most important, he would learn to love and care again, this time about his fellow *Enterprise* crewmembers. He would strive to live according to the concepts of *Bushido,* and always to conduct himself in a way that would honor the love and faith Lynn Mihara had given him.

As the starship *Enterprise* sailed off into its five-year mission, the long and promising career of the contemporary samurai was just beginning.

11.
A BRIEF LOOK AT SPOCK'S CAREER

by Leslie Thompson

After the wonderful fan reaction to Leslie's examination of Captain Kirk's career, we immediately asked her to do the same for Mr. Spock. Les demurred, saying that the character of Spock had been covered in such depth by previous fan writings that she had nothing she could add to the legend. We disagreed, and after much prompting, Les finally agreed to give it a whirl. We think she did an exceptional job ... and so will you.

Fascinating. That oft-used word is very descriptive of how millions of Star Trek fans find the character of Mr. Spock. Probably more has been written about Spock than any other Star Trek character; yet, in actuality, we know very little about him. What were the forces that shaped the uncertain half-breed youngster into the capable and confident Starfleet officer of today? With the few tantalizing hints dropped by the series, and a liberal dose of speculative fiction, this article will discuss in brief the actions and events that molded the character of our lovable Vulcan with the unpronounceable first name.

To fully grasp the elusive character of Spock, we have to go back in time to several years before his birth. The whens, hows, and whys of Sarek's marriage to the Earthwoman Amanda Grayson have been the focus of much discussion in fan circles. Theories given for the marriage range from an ages-old plan to integrate human and Vulcan civilizations to the benefit of the entire galaxy, all the way down to a simple statement of an incredulous Sarek asking, "You're what?!"

We do know that Sarek was assigned to the Vulcan Embassy on Terra when he and Amanda met. It is likely that Amanda, being a teacher by profession, was employed at the Vulcan Embassy to teach the children of Vulcan diplomats something about Earth culture and history. This would explain the constant contact she would have had to have with Sarek, as he would certainly not have socialized on Earth beyond the required diplomatic functions he had to attend.

A record of their first meeting would be fascinating to hear, but we can assume that Sarek was struck by Amanda's native intelligence much more than her beauty or charm. In any case, Amanda would have been the one to make the first approach, as a Vulcan would have considered anything more than normal courtesy between professionals to be an unforgivable breach of manners. Whatever tack Amanda took with Sarek, you can be sure he was shocked. And not for the last time.

Amanda had to be the aggressor in their relationship. She did the courting, so to speak. She had to fall in love with Sarek at first sight, as only a great love would have given her the patience and determination to win a Vulcan. It was probably this as much as anything else that finally caused Sarek to admit that marriage was, indeed, "the logical thing to do."

They were married, probably by the Vulcan ambassador, shortly before Sarek was due to return to Vulcan. The reception that Amanda received from Sarek's family was probably chilly, as all Vulcans are very tradition-bound, and Sarek's family, ruled by the imperious T'Pau, especially so. But Amanda proved herself by wholeheartedly embracing the Vulcan way of life, and we can be sure that she was eventually welcomed as a valued addition to Sarek's clan.

Amanda probably used some sort of birth control during her first few years on Vulcan. Even though she loved Sarek with all her heart (as he did her), it was always possible that things wouldn't work out after all. Raising a child alone would be hard enough, much more one who would be half Vulcan. And there was the very likely possibility that Sarek would not allow Amanda to take a child with her if she decided to leave.

The thought of a child, even if it occurred to Sarek during these busy years when his career was skyrocketing, was not as bothersome to Amanda's husband as it was to her. Both Vulcan and Earth doctors had advised them that conception between human and Vulcan was highly unlikely; but if it happened, it happened. Such was the natural way of things.

(We can speculate that Sarek and Amanda had a normal, healthy, and active sex life. *Pon farr* is not only a time of mating, but a release of inner tensions built up by the Vulcan suppression of emotion. It would be illogical that sex between Vulcans would be limited to this time; it is only during *pon farr* that Vulcans *must* mate or die.)

Eventually (perhaps after the intense sexual activity of their first *pon farr* together) Amanda became pregnant. Amanda would have felt the time had come, her life with Sarek had proved to be happy and secure; and Sarek was probably like any other father—surprised, happy, and proud.

The assumption that the child would be raised as a Vulcan was probably understood between Amanda and Sarek from the beginning. Proud Vulcan that he was, Sarek could not have had it any other way. Any reservations Amanda had on this point were erased when the child was born. His pointed ears and skin tone left little choice. He looked like a Vulcan, would always be treated as a Vulcan, so it was only logical that he should be raised as a Vulcan.

The child was christened (or the Vulcan equivalent) Spock, named after the most famous of Sarek's clan, Spock the Uniter, a disciple of Surak's who brought together the two great nations of Vulcan in the final act of the Reformation. Sarek felt the name appropriate, as his son was the first ever born of a union between human and Vulcan, and perhaps one day his son would help to unite Vulcan and Earth into one great nation.

We can see from Spock's naming that Sarek planned for his son to follow exactly in his footsteps. First, tenure at the Vulcan Academy of Sciences, then some diplomatic training, then back to the Academy, and finally, ambassador to another planet, perhaps even the Federation itself. Although we are never told Sarek's specialty, we can assume that it was the science of psychology, with special emphasis on alien psychology. No other discipline would be so useful to a diplomat, which was Sarek's family profession by tradition.

Spock began to come into his own as an individual at about the age of four. By this time he had learned the rudiments of logic, was able to read quite well, and had a basic grounding in mathematics. Sarek had taught his son logic and math, but it was Amanda who taught Spock to read, and with some very un-Vulcanlike materials indeed.

Books. Real books. And all from Earth. Spock devoured the textbooks which Amanda had brought with her to Vulcan; the histories, the volumes of stories and poetry, and the biographies of great men whose accomplishments made even those of some Vulcan heroes pale. By the time he was ten, Spock had a deep appreciation for the values of Earthmen, and a burning desire to visit the planet of his mother's birth. But that visit was still several years away.

Also by this time Spock had discovered his main field of interest. Science. His grasp of logical theorems surprised even Sarek, and his skill in mathematics was that of a lad twice his age. He was ever curious about what made things work, and on more than one occasion, Sarek had to punish him severely for taking apart one device or another before he knew how to put it back together again.

At the same time, young Spock kept up his interest in the humanities as well. He read and memorized both Earth and Vulcan poetry and song, and became quite accomplished on the "harp."

This did not disturb Sarek unduly, for he knew that his son would naturally seek to learn all he could about his Earthly heritage, and a liberal education in poetry and literature would only help Spock to grasp the finer points of psychology. It was not lost on Sarek that more could ofttimes be learned about a human through his writings than by an endless battery of psychological tests.

What *did* disturb Sarek was the fact that Spock showed little inclination to study the disciplines of his forefathers. Sarek did not understand that his son felt completely alienated from his world, and that an understanding of its people and service to them was the last thing that Spock wanted to achieve in his life.

This is understandable. Spock was always acutely aware of his status as a "half-Vulcan," and the taunts of his schoolmates didn't help matters any. Children being children, Spock was denied the one thing he needed most to feel accepted outside the confines of his own home: a friend. So we can see why Spock would feel little kinship for his fellow Vulcans, and couldn't care less about working with or for them.

Three factors conspired to change Spock's mind: the bonding with T'Pring, his first visit to Earth shortly thereafter, and his discovery of a "friend" upon his arrival back on Vulcan.

The ceremony which bound the youngsters Spock and T'Pring together was most impressive to Spock. It was not only the first time he had been given a glimpse into the majesty and mystery of his Vulcan heritage, it was the first time his latent mental powers manifested themselves to him. The ritual of bonding is so important to the Vulcan way of life that it is the time reserved for the unlocking of Vulcan youngsters' telepathic abilities. The awe of such newfound wonders helps to strengthen the bonding immensely, as the memory of the first person one mind-melds with stays forever strong. It is a feeling which can never again be shared, and is the primary reason why the couple is drawn together at the proper time.

To Spock, it was much more than just his first exhilarating taste of telepathy. For the first time, he had been able to see himself from another's viewpoint, and he found that he was not such a freakish fellow after all. And he was accepted. The ancient rituals and beliefs of which he had heard his father speak so often really were part of his life. By agreeing to the bonding, both the Elders of his and T'Pring's clan had acknowledged that Spock was a true son of Vulcan. The taunts of his schoolmates were forgotten as he listened to his father declare to all Vulcan that his son and the girl T'Pring were forever joined.

As a bit of a celebration of Spock's "engagement," Sarek agreed to allow Amanda and their son to journey to Earth. Spock greeted this news with great excitement, as he had longed to see Earth. He was also interested in meeting his mother's family and seeing if the many interesting—and, to him, almost unbelievable—things the books said about human behavior were true.

Starting the trip with high hopes, Spock returned very disappointed. His mother's family tried their best to make him comfortable and welcome, but he had suffered curiosity and ridicule too long to be unaware of their stares and whispered comments. The children, like those on Vulcan, made fun of him; and this time, a new element was added. For the first time, Spock was teased about his ears. It was almost too much for him to bear, and for the rest of the trip he could not enjoy any of the sights they visited for wondering if people were looking at his ears.

The trip was cut short, as even Amanda no longer felt comfortable around humans, and as their ship approached Vulcan, Spock was amazed to find himself thinking of the planet as "home." And this feeling was reaffirmed by the exceptionally warm welcome he and Amanda got from Sarek. Spock was amazed when his father openly admitted to having been lonesome and having missed both of them very much. It was probably the first time Spock realized that Sarek loved him.

But another important day was due in Spock's life. The time of the *Kahs-wan* was approaching.

Spock had previously felt somewhat afraid of the ordeal. And in his alienation with things Vulcan, he also felt it was somewhat foolish for him to have to take the test. But now, with his dreams of a better life on Earth shattered, and his newly gained acceptance into Vulcan society, Spock looked forward to the test. It would prove once and for all—to others, as well as himself—that he was as much of a Vulcan as any of them.

As he sat with his pet *sehlat*, Spock pondered his probable success. I-chaya had always been Spock's sounding board, listening patiently to the youngster's long and involved soliloquies, offering a friendly nudge whenever emotion threatened to overcome the sad and confused boy. Having no friends, Spock was forced to share his thoughts with himself, through the medium of his pet.

The one doubt that Spock had about the *Kahs-wan* was his father's lack of faith in him. Sarek had as much as told him that he expected him to fail; that to do so was no disgrace. Spock doubted that other Vulcan fathers told their sons that; and he determined to make a "trial run" to convince himself that Sarek was wrong.

The events of that first attempt are well known, and it was at this time that Spock found a true friend. Little did he suspect that the friend (who represented himself as a distant cousin) was himself; but that really didn't matter. For the first time, someone had given him respect as an equal, and that respect helped young Spock to make the most difficult decision of his life: to agree to let the healer put his pet out of its misery, enabling the *sehlat* to die with dignity.

It was Spock's coming of age. The newfound confidence he possessed upon his return was immediately evident to his parents; and, to a lesser degree, to his classmates. Sarek was quietly proud, Amanda wept quietly in her room at the loss of her baby, and Spock's schoolmates ceased their teasing and began to treat him as an equal for the first time. He soon won many friends, and the bitterness he felt toward his Vulcan contemporaries faded and was forgotten.

Not forgotten, however, was his great love of science. Day by day, he found Sarek's instruction in psychology and diplomacy more boring and irritating. He began to feel trapped by the ironclad rules of Vulcan tradition that would force him to take up his father's career. Spock wanted to explore, to learn, to expand the boundaries of his life far beyond the confines of tradition.

Even though he now felt comfortable with his life on Vulcan, it occurred to Spock that he could never escape his father's shadow and become his own man if he remained on Vulcan. Sarek was too strong-willed, too imperious. Spock's human half drove him toward strong individualism, coupled with an inner need to find his own place in life, one that would not only allow him serenity with his dual nature, but would also allow the best of both heritages to come to the fore.

The answer was not too difficult for Spock to find. Starfleet. The first of the great Constitution Class starships were just proving themselves with success in mission after mission, and the limits of space exploration were expanding. To Spock, this opportunity for exploration and adventure was irresistible. And on the logical side of the question, the new horizons opened by the space-warp drive would present a limitless number of new scientific challenges. And in Starfleet, each individual was judged on his own merit. Considerations of family or tradition did not apply. Everyone started equal—only the very best rose to the top. Here Spock could carve his own niche; one which reflected his own desires, needs, and capabilities.

It only remained to tell his father.

Sarek, of course, knew that Spock had little interest in the traditional family vocation. And in a slightly amused parental way, he allowed Spock to spend more study time at the hard sciences than psychology and diplomacy. It was only natural that the boy be somewhat restless. Sarek himself had once dreamed of becoming the greatest of all Vulcan computer experts, but as he grew older, he realized that his father had been correct in directing him to the traditional ways. He was excellent at his work, happy and contented with his accomplishments. His love of computers was now only a hobby, which allowed him to relax and occasionally augment his primary works. He had even gone so far as to explain this to Spock when he gave the boy his first instruction in computers at the age of six.

So Sarek had no idea that his son was seriously planning to enter Starfleet when his instruction at the Vulcan Academy of Diplomatic Sciences was finished. Spock, not yet feeling up to challenging his father, had agreed to spend two years at the Academy. He reasoned that the instruction would help him in the long run, as Starfleet officers had to deal constantly with all sorts of psychological problems, and his degree would help him gain admittance to Starfleet Academy.

Sarek was quite proud when Spock graduated with highest honors, and at an even younger age than he himself had. Spock was assured of a bright future in the Vulcan diplomatic corps; even now, his ability was coming to the notice of Sarek's superiors. Plans were already being made for Spock to be groomed to be the next ambassador to Terra—pleasing Sarek no end, for this was not only a coveted position, but one which Sarek himself had held with distinction and remembered fondly as the place where he met and married his dear wife. It was only the first step in the grand plan to unite Vulcan and Terra, utilizing the talents of the only existing Vulcan/human being.

This, then, was what caused Sarek to be so outraged when Spock calmly announced that he had been accepted into Starfleet Academy, and that he was planning to build himself a career as a Starfleet officer.

Sarek would not—could not—explain to Spock why it was so vital that he follow tradition, as it was necessary that Spock willingly cooperate to be effective in his duties. Sarek simply demanded in a quiet voice that Spock withdraw his Starfleet application and attend the Academy of Sciences as had been planned. Spock just as quietly refused. Finally, Sarek rose from behind his desk. "You will leave tomorrow. Please see that your mother does not unduly distress herself at your departure." Then he strode from the room. Those were the last words he spoke to Spock for eighteen years.

Amanda, however, was not Vulcan, and she spoke quite a bit. She cajoled first Spock, pleading with him to change his mind, then Sarek, using every bit of logic she could muster to get him to at least give Spock his blessing. Neither would give in, and she really hadn't expected them to. But she, as any woman would, could not let her family break up without a battle.

The next morning, however, it was she alone who bid Spock goodbye as he entered the shuttle on the first leg of his voyage to Earth and the Starfleet Academy. And because she was the mother of one Vulcan and the wife of another, she did not cry until she got back to the privacy of her room.

Spock was the only Vulcan in his freshman class at Starfleet. Most of his fellow students were human, as many of the races newly aligned with the quickly expanding Federation had not yet given the UFP the full support they would in later years. An Andorian and a Tellerite entered the Academy with Spock's class; neither lasted through the first year.

That was no reflection on them, however, as less than twenty percent of the class that entered the Academy was present at graduation four years later. Starfleet Academy was perhaps the toughest school in the galaxy, and even Spock, with his years of vigorous Vulcan education, was hard pressed to keep up.

Spock excelled at the sciences, of course, and also got very good marks in administration and tactics. His worst subject, surprisingly, was physical training. Long years of training in the Vulcan way of nonaggression made Spock clumsy and unwilling in unarmed combat and weaponry. It was only his native great strength and coordination that earned him good marks in these classes.

Spock's social life during his time at the Academy was very limited. Still uncomfortable in the company of humans, he spent most of his time in his rooms, in study and meditation. He was fortunate in having as a roommate a taciturn young Greek named Stavros who was more than willing to put up with Spock's grimness in exchange for tutoring in science. Although they never really became friends, Stavros would defend Spock whenever insults or criticism popped up, and Spock realized and appreciated the fact. Several years later, he was surprised to find that he felt a deep sorrow when he heard that Stavros had been killed on Bellerophon II. That realization led to the third—and most disastrous—major decision of his life.

But the second major decision was yet to be made. Spock

stood near the head of his class as graduation neared, and he had been requested by several of his teachers to stand for Command.

It was a difficult decision for Spock. He knew even then that he had no desire to command others; it was not one of the needs within him. Too, he had spent almost his entire life in one kind of schooling or another, and the prospect of two more years in Command School dismayed him. He yearned to be posted aboard a ship, and see some action.

But one thing swayed him. He had caused a seemingly irreparable breach with his father in choosing to join Starfleet. And that action would be unjustified if he did not take every opportunity to make the most of his Starfleet career. Spock felt he would be cheating himself if he did not stand for Command; it would be a waste of his potential, and an indication that he truly did not want to build his own life, but only to escape his father's. So Spock resigned himself to two more years of study, and put in his application for Command. It was immediately granted.

By the time the two years were almost up, Spock was glad that he had chosen Command. He had found within himself the ability to utilize both his Vulcan logic and his own daring and intelligence in simulated combat. He also discovered that the power of command, while not intoxicating and necessary to him as it was to some of his human classmates, did force him to reach ever deeper within himself, and the resources he found there were gratifying. One of Spock's deepest, most secret fears was that his determination and will were not as strong as his father's. But by the time he had completed Command training, he knew that he would always be equal to any task he was called upon to perform.

After graduating from Command School, Spock took time off for a brief visit with his mother at her family's home on Terra. She told him that although Sarek was still adamant about not speaking to Spock, he was following his son's progress in Starfleet with interest. Amanda once again begged Spock to reconsider. Wasn't the fact that he had worked his way through six years of Starfleet training and graduated with highest honors enough? Wasn't he now willing to return to Vulcan with the knowledge that he could make a career elsewhere if he so chose?

Spock was saddened at his mother's words. He had always known that his leaving and the dissension it caused between

A BRIEF LOOK AT SPOCK'S CAREER   127

his father and himself had made his mother unhappy; but he had not suspected it was to this degree. He could hardly bear to tell her that he had already signed aboard his first deep-space mission.

She took the news rather well. She had not expected Spock to come home, but, once again, she had to try. She did, however, get Spock to agree to write to her more often. And as she told him goodbye, she vowed to herself that she would "accidentally" leave his letters where Sarek could find them.

Upon arriving at his new ship, the destroyer *Fomalhaut*, Spock was pleased to discover that his captain was Christopher Pike, a lecturer at the Academy with whom Spock had been most impressed. Pike was an advocate of the "wait-and-see" policy of command, and displayed what Spock thought was an effective use of logic and unemotionalism in command decisions. Spock knew that he could learn much from Pike.

Spock, as a green ensign, was assigned as assistant navigator, the traditional first assignment for Command School graduates.

The science of celestial navigation was constantly changing in those days, as the far-reaching ships of the Federation found new space warps and other means of access to farther distances across the galaxy. It was an exciting time to be in Starfleet, and Spock made the most of it. He performed his duties excellently, and eventually was rewarded with a promotion to lieutenant. He was also allowed to second the ship's science officer.

When a sneak Klingon attack decimated the bridge of the *Fomalhaut*, killing both the science officer and the chief navigator, Spock took over both duties. With Pike at the helm, the two officers managed to overtake the Klingon ship and destroy it, only to find that it had been an advance ship for a large fleet which was on its way to attack the new Federation outpost on Berengaria VII.

In a series of masterful maneuvers designed by Pike and Spock, they managed to get the crippled ship to an area where the Klingons could not jam their subspace radio. Once the outpost had been warned, the Klingons realized they had lost the element of surprise and retreated back to their own territory.

It was on Berengaria VII, while on R&R during repairs to the *Fomalhaut*, that Spock received some good news. He had been awarded a commendation from Starfleet for his actions in the Klingon battle, he was being promoted to first lieutenant, and he was to be reposted to a new ship—the USS *Enterprise*, command of which had just been given to Chris Pike.

A further surprise awaited Spock when he reported aboard the *Enterprise*: He was now chief science officer. Spock was well pleased with the assignment, as it would allow him the time and freedom to pursue his research while still serving in space. And for an officer with only three years of deep-space experience, it was a very prestigious posting.

Pike admitted to Spock privately that he had wanted the Vulcan to be his executive officer, but Starfleet had overruled him. Spock was still considered too inexperienced to be second-in-command of a starship; and although Starfleet Command had agreed with Pike that Spock would be an excellent science officer, they had insisted that he get a more seasoned officer as number one. Pike was rather surprised when Spock agreed with Starfleet. He had heard the Vulcan say many times that he had no desire to command; but, like all ambitious and aggressive officers, he did not really believe it.

The new executive officer proved to be the only holdover from the previous *Enterprise* crew under Captain Robert April. She was a tall, sternly lovely woman of great intellect from a planet where names were a very personal and secret thing. To avoid causing her discomfort, Pike took April's advice and had the crew call her by her rank. But in a bit of sly whimsy, Pike gave her the designation "Number One."

Pike, remembering his tenure as exec and the restlessness he felt, gave Number One the double duty of helm. His reasoning was that the more involved an exec was with the operations of a ship, the more efficient that exec was; and also, it would set an immediate example that everyone aboard his ship would work—and work hard.

Spock admired the cool, emotionless demeanor of Number One. She was one of the few humans aboard who did not feel uncomfortable around the Vulcan, and they worked very well together. She also had a distressing tendency to beat him at chess.

It was at about this time that Spock made his third major life decision—the one that proved so disastrous.

Seeing that Number One was able to live with emotions, control them, and still perform her duties excellently, Spock

A BRIEF LOOK AT SPOCK'S CAREER

decided to try to be a bit more "human." He had always had feelings, of course, but the stern disapproval of Sarek every time he had displayed them had trained him to keep them in rigid check. Now, Spock felt, that he had made a place for himself, it was time to shake off the last vestiges of Sarek—he would allow his human half to surface and see if it would bring him greater happiness.

It worked—for a while. Then the *Enterprise* became involved in the startling events on Talos IV. After the encounter with the Talosians was over, Spock took stock of himself. He had contributed little to the rescue of Captain Pike, and at times was at a loss to know what to do. Spock concluded that he could live with his emotions in normal times, with normal duties; but when an emergency struck, he found that he was too filled with concern for his fellow crewmembers to perform his duties efficiently. It did not occur to Spock that this was simply a sign of his emotional immaturity, and something he would "outgrow" in time. To him, it was a serious failure in his duty, and he would not countenance it again. After leaving Talos IV, Spock reverted to his old self—at least on the surface.

Several more years passed. Spock grew ever more content with his place aboard the *Enterprise*. Perhaps, he thought, as the ship neared the end of its first five-year mission, he was too content. Science officer was a responsible position, but for one who did not actively pursue command, it was a dead end.

So when Number One announced that she was leaving Starfleet (no doubt angered over her failure to achieve command), Spock was invited by Pike to take over her position. The ship was due for a refitting, and everyone was given six months leave, so Pike gave Spock this time to decide.

Another visit with Amanda followed. Sarek was at this time ambassador to the Anaxar Peace Missions, so it was an easy jaunt for Amanda over to Starbase Eleven to visit her son. This time, Amanda did not ask Spock to come home. Instead, she told him of the pride that his family felt in his achievements—including Sarek. She knew that this, more than anything, would eventually bring her son back to Vulcan. Once he was satisfied that he had proved himself beyond a doubt, he would accede to Sarek's wishes, and all would be well.

Amanda did not come to Starbase Eleven alone. She was

accompanied by T'Pring, whose father was also on the peace mission. This was Sarek's wish, as it was long past time for Spock and T'Pring to make plans for their eventual marriage.

It was a miserable time for poor Spock. He and T'Pring had not been close even as children, and now he was required to be almost constantly with a person he hardly knew. It did not help matters that she announced to one and all that she was his betrothed—usually in a quite loud voice to any unfortunate female who happened to be speaking to Spock, for whatever reason.

Too, Spock found a coldness and ruthlessness in T'Pring that was rather frightening to him. She constantly questioned him about Starfleet, and made it quite plain that she felt Spock should actively seek a command. Her entire universe revolved around what was best or most advantageous for T'Pring, and Spock was very relieved when she finally left. Her parting words to him were—naturally—a request that he seek higher rank, command, and honors. It had been some time since Spock had smiled, but he gave a grin of relief as she sped away.

It was that grin that led him into his first "love affair." As he turned from the spaceport to go back to his quarters—and some well-deserved peace and quiet—he was accosted by a beautiful young woman who smiled at him. "I thought," she said quizzically, "that Vulcans never smiled."

Having by this time become used to the strange ways of humans, Spock merely gave her a nod and continued on his way. But she was not to be denied, and followed him. Taking his arm for all the world as if they were lovers, she ignored his glare of protest and chatted gaily as they walked along. Extricating himself as soon as possible, Spock fled into a shuttle, and this time gave a gasp, not a smile, of relief. Glancing back, he saw her happily waving goodbye.

Spock reported the next day to the starbase computer central, where he planned to spend his remaining leave in learning the latest developments in computer technology. Assigned an office by the overjoyed administrator—who felt he could learn as much from Spock as Spock could from him—Spock discovered that he had his own secretary. And that secretary, one Leila Kalomi, was the same girl who had teased him the day before at the spaceport.

Leila was naturally embarrassed, and made profuse apologies. Spock told her to forget the incident, that he already had. In this he lied, and he found that it was not to be the first time he would be forced to lie to this sensitive young woman.

As the weeks passed, Spock realized that Leila was falling in love with him. He did not encourage it, but neither did he take the obvious solution and have her transferred to another office. He gave himself many logical reasons for not doing so—it would damage her career; it would lend credence to the rumors already spreading about them and embarrass her; it would hurt the progress of his work.

That he cared for Leila never occurred to him. Or if it did, he never admitted it to himself. The only people who realized he was falling in love with his beautiful assistant were Leila herself, and his mother, who read much into the glowing descriptions of his assistant which Spock included in his letters. Spock considered the things he told Amanda about Leila to be quite dispassionate and proper, but he failed to take into account that his mother was not only a human, but a woman as well. Sarek, of course, never noticed a thing. And reading Spock's letters on the sly (as Amanda knew he had been doing for years), he could not discuss with his wife the fact that Spock's young assistant reminded him strongly of someone he knew, though he couldn't quite recall who.

As the time approached for Spock to decide whether or not to accept Pike's invitation to become second-in-command, Leila forced him into a showdown. She told him outright that she loved him, and demanded to know if he loved her in return. Naturally, Spock was rattled at this blatant declaration and found refuge in his Vulcan shell. He told her he did not, and could not, love her and that it would be hopeless for her to think things would ever change. When she began to cry, Spock left. He went immediately to Pike and told him he would accept the offer. Spock committed himself to five more years aboard the *Enterprise,* hoping that in that time, Leila would forget him. And that he could forget her.

Time passed quickly. The ship saw much action, the most important of which was the discovery of a rich vein of dilithium crystals on Rigel XII, and the first test of Spock's new method of mining via sonic disintegration. The method was successful, allowing an increase of more than thirty percent in crystal recovery. For this development, Spock was awarded the Vulcan Scientific Legion of Honor. It also almost cost him his life when a mine shaft caved in. It was only due to the quick efforts of Chris Pike in pulling Spock from the debris that the Vulcan was saved, and it was a debt that Spock made a vow to repay.

The mission was cut short when Pike was named fleet captain, and the *Enterprise* was recalled to Earth. Pike wanted Spock to go along with him as his deputy, but this time Spock had little difficulty in saying no. He was happy in deep space, happy in his duties, and mostly happy that the new captain of the *Enterprise* would be bringing along a new executive officer, so that Spock could return to his post as science officer and his beloved research.

But Spock was a bit worried. He had heard of this new captain, James T. Kirk. Kirk had risen meteorically in Starfleet, and it was rumored that he was brash and cocky. Having served over eleven years on the *Enterprise* with Pike, Spock was used to Pike's cool and cautious way of command. He did not know if he could work with a captain who based all of his decisions strictly on emotion. So it was just as well that Kirk would be bringing Commander Gary Mitchell on as exec.

Spock, however, was in for a surprise. In a few short weeks, Kirk amply demonstrated that he was a superb commander. In a confrontation with Orion pirates, Kirk used one of the neatest bits of logical deception that Spock had ever seen to lead the pirates into a trap and force them to surrender without a shot being fired on either side. Spock relaxed. Kirk's rise to the top hadn't been an accident—he knew what he was doing.

Spock was also pleased to find that Kirk was an avid chess player, although his style was often irritatingly unorthodox. And it was not lost on Spock that Kirk used the time between moves to question him on every aspect of his life—both private and professional. Spock realized with a start that several of the crewmembers had also been playing chess with Kirk, and answering his questions. And some of these had been quietly, but quickly, transferred out. Again, Spock's estimation of Kirk rose.

He politely rebuffed the captain's overtures of friendship, however. Kirk made no mention of it, except to refrain from asking as many personal questions after he was satisfied that he could work with Spock. Spock appreciated the gesture very much and did not forget it.

During the events that occurred after the *Enterprise* had

attempted to cross the barrier at the edge of the galaxy, and Kirk was forced into killing the man who had been his best friend, Spock made a small gesture of friendship to Kirk when he called him "Jim."

It meant a lot. To both of them. Never before had Spock called his superiors by their given names, and Kirk knew that it was a major concession from a Vulcan. For Kirk, it was a hand to help him through his loss, and he accepted it gratefully.

After Gary Mitchell's death, Kirk was without an exec, and offered the job back to Spock. Spock accepted without reservation, as he knew Kirk needed him—especially since the failure of the mission was not being taken too well in some areas of Starfleet Command. Kirk got an unofficial reprimand for not having acted against Mitchell sooner, and many of the crewmembers were transferred. It was in this shakeup that Dr. Piper was assigned to a starbase, and a new chief surgeon was assigned—Dr. Leonard McCoy.

Kirk and McCoy had met before, and soon became fast friends. McCoy, being the superb psychologist, soon discerned the growing relationship between Kirk and Spock, and assigned himself the role of gadfly. He would serve as Kirk's brake, keeping him from being too rash. And he would serve as Spock's prod, forcing him to look at the emotional side of a question. It was a role he enjoyed, and he relished playing it.

So the three became the heart of the Starship *Enterprise*. And Spock, at last, was content.

12.

STAR TREK: THE MOTION PICTURE—A REVIEW

by Walter Irwin

As the most important event to occur in the Star Trek saga since the premiere of the series fourteen years ago, the Star Trek movie was eagerly awaited by both fans and the general public alike. But the question in everyone's mind was: Would the picture succeed? In the following review, editor Walter Irwin explains the reasons why Star Trek: The Motion Picture *did succeed, and how it succeeded on more than one level.*

Star Trek: The Motion Picture must be considered by all Star Trek fans to be the ultimate expression of Gene Roddenberry's philosophy. In the reputedly $40 million effort, Roddenberry finally had the time, the money, and the means to give full rein to Star Trek. He has succeeded admirably. *STTMP* is an enthralling two hours.

But as Star Trek *fans*, we must look beyond the philosophy of this one effort. We must view the movie as "episode eighty," placing it within the context of aired Star Trek, and judging it by that criterion.

The most important facet of the movie to fans is, of course, the characters and how they are handled in the film. If the movie had failed on this one point, nothing else would have mattered to us. Fortunately, all of the characterizations are superb.

The intervening time frame which the movie sets up is reputedly two and a half years from the time of the final aired episode to the appearance of V'Ger. Although this allows for better continuity in characterizations (as less had to be explained about the actions and career advances of the crew), it makes for a somewhat strange feeling when we *know* these people are ten years older—and in some cases, we can tell.

But this is a minor point, and one which has been discussed over and over since the film was first planned. In actual fact, it has little or no effect on the story itself.

However, the characterizations in the film are based on the two-and-a-half-year hiatus. As this affects only the three major roles to any depth, it is on the characters of Kirk, Spock, and McCoy that the success of the film turns.

Most important to *STTMP* was Kirk. This reviewer feels he can say without rebuttal that *STTMP* is a "Kirk" movie. At each juncture, the focus is on Kirk: his decision to retake command of the *Enterprise;* his confrontations with Decker, and later, McCoy; his determination to find the secret of V'Ger; and, lastly, his decision to take the *Enterprise* "Out there . . . thataway."

The role was very well written. Kirk is a man torn between his desire for power and glory and the responsibility to his ship. We have seen this facet of his personality before, but never in such a graphic illustration. In the early part of the film, Kirk is almost cold and arrogant in his efforts to usurp command from Decker. It is only after his unfamiliarity with the ship redesign, and the following spat with McCoy, that Kirk begins to loosen up, and show flashes of the captain that we know so well.

Much of the credit for the believability of the "new" Kirk must go to William Shatner. Gone are the familiar (but somewhat tiresome) "Kirkisms" that often cropped up in aired episodes. Shatner brings a certain amount of dignity to the role which had escaped him in the past, as well as a very definite tension that said much more than the words he was given to say.

Leonard Nimoy also performed well as Spock, but unfortunately, his was the lesser part. Unlike Kirk, we learn nothing new about Spock in *STTMP*, and it seems as if Spock learns nothing new as well. Many fans have exulted over the scene in which Spock "accepts" emotionalism as necessary to life; but if this was such a startling revelation to Spock, then why didn't it seem to affect him more in the final scenes of the film?

One feels that this is more a failure of the script than of

Nimoy, however. In the earlier scenes, Nimoy is unbelievably good. The entire bearing of his Spock differs from anything we have ever seen before. Even his voice is deeper and colder. The effect is somewhat chilling, and for a while we almost come to hate Spock.

One can only hope that in the sequel, Spock will be given more to do. There are as yet myriad depths to the character, and it would be exciting to see him faced with such a life and career crisis as was Kirk in this film.

McCoy was also given little to do, but such are the acting skills of DeForest Kelley that he absolutely "stole" every scene in which he was featured.

From the time he appeared grumbling from the transporter to the final confrontation with V'Ger, Kelley was always comfortable and believable. Like an old friend, he often brought calm and sanity to the proceedings. If only they had let him keep the beard!

As they played such pivotal roles in the film, the characters of Decker and Ilia must be discussed. Both were, of necessity, somewhat two-dimensional, and we were often left guessing about the past association that bound them so strongly together. Surely it would not have strained the budget too much to present a quick and simple flashback to their romance—or at least their parting. So much would have been gained, both for the film and the characters. But we take what we are given.

Decker did not impress this reviewer overly much. He seemed a bit too young to attain the captaincy of a starship, as well as seeming not nearly forceful enough for the post. It is hard to believe that he could have made some of the difficult decisions and run some of the daring bluffs that Kirk has performed. His decision to merge with V'Ger seems more of a cop-out to responsibility than an overriding desire to explore the unknown.

It is interesting to observe that no one aboard the *Enterprise*, including the crew which he had worked with for over two years, was overly distressed by his "demise."

Ilia was also a disappointment. The much-heralded sexuality of the character simply didn't come across, even though quite a bit of dialogue was directed toward it. Perhaps some of those powerful "sexual pheromones" should have been wafted across the theater whenever she was onscreen.

It is perhaps unfair to discuss a character when that character is killed off early in the film and replaced with an android double. This was indeed an unfortunate plot device, as we immediately lost all real interest in Ilia, and lost even more sympathy for Decker.

His clumsy attempts to "find" the "real" Ilia within the V'Ger construct did little to impress us with the tragedy of a man being forced to work with the exact double of his lost love. Had Ilia simply been taken over by V'Ger in some way, it would have provided much more suspense and drama for the film. We would have then applauded Decker's efforts to bring her true personality out, rooted for Ilia to conquer V'Ger's influence over her, and had a literal life-or-death problem to lead to the climax of the film.

The supporting characters were all very good. Of them all, only Scotty and Chekov were featured for more than a few lines, and this will also be something to correct in the future.

So much for characterizations. In this aspect, the film did not fail us. No, we did not get as much as we wanted, but by no conceiveable means could Roddenberry and crew have matched the development that fans have created for the *Enterprise* crew over the past ten years. But neither were there any major changes. For that we can be thankful.

The second aspect on which the success of *STTMP* hinged was the special effects. Not only did we fans expect the extraordinary, so did the average moviegoer. Viewers fully expected to be "knocked out of their seats." Luckily, the special effects in the movie were ample in number and impact for even the most jaded or casual man-on-the-street; and for those of us who know the time, effort, and expense involved in such work, they were simply amazing. (This is especially true when one considers the fact that the effects teams were working under an agonizingly tight deadline.)

Most impressive of the effects were those involving the *Enterprise* in "drydock." The long, lingering look taken by Kirk and Scotty at their ship was more than deserved. It is perhaps the finest model miniature ever constructed for films. The matching on these shots was masterful. At no time could one find any "blue line" or discrepancy of relative sizes; nor were there any "cheats" used, such as reversing angles or shooting from one side of the ship only. And did you notice the worker turning a backflip as the *Enterprise* pulled away? Wonderful!

The Klingon ships were also exciting, shot as they were in

constant movement and from a variety of angles. But it was the method of their destruction that was really impressive. The gradual disintegration of the Klingon ships by V'Ger's beam was terrifying, and one of the most enthralling special effects this reviewer has ever seen.

The interiors of the Klingon ships were also very good, though seen all too briefly. The use of subtitles as the Klingons spoke was a nice touch, harkening back to those great documentary-style war films of the past.

The *Enterprise* interiors were also well done, with three exceptions: The corridors seemed too sterile and cold for deep-space comfort (one would expect a variety of color, murals, pictures, etc.); the recreation hall (as it was seen in the scenes with Decker and Ilia) did not seem to be the intimate, cozy area it was in the series; and the bridge lighting was much too dim.

But the successes far outnumbered the lacks. The functional-looking transporter chamber, the spacious and plush captain's quarters (the kind we always *knew* Jim Kirk deserved!), the vastness of the cargo bays, and, of course, mind-boggling Engineering! All totally realistic. All superbly designed, constructed, and utilized.

As beautiful and as impressive as was V'Ger itself at first glance, it is sad to say that here the effects work failed. At no time could we get a comparative feeling of the vastness of the Intruder; nor at any time did we see any part of V'Ger which could have served as a red herring to lead us to believe that an alien crew could have been aboard. This severely hampered the suspense of the film, as it was evident from the very beginning that V'Ger was a machine of some sort.

If we could have seen a recognizable ship of immense size, or at least an interior "command area," we would have had a much more exciting comparison of the relative sizes of the *Enterprise* and V'Ger; and the time spent with *Enterprise* flybys across the V'Ger surface would have been of stronger advantage to the film. As it stands, the effects are repetitive and confusing, and much of this time could better have been spent developing story and characters.

Thus, we come to the story—the third, and final, component of *Star Trek: The Motion Picture*. Did the story work? Was it deserving of the long wait? Was it a "Star Trek story"?

The answer to all of these questions is yes. The story

STAR TREK: THE MOTION PICTURE—A REVIEW 139

worked very, very well. It was of sufficient magnitude to warrant feature-film length, as well as the amount of time and money spent. And yes, yes, yes . . . it was a Star Trek story. Everything in it reaffirmed the elements that made Star Trek such a success and an enduring legend.

The story itself is a relatively simple one. An immense, unbelievably powerful object of unknown origin and purpose enters our galaxy. It destroys several Klingon ships and a Federation outpost. Nothing seems to be able to stop it, and it is heading directly for Earth. Only the starship *Enterprise*, currently under the command of Willard Decker, is in a position to intercept the Intruder before it can reach Earth. However, the *Enterprise* is not yet quite ready for action, and in steps her former commander, Admiral James T. Kirk. Kirk assumes command from Decker, and rushes the ship into space. The resultant problems this causes (bitterness from Decker, trouble with the ship, the necessity for gathering together the "old crew") are many, but Kirk finally manages to intercept and confront the Intruder, which proves to be an incredibly advanced machine, based on an early Earth space probe.

Nothing terribly startling or original about that. The theme of the wise old commander, still hungry for battle, glory, and responsibility, taking over from the younger replacement is an old one. So is the "man vs. machine" plot ("The Changeling," for instance), the "immensely powerful threat to Earth" plot, the "malfunctioning equipment" plot, and many other elements of the film.

But try to think of a *new* plot, people. Just try.

What *was* original or startling about the plot of *STTMP*, then? Simply the way the Star Trek characters, people we know and love, reacted to the plot elements. Any experienced writer will quickly tell you that there are no new stories, only new characters reacting to old stories in new ways. And in this area, *STTMP* was a success.

It was a question of *verisimilitude*. Not whether we could believe that V'Ger was threatening twenty-third-century Earth, but whether we could believe that Kirk, Spock, McCoy, and all the rest were *reacting* to a threat by V'Ger.

That is the story of *Star Trek: The Motion Picture*. Not the attack of V'Ger, but the crew of the USS *Enterprise*. Any plot device, any reason would have served to get the *Enterprise* back into action again as long as viewers of the film *be-*

lieved that it was necessary for them to do so. And once having done so, they must needs perform as our unavoidably preconceived ideas say they must. This the *Enterprise* crew did, and in so doing, made the rest of the story believable and exciting as well.

No amount of window-dressing could have saved the plot of *STTMP* if the characters we know so well had not come alive once again for us. This was the success of the story, in that it recaptured the spirit and reality of the ship and crew and gave us new insight into the Star Trek universe.

Yes, in some individual instances, it failed to offer enough, and much went unexplained, forgotten, or ignored. But we were able to see advances in all areas, and this was enough.

Magnitude. Current definition in film parlance means bigger and better. And *STTMP* did quite well in those areas. Mind-blowing special effects and sets, superior production, excellent performances.

But some have carped that the basic story of *STTMP* was nothing to crow about, that it was simply a rehash of several television episodes and other films, and not the overwhelming blockbuster they expected it to be.

The tale of V'Ger was not meant to be overwhelming in scope. Neither was it meant to be much different from themes already presented on the Star Trek series itself, or in other areas of science fiction films or literature. *Star Trek: The Motion Picture* was a reaffirmation of the principles of Star Trek: individualism, harmony between races, the necessity of exploring and understanding space, and the overriding need for man to control his technology, not to be controlled by it.

This is not only the message of Star Trek, but the heart and soul of Star Trek. And as much as Gene Roddenberry may have wanted to present the Federation-Klingon War, or the return of the Tribbles, he *had* to take the opportunity of this feature film to restate his principles. It would have been impossible for him to have done less, and shameful for us to have expected or accepted less. If there is anything "familiar" about *STTMP*, it is mainly in ourselves we find it, not in the story.

So it was a "Star Trek story" after all. How could it be less?

Overall, *STTMP* must be seen as a rousing success. And current box-office figures back up that opinion. A sequel is sure to be in the works soon—one report to this reviewer has filming set to start in June 1980. A rumor, to be sure, but an encouraging one. And it is good to finally hear an encouraging rumor after all of the months of *dis*couraging ones before *STTMP* was released!

We think it only fair to note at this point that even if Paramount does not make money with *STTMP*, a sequel is almost a certainty, as it could be filmed much more cheaply, and make almost as much money, thereby showing an overall profit against the cost of *both* films.

It would be agreeable to end this review at this point with a ringing declaration of the success of the film, but the one major flaw of *Star Trek: The Motion Picture* must be pointed out: Too many changes were made in the *Enterprise* simply for the sake of making changes.

One would expect the matter of the uniforms to crop up here, but that is not the case. The new uniforms, as much as they were despised and ridiculed by fans before the release of the film, proved to be eye-pleasing as well as functional. After a few moments, it seemed as if they had been around forever.

The point of dissension is that in making the film, the producers seemed to feel as if they had to change everything about the *Enterprise,* if only slightly. This was a major mistake, as it left almost nothing for the viewer to relate to the series, and kept one constantly on the edge of the seat squirming in unfamiliarity.

A good example of this is the transporter effect. It was established on the series that the transporter was an efficient piece of machinery that could operate only under stated conditions and in a stated manner. Yet, in the film, the "beaming" effect was radically different, in look and sound, with no explanation and no justification.

Surely, if this change was made, it was for a reason, but the transporter on the new *Enterprise* operated no more quickly and even less efficiently than the one on the series. It would have been good to see the familiar shimmer and hear the beloved whine once again, but we could have foregone the pleasure if crewmembers would have appeared in the wink of an eye or some other such visible improvement.

In short, the overall changes may have made for a somewhat more realistic-looking *Enterprise,* but left the viewer feeling that he was on the outside looking in.

The effect was like returning home after a long absence, only to find that someone has completely rebuilt your house.

But this feeling, while a shock and a distraction at first, is quickly dispelled by the overall success of the movie's elements. The *Enterprise* may be a "rebuilt house," but the same old warm and loving family is still living there, and we are most certainly welcomed home.

Perhaps this is one of the major reasons why *Star Trek: The Motion Picture* gets better with each subsequent viewing. (Yes, normally a review is no place to discuss seeing a film more than once, but as Star Trek fans will definitely see the movie several times, it is right and proper in this case.) This is the utmost rarity in film. Many movies stay just as enjoyable when seen again, but very, very few improve. *STTMP* definitely improves, and to an astonishing degree each time.

Why this should be so is a mystery. Perhaps it has something to do with the viewer's being able to overlook the anxiety of waiting for each character to be introduced and the unfamiliarity of the surroundings at a second viewing, and being able to concentrate instead on the characterizations and subtleties in the movie.

In any case, *STTMP* is an eminently watchable movie; no matter if it be for the first or the fourth or the fortieth time.

And that, my friends, is the measure of success for a film. Not in profits, or box-office records, or awards, but in the place a movie holds in the hearts of viewers. *Casablanca, Gone with the Wind, Mary Poppins, Star Wars,* and too, too few others hold that special place in moviegoers' hearts, where a movie can be watched again and again, and be found more exciting and more enjoyable each time. It is thrilling to know that *Star Trek: The Motion Picture* will now be joining that select list.

13.

THE PSYCHOLOGY OF CAPTAIN KIRK'S POPULARITY

by Gloria-Ann Rovelstad

One of the most popular articles we have ever published was Gloria-Ann's "The Psychology of Mr. Spock's Popularity," and it was collected in The Best of Trek (#1). *Upon our request, Gloria-Ann quickly followed up with this examination of our favorite captain, and some of the reasons why he is so dear to us. Gloria-Ann, by the way, is also an accomplished sculptress, and fashioned the Spock sculpture featured on the cover of* Trek No. 14 *that is so widely admired by fans.*

Why is the character of Captain James T. Kirk so loved by millions of Star Trek fans? And more, what are the elements that make up a starship commander? The answer to both of these questions is the same—the things that make Jim Kirk an excellent starship commander are the very same things that cause Star Trek fans to admire him so.

We wish to see some of the same elements in ourselves. We, too, want to be brave, loyal, resourceful, quick of wit, respected, and admired by all who know us. That is why we admire Jim Kirk so. He is all of these things—and more—yet he is also humanly flawed, just as we are.

In this article, we will examine the things that make James T. Kirk such a fine starship commander, and also briefly examine what those things represent to us.

Above all else, as the commander of the USS *Enterprise*, Jim Kirk is alone. His is the final responsibility for decisions that can often mean life or death for everyone aboard his ship. And whatever the consequences of his decisions, he cannot evade the blame or pass it along to someone else. He is the captain—he stands alone.

True, he may ask others for opinions regarding their specific areas of scientific or technical expertise (as he should), but he must always bear in mind that his officers may have incorrectly received or computed information. Therefore, he must be knowledgeable enough in all areas of starship command to assimilate data from his officers and use it in making his final decision.

This is perhaps the outstanding element of Kirk's popularity: his aloneness. We are often alone in making difficult decisions; and we can appreciate how very much more difficult it is for Kirk to do so with the lives of over four hundred people in his hands.

The *Enterprise*'s mission often takes the ship far from Starfleet Command, and Kirk can rarely ask or inform his superiors about situations that require immediate decisions.

Many viewers who are in positions of leadership understand what it is like to have such responsibility, and so empathize with Kirk. Even the majority of us who are not in such a position can respect him for his courage in taking on such a lonely job. Most of us have a hard enough time running our own family lives and directing those of family members, using all of our tact, experience, logic, emotions, and sometimes force. Consider what is needed to run a starship with over four hundred highly independent, strong-willed crewmembers!

Jim Kirk has all of the requirements to be a starship captain: He is very capable, and has the good judgment, intelligence, and courage to lead. He is respected and well liked by his crew. He has been given many honors and awards.

Therefore, he must of necessity have a large ego, and is proud and possessive of his ability and position. We see this in "The Ultimate Computer," in which Kirk must give over command of the *Enterprise* to the M-5 computer unit. Even though the machine will control the ship for only a short while (it is being tested), Kirk is resentful. He has spent a great deal of his life in training for his position, and after making a spectacular success in his chosen career, he certainly will not take kindly to having his ship run by a computer—no matter how superefficient and accurate it might be.

We share Kirk's frustration. He knows that to command a ship, one must have both knowledge of technology and an understanding of human traits. The M-5 computer, while great at the former, would be forever lacking in the intricate and intuitive knowledge needed to deal with the latter. M-5 could never have come up with a bluff such as the "Corbomite Maneuver." Only a human can play a hunch.

A good leader must be just and often stern, but he must temper his command with humanitarianism and humility. In "Arena," Kirk is forced to battle the Gorn captain to the death, as the alien Metrons have declared that the loser's ship will be destroyed.

Kirk disables the Gorn, but refuses to kill it. He will not kill for others' sport, not even at the risk of his ship. And he refuses to violate the spirit of his mission: peace. We admire him for this, as few of us would have the courage *not* to kill the Gorn, and risk annihilation of ourselves and our comrades.

"The Enemy Within" demonstrates the two sides of Kirk's nature—and those of all humans. Split by a faulty transporter into two beings—one passive and gentle, one violent and aggressive—Kirk demonstrated the many opposing factors of personality that must be integrated into one complex, but controlled, being. Neither extreme could function effectively separated from the other, and we see how both strength and gentleness are necessary to make up a complete person.

As a commander, Kirk is often among the first to enter a dangerous situation. In a great majority of episodes, it is Kirk and his top officers, Spock and McCoy, who beam down to a planet and take the brunt of action and danger. We enjoy seeing Kirk take the initiative in such a way, even though it exposes a flaw in his character.

In all logic, Kirk should stay aboard the ship to direct events, as he is the most important person aboard, and the most necessary to the successful completion of the ship's mission. (And he often does so, as seen in several episodes.)

But more often, Kirk goes ahead, sometimes even to the point of ordering everyone else back to the ship while he alone stays to face the danger ("The Doomsday Machine," "The Tholian Web").

The fact that Kirk could stay aboard and order others to face the unknown but chooses to do so himself is perhaps his major failing as a starship captain. But it endears him to us.

We see that Kirk is somewhat headstrong and stubborn, and that he also cares deeply about his crew. How many of us live by the philosophy of not asking anyone to do something we would not do ourselves?

Perhaps the hardest part of command for Kirk is when he must go against the advice of his officers, often on "just a feeling." It is part of their duty to offer advice and opinions, and they are competent at their jobs. So we can see how terribly difficult it must be for Kirk to do what he feels is right even when his officers disagree.

"Obsession" is the best example of this. Kirk's officers feel that he is obsessed with the cloud creature because of guilt feelings, but he is convinced that it is intelligent and evil. He is eventually proved right, and his officers find that Kirk was correct in this case to listen to his intuition. But he did suffer doubts about his conviction, just as any of us would when pursuing an action that our friends and family thought foolish or wasteful.

One of the most popular Star Trek episodes concerning Captain Kirk is "The City on the Edge of Forever." It demonstrates to the fullest the painful choices that are Kirk's to make. Not who will live or die this time, as either choice will result in death, but the balance of the life of one woman against the existence of Kirk's entire future galaxy.

Not such a difficult choice. Letting the woman die would be for the good of all humanity—preventing a disastrous reversal in the outcome of World War II which would change all future events.

But the price of putting things right is almost too high for Kirk, a price that is the death of an innocent and brave woman whom Kirk has come to love.

How deeply we empathize with Kirk! And yet, we cannot fully understand the choice he faced. We cannot balance the life of a galaxy against a loved one—we can't face the knowledge that saving the one nearest to us will cause the death (or nonexistence) of countless millions in the centuries to come. But Kirk had to. And he made the only choice he could.

In "City," the choice for Spock was easy. Although he sincerely regretted the fact that Edith Keeler had to die, it was only logical that she do so in order that millions more might live.

But Captain Kirk isn't the logician that Spock is. He arrives at his conclusions by a combination of intelligence, experience, intuition, and deeply felt human emotions. As much as we may love Spock, we can identify much more easily with Kirk.

Yet Spock is Kirk's closest friend. Together, they make the most efficient commanding team in Starfleet, while still operating on different "wavelengths" and basing their decisions on often wildly varying reasoning. But those decisions are more often than not identical.

All of us would like to have Spock as a friend, but in actuality, how many of us could win that friendship? It took Kirk quite a while to do so, and we admire his patience. But we must also remember that in making a Vulcan his closest friend, Kirk displays a refreshing lack of prejudice.

Yes, prejudice still exists in the time of Star Trek. Take, for example, Lieutenant Andrew Stiles in "Balance of Terror." His deep-seated animosity toward Romulans spilled over into prejudice against Spock and all other aliens.

Even though the many different species of beings encountered in the galaxy have taught Starfleet crewmembers a great deal about tolerance of others, acceptance of the seemingly bizarre, and the need to keep an open mind, many beings still feel uncomfortable with members of another race. "Journey to Babel" showed us that even the members of a diplomatic corps could harbor animosity to others and cast racial slurs among themselves.

As well as a lack of prejudice toward aliens, we are pleased to find in Jim Kirk a fine understanding of his fellow man.

A superior captain must like and be liked by his crew. It is easy to command people by right of rank, but to get them to do that little extra that is often the difference between success and failure, you must have both respect and love.

We see many examples of this. Spock is called upon to get information, formulate theories, and find answers—usually with insufficient data! McCoy must cure incurable maladies. Uhura is always asked to get through unbelievable interference and static.

But the best example is Scotty. He is always being called upon to coax a little more power from his failing or overloaded engines, or to make amazing repairs on the phasers or transporter—just in the nick of time.

What would happen if he wasn't quite so concerned with

succeeding for his captain? After all, the engines are his primary responsibility, and he would be within his rights to demand that Kirk work within the safe parameters of engine design.

But like all of the *Enterprise* officers, Scotty is willing to risk his life (or, more important, his engines!) for Kirk—not just because it is the logical or humane thing to do or because it is his duty, but because he *likes* him. All of the crewmembers want to do their best for their captain, with no more reward than a sincere "Well done."

Most episodes show some sort of interchange between Kirk and his crew. He is one with them in friendship, yet apart in duty. As commander, he may be on close and intimate terms with only a few; and in times of distress, he turns to Spock and McCoy.

As we have close friends who share our lives, Kirk must have his. Spock and McCoy accompany him most often; they share his dangers and adventures equally, saving him from death as often as he saves them. They also share in his social life, if only in a brief moment of bantering humor.

Captain Kirk's presence in times of stress instills a feeling of confidence in his crew, for they believe unquestioningly in his judgment and ability. We, the viewers, like and admire such a person, and wish we could be looked up to by our friends in such a way.

It is Uhura who usually voices their need for reassurance when the ship is in a touchy situation and the outcome seems dubious. Kirk then has to give an appearance of confidence, even if he is secretly in doubt himself. In return, their reliance on him intensifies his desire to succeed.

But their unquestioning loyalty to him sometimes backfires! In "Turnabout Intruder" and "The Enemy Within," the lesser officers and crew who didn't know Kirk well were ready to obey the orders of what appeared to be their captain, even though they might have doubted his sanity.

In instances such as these, it is very important to Kirk that he have close friends who know him well so that they can see a difference in even little things, and question and investigate the reasons for his behavior. For example, in "What Are Little Girls Made Of?" the insult to Spock that Kirk manages to instill into his android double warns the Vulcan that something is amiss.

Luckily, Kirk has a few good friends among his officers

THE PSYCHOLOGY OF CAPTAIN KIRK'S POPULARITY 149

and gets along well with his crew; otherwise he would be very lonely indeed. For Kirk is "married to his ship," and the dedication he brings to his work does not allow for a woman in his life. Kirk has a reputation as a womanizer, and it is a reputation he both enjoys and tries to live up to. But rarely does a relationship go beyond that stage, since in no way is Kirk going to relinquish his ship and captaincy for a home and family at this time in his life.

We can appreciate the turmoil this situation brings about in Jim Kirk. He is lonely, yet to form a lasting relationship, he would have to give up his life as a starship captain. So almost every relationship he enters into is doomed from the start, as he cannot win, and always opts for the status quo. Many viewers have that in common with him.

Kirk's loyalty, above all, is to the *Enterprise*—not just to the empty shell, but to what makes it a living, active entity: its crew and the ideals of peace and exploration that crew represents.

Although he is responsible for the lives of over four hundred crewpersons, Kirk often takes great risks to save just one or two crew members. We like him for this, and it shows the great emphasis placed on an individual life, both by Kirk and the Federation.

So we see that the qualities that make up a superior starship captain are the same qualities that we would like to bring to our own lives. That is why we like and admire James T. Kirk so much: He is the embodiment of the best in humanity—and the best in us and our children yet to come.

That is why Captain Kirk is so popular, and why Star Trek would not have worked without such a "superhuman" model of our own aims and desires as the commander of the USS *Enterprise*!

14.

CHANGES IN *STAR TREK:*
THE MOTION PICTURE

by G.B. Love

One of the greatest fears fans had about the Star Trek movie was that their beloved Enterprise—*and perhaps even the characters!—would be changed beyond recognition. Those fears proved to be groundless when the movie appeared, but there were substantial changes made from the series. In this article, G.B. Love explains why some of the changes worked and why others did not.*

As *Star Trek: The Motion Picture* begins, we learn that two and a half years have passed since the completion of the *Enterprise*'s original five-year mission to seek out new life and new civilizations. Thirty months is quite a long time even by our standards, but in the fast-paced world of the twenty-third century, many things can happen in this span of time, bringing many seemingly drastic and radical changes. As the movie unfolds, we see many of these changes in the *Enterprise* crew and even in the ship itself. Some are expected, some are shocking, but all are logical.

In this article, we will discuss some of these changes, and the relationship they have to Star Trek as we have known and loved it.

Perhaps the most shocking development as the film opens is that Kirk has now been promoted to the rank of admiral, and is no longer in command of the USS *Enterprise*.

Kirk has bowed to the pressures of Starfleet Command, and accepted a rank and post which is—in simple terms—a public-relations job. Even in the twenty-third century, it appears, there is a crying need for heroes; and Kirk, as the only commander to successfully bring his ship back from a completed five-year mission, is lauded as a hero by the citizens of the Federation. But, as Emerson said, "Every hero becomes a bore at last," and Kirk soon found himself in an aimless, boring desk job.

We can assume that Jim Kirk, being the man that he is, accepted the adulation for higher purposes than personal aggrandizement (most likely he saw the chance to speak of his deep commitment to space and by doing so, to upgrade and enhance the public's enthusiasm for space exploration, as well as enticing young people into joining Starfleet), but there is a part of Kirk that reacted to fame in quite a bad way. You can be sure that he didn't mind at all having himself flattered and feted, and often seduced. This is a small part of Kirk, however, and his desire for action and a purpose would soon lead him to tire of the constant "good life." If he became a boring hero, then it was because he himself was bored long before.

Once having accepted the promotion and fame, Kirk found himself trapped. Starfleet was not about to let its "model starship captain" go back out into space and maybe get himself killed. It would be bad for business. So young Admiral Kirk found himself at a loss. His career, for all practical purposes, was over, his friends left far behind in both rank and duties, his ship in the hands of another man, ironically a man Kirk himself had chosen to take over.

We see a sad and disillusioned Kirk in the opening scenes of *STTMP*. His eyes are haunted by his failure to utilize his fame to make any decisive or lasting changes in Starfleet. (It is another indictment of Kirk that he truly felt he could overcome the Establishment, due in part to both his ego and the empty praise that fell on his head.) He is no longer the cocky, striding Kirk of the past. It seems sad to say it, but James T. Kirk was on the verge of being a broken man when the Intruder appeared to save his career—and probably his life.

The same faults that led Kirk to accept the admiralcy caused him to pull strings and retake command of the *Enterprise*: an overriding conviction that only *he* could get the job done, the need for power and glory once again, and his always-ready response to a challenge. By this action, which was due only to self-interest, we can see how truly desperate Kirk was. True, an experienced and superbly competent commander was desirable for such an important mission, but to Kirk it was a means of escape. It is safe to say that he would have literally killed for the chance.

Kirk knew that he would have to ride roughshod over Decker when taking command from him. If he had been the kind of man to meekly accept Kirk's coming aboard, Willard Decker would not have been the kind of stuff that starship commanders are made of. And to make matters worse, Kirk had personally given him the position, and was an old and trusted friend. In his determination to command once again, Kirk cared little for Decker's feelings; and worse, seemed to care even less about the resentment his action would cause in Decker, as well as in a great number of crewmembers who had never served with Kirk and knew and respected Willard Decker as their captain.

If a case can be made for Kirk's actions being in the best interests of Earth, the Federation, and the *Enterprise*, that is the major flaw in it. A commander must be respected and trusted by his crew to get the maximum out of them, and even in the holdovers from the original mission, there is some doubt and consternation seen. Kirk may have been much, much wiser and more experienced, but Decker would have commanded the crew as a whole.

The unfamiliarity that Kirk shows with the changes and improvements in the *Enterprise* is somehow startling. We would naturally assume that wherever he was, he would keep tabs on every minute detail concerning his beloved *Enterprise*. Not to mention the fact that as an admiral, he would be informed of any major changes in starship design and performance as a matter of course.

How then can we explain Kirk's ignorance? First, in the novel, Kirk remembers that the question of the warp power's being connected to the phasers came to his attention, and he forgot all about it after voicing his objections. This is a perfect example of the malaise that Kirk fell into during his stint as an admiral, for with his wits about him, he would have fought to the end to protect not only the *Enterprise*, but other ships as well.

Secondly, as Kirk's dissatisfaction with high rank increased, he probably found it increasingly painful to think of the *Enterprise* and the freedom he had left behind when he gave her up. So it is not then so mystifying that he should not know what was going on aboard her when he purposely locked himself away from the world of starships.

For perhaps the first time in his life, Kirk is unsure of himself and his motives as he takes command of the *Enterprise*. We can see this by the way he so desperately seeks approval and acceptance from both Spock and McCoy. As events unfold, Kirk realizes that he has perhaps bitten off more than he can chew, and it is not until his confrontation with McCoy that he begins to ease up.

Kirk is the sort of person who can accept and conquer doubts only by first verbalizing them, even if it means having someone else broach the subject first. It is interesting to note that as Kirk regains his confidence, we can see Decker's resentment lessen and his respect for Kirk rise again. It is a question of will and of bearing, more than one of any overt actions on Kirk's part. One almost gets the feeling that the more Kirk *acts* the captain, the more his crew accepts him as the captain.

By the time Spock comes aboard, the question is just about settled. Kirk is in command, flaws and all, and everyone knows it. Only one other element is needed to complete the transformation of a disillusioned and unsure man into an efficient and confident captain; and that is Spock.

Millions of words have been written about the relationship between Kirk and Spock, and it would serve little purpose here to try to cover every aspect that fans have either discovered or invented. But it is important to describe, in brief, how this relationship affects the events of *STTMP*.

We all know that neither Kirk nor Spock is complete without the other. As stated above, Kirk could not again become the commander he once was without the presence of Spock. The reverse is also true. Spock could not be successful in returning to Starfleet without Kirk.

Our first view of Spock in the movie is on the planet Vulcan. Spock has returned there in an attempt to conquer his emotions, and to be accepted into *Kolinahr* by the Masters. Because of the mental infringement of V'Ger, Spock fails in his quest, and leaves to join the *Enterprise* as it rushes to intercept the Intruder.

We wonder why Spock has chosen to completely rid himself of his human half. It seemed in the aired episodes that he had not only accepted his role in life, but had actually come to enjoy and appreciate his work and constant contact with humans. In only a few instances did we have the feeling that Spock was incomplete or unhappy.

His return to Vulcan after the end of the original voyage was no surprise. His original purpose in joining Starfleet had been served. He had found that he could function and be successful in both societies, the rift with his father had healed, and he was no longer ashamed of his heritage. His exploits had also become something of a legend on Vulcan (we can assume that his scientific discoveries and uses of logic are what would have impressed Vulcans more than heroics), so his acceptance in all circles would have been assured. It would be completely natural for him to join his father at the Science Academy, or else to use his experience in a diplomatic or governmental post. Most of us have always had a sneaky suspicion that Spock would end up running Vulcan someday, anyway.

By his endeavor to join the Masters and devote his life to logic, we can see that Spock was indeed not quite so contented as we thought he was. Although Vulcan philosophy is based on logic, the Masters could be little more important to day-to-day Vulcan life than the Dalai Lama is to us here on Earth. In effect, Spock was removing himself from all contacts with others, both human and Vulcan, and was quite prepared to waste his talents and achievements in a futile quest to change what he was.

Obviously, the thought impulses of V'Ger did not reach out to Spock, or else other Vulcans and the hundreds of other vastly superior telepathic races in the galaxy would have "heard" from V'Ger as well. Spock was *looking* for something without really knowing it, and V'Ger was as happily forthcoming for him as it was for Jim Kirk. Both needed a form of escape; both found it in the threat of the Intruder.

Spock, heeding the call without really knowing why, still felt that he had to suppress his human side. The effects of thirty months of studying the tenets of *Kolinahr* also came into play, as Spock had managed the most successful suppression of his emotions in his life. Such discipline is very hard to shake off, even if one wants to.

When Spock comes aboard the *Enterprise*, he is almost overwhelmed by the impact of the emotional attachments the ship and crew hold for him. Seeing this as a failing in himself, he becomes even more cold and aloof, as we must remember his stated reason for joining the expedition was to find the Intruder and discover its secrets of flawless logic. To give in to the rush of feelings at such a time would be unthinkable to Spock, although he does admit their existence to himself.

McCoy's fears that Spock would either be "taken over" by the Intruder or betray his ship in any way to gain the perfect logic he sought were completely unfounded. Spock was not looking for logic, per se, he was looking for escape from the torment his half-breed soul caused him. Once Spock discovered acceptance of emotion, and its necessity to a complete life, his quest was over. His interest in V'Ger beyond that point was only how to stop it.

Spock, like Kirk, was not complete until he was once again part of the crew of the *Enterprise*. Only the methods of their realization of that fact were different. Kirk forced himself to see that his desire to command the mission was essentially selfish; Spock was forced by the sterility of V'Ger's logic to see that his human half was right and valuable. Spock did indeed complete his task on Vulcan; it was completed not on the arid sands of Gol, but aboard the *Enterprise*, as we always knew it would be.

The intervening years seem to have had little effect on the rest of the crew. McCoy had become something of a recluse during his stint researching ways to apply Fabrini medicine to surface dwellers, but that was to be expected. His tolerance for humankind in general was always pretty low. McCoy has seen too many people die and too much suffering to allow himself to form any new lasting relationships.

It is also not surprising to us that his opinion of Kirk drops a bit when he learns that Kirk has not only forced him to serve on the mission, but has also usurped command from Decker.

The cynicism McCoy has always harbored in large measure is only reinforced by what he sees as a grandstand play by Kirk, and the seeming confirmation of all his fears about Spock. Beyond a little bit of goading of Spock for old times' sake, McCoy's heart never really seems to be in the effort. It is interesting to note that only the creation of a new life form brings him back to his old self, showing us that while he is cynical, he is not completely jaded. He still cares. Very much.

Scotty, now sporting a mustache, is relatively unchanged,

and that is completely as it should be. He lives only for his engines and his ship, and it would have been unthinkable for him to allow anyone else to install the improvements aboard the *Enterprise*. As a person who works with machinery and leaves policy to others, Scotty would probably be the same person after thirty years, much less thirty months.

Sulu, Rand, Uhura, and Chekov have new ranks and duties, and that is about all. It is a shame, however, that there was simply not enough time to delve into what has happened to them in the interim. As a thumbnail basis: Uhura has given up all hope of command and is content to operate as communications chief, while still taking advantage of every opportunity for action and excitement. Chekov's duties as weapons control officer are only part of the overall training for command, and not indicative of any special desire or aptitude. Sulu has probably had a hundred new hobbies and interests, as well as serving as second officer to Decker. Rand moved up in rank as quickly as possible for an enlisted crewperson, and she accepted reassignment on the *Enterprise* only after having established that Kirk was no longer in command.

Christine Chapel, we learn, has finally gotten her full medical credentials, and is serving as chief medical officer when McCoy arrives and takes over. She could have been chief surgeon as well, as she certainly would have learned much from assisting McCoy for so many years.

In *Star Trek: The Motion Picture* we get our first look at twenty-third-century Earth and the United Federation of Planets Starfleet Command Headquarters, and they are indeed impressive. However, the only things we have from the series we can remotely connect them to are starbases and such, so there is little profit in discussing their relationship to the series' sets.

When we first see Admiral Kirk, he is clad in a simply beautiful two-tone form-fitting uniform. And we breathe a sigh of relief, as we feel that all of our worries about the appearance of the new uniforms have been unfounded. Unfortunately, not so. Although the new uniforms look much better onscreen than still photos would indicate, they still lack the style and color of the series uniforms. Also, on certain of the actors, the uniforms look ludicrous. Decker is a good example. His shoulders and chest are too narrow for a form-fit-

CHANGES IN *STAR TREK: THE MOTION PICTURE*

ting outfit. Also not quite flattered were several of the ladies, but let's mention no names. . . .

Natural progression could cause a change of this sort in Starfleet uniforms in a couple of years, and cost is no object when the style and color of a garment can be synthesized from a materializer. Pop in an old uniform, pop a new one out. Only in the case of the women could one say that the new uniforms were any more efficient, and that is nothing new, as they wore slacks in the early television episodes. Just one of those bureaucratic decisions that somebody makes to justify his position, most likely.

The only uniform changes that made sense were the protective suits worn by engineering crewpersons and the armor worn by security personnel. It is only logical that security men would have more protection and better weaponry than the average crewmember. Perhaps it finally got through to the people upstairs that fewer security people would be killed if they had a better chance going into dangerous situations.

The travel pod has apparently replaced the shuttlecraft as a means of getting to and from a planet without the aid of a transporter. However, we can assume that they vary in size and shape, as the one which Scotty used to bring Kirk to the *Enterprise* looked too small to hold more than a few people. And remember the Aquashuttle from the animated series? An exploration ship such as the *Enterprise* would have a number of such specialized shuttles and pods.

The shuttle which delivers Spock to the ship is called a shuttle, but it is obviously quite beyond what we have known as a typical shuttlecraft. Perhaps it is a strictly Vulcan ship (which would account for the Vulcan writing and the name "Surak" on its side), or a special diplomatic craft. Spock, as the son of a very influential ambassador and famous in his own right, could likely command the use of such a ship in an emergency.

Remember that the *Enterprise* had already entered warp speed for a few moments before the wormhole disaster, and even in that brief time it would travel far beyond the range and speed capabilities of the television shuttlecraft. So Spock's shuttle must have been equipped with warp drive. Even though it was quite a bit larger than the TV shuttles, it was still tiny compared to the *Enterprise*, so one of the major advances made by the Federation during the hiatus must have been miniaturization of the warp-drive engines. Such an occurrence could lead to exciting things, as small ships could be used as adjuncts in battle and exploration.

As the "world" around which everything in Star Trek operates, the believability and detail of the *Enterprise* is a necessity. And to the delight of many—and the consternation of some—the *Enterprise* is almost completely different in every way.

When some viewers point out that two and a half years is not nearly enough time for so many advances and changes in starship design to take place, it must be considered that from the time we got our very first look at the *Enterprise* as she appeared in "The Man Trap" until the beginning of the motion picture was over *seven* years ... Star Trek time, that is.

The *Enterprise* never went in for a major overhaul during the aired episodes, so we never got a look at the ongoing Federation technology. It seems like a lot when we see it all at once, but the total is actually the result of years of planning and modification.

Too, it should be remembered that the *Enterprise* is somewhat of an experimental vessel in *Star Trek: The Motion Picture*, and many of the new innovations on board may not yet be Starfleet standard—or may never be.

The exterior of the ship is the first thing we see, and it really isn't so different. The saucer edge is curved a little differently, the nacelles have obviously been completely replaced in order to accommodate the new engines, the rear part of the engineering section has been changed, and the sensor disc is gone, replaced by a giant spotlight. (It was obviously replaced by better, more strategically placed equipment.)

Aside from these changes, the ship has an overall "different look" to it only because we have never seen its exterior skin in such detail before. Protrusions, vents, lights, pods, antennae, etc. are all easily seen, and are at loggerheads with our previous notions of the exterior of the ship as being smooth and sleek. But in airless space, it doesn't need to be. The basic design of the ship has not changed, nor would it be expected to, as it is perfectly balanced for the optimum performance of the engines in moving the ship's mass, which is the only thing one has to worry about in a gravity-free environment.

Inside, however, is a different story. As with Starfleet HQ and Earth, the areas which we have never seen before are interesting and exciting—the cargo bay, the rec hall (and the rec room, which is an obviously different area), Engineering (we saw only the command center before, not the engines themselves), and myriad hallways, anterooms, offices, quarters, etc.

The changes are mostly cosmetic, when you get right down to it. The turbolift has a "map" of the ship in it. The corridors were lit differently, and paneled in metallics. Doors were enlarged. And hundreds of other small differences, the like of which you could make in your own home without too much effort.

In fact, the only areas that looked quite different from their series counterparts were Engineering and the bridge.

As stated above, Engineering was simply a section of the ship that we had not seen before. True, those were new engines in the movie, of a slightly different type than those on the ship during the original mission. But they had to be very similar in design, as the areas in which they are placed and operate would have to be the same—the nacelles. This would account for the long, tubish appearance of the matter-antimatter mix chamber—and there should be an identical chamber in the other nacelle. The "mix" of the engines may be the need to get equal amounts of propulsion from both nacelles.

All new equipment has been placed on the bridge, so naturally the entire area will look quite different. The only major differences in bridge layout are: Spock's station is now to the captain's left, Chekov's weapon station has been added, and the lighting is much dimmer—required so that the rear-projected displays would show clearly on film. Again, it was mostly cosmetics that made such a seeming difference.

The single most noticeable change onboard ship was in the transporter chamber. Instead of the cozy room it was on the series, it has now become a stark, functional place that would only help to make McCoy's distrust of the machine more understandable. Beaming up or down doesn't seem like such a casual affair in a room where machinery lines the walls and the operator is behind a sheet of protective glass! The transporter itself is also a new model, as the sound and shimmer are different. But it doesn't seem to be any faster or more efficient than the old one. Perhaps its range or overall load capacity is greater. (Still breaks down, though!)

Overall, the passage of time from the end of the five-year mission to the beginning of the movie has not made too much difference for our purposes. The characters, while looking a little older, are still viable and true to aired Trek. The ship is newer and refitted, but it didn't take us long to get used to that. And the only major new characters introduced in the film are gone, so we don't have to concern ourselves with wondering how they will fit into the scheme of things.

We can be thankful that the changes were not damaging. It would have been so easy to kill off Spock, as so many of us feared. And it would have been easy to have the *Enterprise* transformed into a dreadnought, as many fans insisted. Or we could even have had to put up with the all-star, "big-name" replacements for the original actors that Paramount reportedly wanted to play Kirk and Company. (Whew!)

The changes in the film are many, but they are all true to the premise of Star Trek. And that means that nothing has really changed at all!

15.

THE OTHER FEDERATION FORCES

by Walter Irwin

In the vast Star Trek universe, there are literally billions of beings whom we never saw on our television screens. And many of these persons are involved with the day-to-day workings of the Starship Enterprise. *In this article, the first of several, Walter looks at some of the Federation support personnel.*

One of the most regrettable aspects of Star Trek as a limited-budget television production is that viewers were never allowed to see more than a small fraction of the vast inner workings of the United Federation of Planets. How fascinating it would have been to see the free-space "drydock" where the *Enterprise* was built, or the vast command center of a starbase (both promised in the movie), or the colonization of a planet, or a full-scale diplomatic conference on Babel!

But as we were never shown these wonderful sights, we can only speculate on how they operated on a day-to-day basis, and, more important, what sort of Federation officers and crewpersons were involved in making it possible for the *Enterprise* to voyage off to worlds unknown.

Speculation leads to more than just outlining the duties of the above-mentioned areas. It also leads into new areas of Federation activity. Among these are peace-keeping forces and supply forces.

These are all militarily controlled spheres, which makes them much more important to the missions of the *Enterprise* than, say, colonials. And all are constantly active in deep space, which would make their duties inherently more exacting and exciting than those of starbase forces.

In this article we will examine these forces, and how they relate to and aid in the operations of a starship such as the *Enterprise*.

The Starfleet Marines

One of the most overlooked aspects of the Star Trek universe is the need of the Federation to have a peace-keeping force which is fast-moving and hard-hitting—troops which are essentially "ground-based" and designed to handle situations that cannot be efficiently solved in any other manner.

Starships of all types are superb for exploration and defense, but there are often times when they supply simply too much power for the job at hand. Power enough to devastate a planet is horrifyingly wonderful, but when something is needed to settle a simple planetary dispute, calling in a starship is like burning down the barn to get rid of rats.

So the Federation must have a force of men and arms which can operate efficiently on a relatively small scale, in a short amount of time, and within the laws and guidelines of the Federation Articles. This group is the Starfleet Marines.

The Marines are an integral part of the Federation forces. Acting under Starfleet Command, they work with starships and other vessels in exploration, defense, and security. But they are also quite autonomous, as Marine exercises are often undertaken far from the nearest starbase or command center.

In fact, most of their duties are those which are simply too small, on a galaxy-wide scale, to be of primary importance to Starfleet. But the Marines' operations are no less important for all that, as allowing small disputes and emergencies to get out of hand could quickly cause the collapse of the entire Federation from within.

What, then, are the duties and responsibilities of the Federation Marines? It is an open question, as the force is rather loosely organized, enabling them to meet any contingency with a maximum amount of flexibility. True, many Marines have assigned posts as security and containment forces, but such duties are outside the norm.

The elite of the Marines are ready at any time to move in on trouble; consequently they cannot be sequestered to permanent duties. The entire idea of a quickly activated strike force is defeated if they are tied down. For most purposes, we can assume that all Starfleet Marines are among this "ready" force, no matter where they are billeted.

The Marines are a hand-picked group of tough fighting veterans. They hold immense pride in being Marines, and rightfully boast that it is harder to join their number than it is to get into any other branch of Starfleet.

Each member of the Marine force is chosen for outstanding qualities. Intelligence, fighting prowess, and bravery are among the primary considerations, but Marines are also chosen for their leadership abilities. Another boast of the Marines is that any one of them would be in a position of command elsewhere in Starfleet, and this is often true.

In many instances, when a member of the fleet is accepted for Marine training (several years of deep-space experience is a prerequisite), he has already begun his rise in the ranks. In almost every case, the aspirant accepts his demotion cheerfully, as each Marine candidate goes into training as a basic crewmember, with no consideration given his previous rank or service. One can find many ex-lieutenants and ensigns proudly serving as Marine corporals and sergeants.

Federation Marines are constructed around squads, each squad being composed of five men commanded by a lieutenant and a sergeant. Most squads are part of companies, which in turn make up divisions, and these divisions are elements of armies. Starfleet Marine Corps consists of five armies, each comprising a command personnel of twenty-five divisions. Divisions are divided into twenty-five companies, with each company composed of ten men. So at any given time, the Marines' total complement is roughly thirty thousand troops. Not seemingly a large number for all the space they have to cover, but because of the caliber of the men and the throughness of their training, quite sufficient.

As the Marines are basically a strike force called in for policing and peace-keeping action, not more than one division is usually needed for a specific job. In fact, many Marine assignments are handled by an even smaller number of troops, sometimes as few as two or three squads. Doing the job with the least amount of manpower possible is a basic tenet of Marine practice and tradition. An old Marine joke goes like this: A colony governor called the Marines for help in quelling a miners' riot on his planet. When a Federation ship arrived, the governor was aghast to see only one Marine beam down. When the governor sputteringly demanded to know why Starfleet only sent one man, the Marine answered, "There's only one riot, isn't there?"

As you can see, the Marines pride themselves on their efficiency in peacekeeping. They hold a haughty disdain for their brothers assigned to starship duty, referring to it as "milk runs"; and they have even less regard for regular starship crewmembers, whom they scornfully call "space jockeys." Many a barside brawl has started when Marines and regular Starfleet troops get together, and the Starfleet hierarchy often goes to great lengths to keep them apart. As one beleaguered commodore put it, "I only wish our boys would fight the Klingons with as much gusto as they fight each other."

But such brawls usually end up with the Marines and starshipmen allied against a common foe: security. "Spoilsport" is about the nicest term that has ever been hurled at security forces when they move in to break up an altercation; and this usually leads to the hurling of other objects, such as fists, bottles, and chairs. Although security troops are specifically chosen for their toughness, even they think twice about taking on a Marine deep in his cups, and ready for a good fight.

It is not surprising, however, that a large majority of Marines transferred in from security. It makes an excellent training ground.

Marines are constantly drilled in the use of the latest and most deadly weapons that Starfleet can devise. One of the first requirements for admission to Marine training is to qualify as an expert marksman. To do so is very difficult, as it requires pinpoint use of a phaser (both hand and rifle) at distances of up to a quarter of a mile.

One of the simpler exercises is to disintegrate a Federation one-credit coin at a hundred yards . . . as it is launched like a clay pigeon. Others are much harder, such as stunning one person as he runs through a crowd. This is done at a hundred feet, in twilight and under the worst possible atmospheric conditions.

As situations do arise that require Marine action on a planet whose conditions are too severe for standard atmosphere belts, trainees must perform all exercises in full space suits before graduation. It is not uncommon for the rookie Marine to find himself in the simulated conditions of a methane-gas atmosphere with a suit that suddenly malfunctions. If he cannot repair his suit before he succumbs, he

THE OTHER FEDERATION FORCES 165

washes out and is transferred back to his old outfit . . . after he gets out of the hospital, that is.

Basic weaponry carried by a Marine into action is a hand phaser Type II, a rifle phaser of the newest Mark 4 model, a vibroblade knife, communicator, and several small-scale photon grenades. This is in addition to survival gear and rations, although not a great deal of these items are needed, Marines preferring to "live off the land" whenever possible.

Other kits carried by Marines with specific duties includes a scouting tricorder, medical supplies, long-range communications equipment, photon mortors, laser cannonry, and limited force-field generators.

A Marine action uniform consists of lightweight body armor (with helmet), belt and waist supply packs, and atmosphere belts and special boots which compensate for gravity extremes when conditions require. A small jet pack worn on the back allows a Marine to make short hops into the air.

The jet packs enable the Marines to use their favorite combat maneuver: Half of the troops form a defensive firing line, while the remainder leapfrog over them. Once they have gained ground, they in turn become the defensive line, and the troops behind repeat the action. With this combination of constant advance coupled with the deadly accuracy of Marine weapons, most foes can be overcome before they have a chance to set up any kind of efficient counterattack.

The use of Marines on a starship of the *Enterprise* class is rather limited, as such a ship carries a large and well-trained number of security forces. However, at least one squad of Marines is always aboard. When their skills are needed, they are usually needed desperately, and it is not unusual for a captain to give the ranking Marine temporary control over all of his able-bodied men in a crisis situation. This need for ground-trained combat experts among a starship complement was quickly discovered in early deep-space explorations, such as the events which developed when the *Enterprise* landed on Rigel VII, and three crewmen were killed and seven injured.

Let's hope as Star Trek goes on to a series of films we will get a chance to see the Starfleet Marines in action alongside Kirk and his crew. It should be a most interesting story.

Starfleet Supply Forces

The Federation military supply forces are the lifeblood of Starfleet, and although they face as much adventure, excitement, and physical danger as starship forces, their efforts are often overlooked.

The majority of supply troops are given fairly standard duties, such as ferrying needed goods to Federation colonies, starbases, and the better-protected planetary systems.

But a number of supply forces have to travel into regions of space which are less secure. For example, the transportation of material to the Neutral Zone Outposts under constant threat of Romulan attack is quite hazardous, especially for the slow-moving and undergunned supply ships and large-scale transports. Starships such as the *Enterprise* must also make occasional stops for necessities, and as it would be a waste of time and fuel to travel perhaps millions of miles to a starbase, supply ships are sent to prearranged rendezvous to meet with the starships. These are usually in unexplored territory, always fraught with danger.

But even among the supply sections which do not venture into hazardous territory, there is a tremendous amount of pride and *esprit de corps,* as they fully realize that without Supply, the Federation would soon come to a grinding halt.

"Can do!" is the motto of Supply. Not only are supply forces supremely confident of their ability to go anywhere, do anything, and fix anything; they are always ready to take on a new challenge. Some of the major advances in Starfleet technology and operations have come about through Supply's efforts to find a way to get a job done easier and faster.

Members of Supply are usually hard-bitten space veterans. Most feel uncomfortable planetside, and find the long hours of routine and comparative solitude preferable to the bustle of civilization. As supply ships and bases are usually informally run, a large measure of independence and personal freedom is allowed the supply workers, and they cherish this as well. As a result, Supply has a low opinion of "the brass," and its members can effectively work outside normal chain of command.

This ability to circumvent higher-ups makes for a good working relationship between Supply and the fiercely independent starship captains. Both realize that battling their way through red tape could often mean the difference between life and death in space.

Let's hope we will get a chance to meet some of these extraordinary people in further Star Trek adventures. Only by seeing the actual operations of the supply forces will we be able to grasp the incredible amount of work and planning that is necessary to keep the Federation working.

16.
VULCAN AS A PATRIARCHY

by Rebecca Hoffman

The inner working of the planet Vulcan is one of the most popular subjects for speculation by fan writers. Because we actually know so little, we can speculate a lot. This article by Rebecca Hoffman is one such speculative look at Vulcan, but the conclusions drawn are firmly based on evidence from aired Star Trek episodes and scripts. We think you will find it ... fascinating.

During Star Trek's second season, two of the most popular episodes dealt specifically with Vulcans. One, of course, was "Amok Time," wherein the unrelenting mating drive of the Vulcan male forced Spock to return to his native planet to take a wife, or else die. The other episode was "Journey to Babel," in which the viewer met Spock's parents, Ambassador Sarek and his human wife, Amanda.

Both of these episodes raised many questions, and the discerning viewer may answer many of those questions on the basis of evidence contained within the episodes.

The question discussed in this article concerns the structure of Vulcan society: Is Vulcan life built around a patriarchal society (one in which males are dominant, and are heads of the clan/family group), or a matriarchal society (one in which females dominate)?

Although the answer to this question is revealed in the title of this article, the process of arriving at that answer was relatively complex.

Proponents of a matriarchal society point to T'Pau, the Vulcan woman who presided over Spock's "marriage ceremony" in "Amok Time." In the script, we are told that she "is an Elder, a great force in the land. She is a woman of immense dignity, and her authority is obvious."

Even the undauntable Captain Kirk stands in awe of her. He tells Dr. McCoy that T'Pau is "the only person who ever turned down a seat on the Federation Council." A bit later, he describes T'Pau as "all of Vulcan in one package."

At the end of the episode, it is T'Pau who gets Kirk out of the trouble he has made for himself by taking Spock to Vulcan against orders when she intercedes with Starfleet Command. Command's official reply to Kirk was, "T'Pau of Vulcan has requested that the *Enterprise* divert here. Any reasonable delay is approved." McCoy's response to that was, "They just couldn't turn her down."

An immensely powerful figure. On the surface, the very existence of one such as T'Pau is credible evidence that Vulcan society is matriarchal. But, even on Vulcan, the obvious is multifaceted, and a bit deeper digging uncovers facets not readily discernible from the top.

Before we further examine "Amok Time" and the aspects of a patriarchal society inherent in a physiology dependent on a male rut cycle (which is fatal if not completed) for reproduction, let us turn to "Journey to Babel" for a closer look at the Vulcan male/female relationships exemplified by Sarek and Amanda.

In "The Corbomite Maneuver," Spock remarks that Balok reminds him of his father. It is not, of course, a physical resemblance, but rather one of personality. Balok is a commanding individual, and at Sarek's first appearance in "Journey," the viewer is struck with that same aura of command. Sarek is an elegantly forceful man, obviously accustomed to obedience from both women and men, and as such is an unlikely candidate to have been raised in a matriarchy where women rule the family and are the prime movers.

From the beginning of "Journey to Babel," we see Sarek's commanding stance carried into all aspects of his life. Even his scenes with Amanda in private serve to point up the fact that he can, and does, take the same commanding demeanor with her.

Shortly after the arrival of Sarek and Amanda aboard the *Enterprise* we see one of Vulcan's customs wherein Amanda (or any woman, the script tells us) "habitually walks behind and to the side of any man, but especially her husband." It is probably a holdover from pre-reform times when men walked ahead of their women to protect them. The custom is a quaint one, which while useful at one time, seems to serve no practical purpose now—though it is one which even many human women would appreciate, for it is an outward expression of courtesy and appreciation. It is also extremely unlikely that a matriarchy would retain such a custom.

Whenever Sarek wishes Amanda's presence, he says, "My wife, attend." An order, and a rather curt one at that. Again, an action which would seem incongruous if Vulcan society were matriarchal.

It has been argued in fandom that Sarek's actions are atypical of Vulcan's, and that Sarek treats Amanda as he does because she is an "inferior" human, not because it is Vulcan custom for women to be treated thus.

This argument, however, has no basis in fact.

In the first place, Vulcans are ruled by logic, and it would be extremely illogical for Sarek (or any Vulcan) to marry someone inferior.

An important point, but moot in the light that Amanda is *not* inferior to Sarek. A Vulcan may be stronger mentally and physically than a human, but that does not automatically make the human inferior. Indeed, a greatly inferior being could not adapt to a radically different life-style such as the one Vulcan must have presented to Amanda. Inferior? Hardly. One chooses a life's mate on the basis of complimenting one another, and an inferior being does not complement a greatly superior being.

Further, since Vulcans seem to be tradition-bound, it is hardly logical that Sarek would treat Amanda any differently than he would a Vulcan female who was his wife. Privately, of course, he must treat her as a human, for she has needs which a Vulcan woman would not. But in public, Sarek would treat Amanda exactly as other Vulcan males treat their women. To do otherwise would not only go against tradition and social mores, it would call attention to the fact that Amanda is "different," and it would be illogical to deliberately—and constantly—emphasize the fact that he is married to a human. Since Vulcans know this, there is no reason to—as humans say—rub everyone's nose into obvious facts. Amanda is Sarek's *wife*. That is her status, and therefore he treats her the way all Vulcans traditionally treat their wives.

Amanda makes this very clear after Sarek decides to ex-

VULCAN AS A PATRIARCHY

cuse himself from the tour of the *Enterprise* which Captain Kirk is conducting. Sarek's last words to Amanda are: "Continue, my wife."

The script then states, "She bows her head in characteristic acceptance," and such a action would be extremely out of place in a matriarchal society.

After a few lines of conversation, Amanda says, "Shall we continue the tour? My husband did request it."

Kirk replies, "It sounded more like a command."

Amanda's rejoinder is a most telling comment. "Of course. He is a Vulcan. I'm his wife."

This situation would not exist in a society where a woman is the family head, but it would certainly hold true in a society where the family or clan is headed by a man.

A bit later, Sarek is reprimanding Amanda for her conduct at the formal reception. This is in reference to the famous "teddy bear" Spock was so fond of as a boy. Sarek had hastily pulled Amanda away from the reception, and once in their quarters, he proceeded to lecture her on the proper way to treat Spock.

Sarek opens the conversation by stating, "You embarrassed Spock this evening. Not even a *mother** may do that. He is a Vulcan."

Again, an unlikely restriction in a matriarchy.

In Sarek, we have seen a man who seems to be the product of a patriarchal society—a man who is used to commanding others and expects obedience.

In his relationship with Amanda, we see that Sarek is obviously the head of his family (in fact as well as in title), and that Amanda submits to his authority in a manner uncharacteristic of a woman living in a society based upon matriarchy.

What of "Amok Time"? In that episode, we see an entirely different side of Vulcan life, which also deals with Vulcan male/female relationships. While providing us with a puzzle piece (in the form of T'Pau) which is seemingly out of place in a patriarchy, "Amok Time" only serves to bolster the conclusions drawn from "Journey to Babel."

Before discussing the specifics of that particular episode, it may be wise to backtrack in time, before the reformation on Vulcan, and try to glimpse Vulcan life before the reforms of Surak and the institution of logic.

---

* Italics are the author's and not included in the script.

To begin with, Vulcans are not native to the world they call home. This fact was brought out in "Return to Tomorrow," wherein the crew of the *Enterprise* discovered a dead world inhabited by the essences of a few individuals whose life forces were contained in small globes. The leader, Sargon, calls the *Enterprise* crewpersons "my children," and when asked why, he proceeds to inform them that six thousand centuries before, his people were star travelers and had colonized the galaxy.

While Dr. Anne Mulhall tells Sargon that Earth humans evolved independently, Spock says that Sargon's explanation of colonization "would explain many enigmas in Vulcan prehistory."

There is, of course, no way to determine what these ancient Vulcans were like. Even Vulcans of Spock's time do not know, for it was so long ago that all records and memory of that time are lost. What is known is that Vulcan is a moonless world—now. It may not have been so at the time of colonization, and chances are good that the original colonists came from a world with one or more moons.

In humans—and it can also be assumed to hold true for other humanoid species as well, as most of them come from worlds with satellites—the reproductive process is controlled by the woman's cycle, which in turn is controlled by lunar influences. On starships, birth control is necessary, not so much to keep pregnancies from occurring, but to regulate a woman's cycle. For without the lunar influences, those cycles become totally out of kilter.

If those ancient Vulcan colonists settled on a world without a moon, they likewise would have had to continue to use some form of artificial control—probably the same method they used while in transit across the galaxy. But these early Vulcans were emotional beings, and eventually fell into the old ways of conquest. Devastating wars occurred, and knowledge of their beginnings was lost, along with most of their technology.

Without the knowledge of a need for artificial means of controlling the woman's cycle (much less the technology to produce it), the species adapted to a different way of controlling reproduction, one which did not depend upon a woman's cycle. In time (and rather shortly by evolutionary standards of humans), the male developed a cycle of fertility—one which erupted in a rather forceful manner.

VULCAN AS A PATRIARCHY

(A note: Perhaps Vulcan *did* possess a moon at the time of colonization, for it seems unlikely that the members of Sargon's advanced race would allow colonists to populate a planet that required constant treatment to maintain the female cycle. One can speculate that the same disaster that decimated Sargon's people caused havoc throughout the galaxy, destroyed Vulcan's moon, and caused the Vulcan colonists' regression to barbarism. In either case, the loss of the lunar influences caused the development of the male rut cycle.)

No doubt the pre-reform Vulcans had problems with males going into rut cycle and grabbing the first female that came along. But it is unlikely that the cycle was as destructive to individuals as it is today, simply because the Vulcans at that time were a highly emotional race. The rut cycle was probably more of an aggravation than anything else, though it is likely that some indiscretions occurred and ended in feuding and bloodshed.

Then, during Vulcan's darkest days, at a time when they had nearly destroyed themselves through war, a figure of reason emerged: a philosopher, a man of peace named Surak.

In "Savage Curtain," Spock describes Surak as "the greatest who ever lived on our planet. The *father** of all we became."

(Another note: As Surak is revered as the father of modern Vulcan, and since Vulcans are so tradition-bound and revere Surak so highly, it is unlikely that they would do a complete turnabout and institute a matriarchy, when it is a father figure whose tenets form the basis for their society.)

Surak initiated the reforms which led to peace and to the containment of emotions. A person's actions were predicated upon logic, emotion was suppressed—even denied—and, once again, nature caused changes.

If for every action there is a reaction, then Vulcans got a stronger reaction than they bargained for when they tried to excise emotions from their daily lives. In attempting to follow Surak's reforms, they went too far in the suppression of emotion, and nature repaid them.

Instead of just a period of intense mating, the male rut cycle—*pon farr*—became a far more violent time, when all those suppressed emotions boiled to the surface and spilled over. *Pon farr* is more than just "the time of mating," it is a

---

* Again author's italics.

time when bodily functions become unbalanced, as if (in a human system) huge amounts of adrenaline were constantly being pumped into the bloodstream. Hormones go wild, the emotional and physical pressures become unbearable, and the male loses all self-control. If he does not mate, he will die.

A most distasteful time for the fastidious Vulcans—not because the sex act is involved, but because they lose their self-control, their logic, their identity. As Spock tells Kirk, "Vulcans understand, but even we do not speak of it among ourselves. It is a deeply personal thing."

Deeply personal, private, embarrassing . . . and deadly. The inventive Vulcans came up with a way to neatly handle the entire mess as efficiently as possible, assuring at the same time that all males would have a wife to turn to, and that no male would run amok and rape the first woman he got his hands on. As is to be expected, it does not always prove to be as perfect in practice as in theory.

As we have seen in numerous examples on Star Trek, Vulcans are telepathic. And telepathy plays an important part in the relationship between husband and wife. Parents choose mates for their children, and at around seven years of age, the future mates are mentally bonded together. As Spock describes it, "One touches the other to feel another's thoughts. In this way, our minds were locked together so that at the proper time we would both be drawn to *Koon-ut-kal-if-fee*."

A perfect solution? The translation of the Vulcan term into English is "marriage or challenge." Vulcans seem to equate the two—and the phrasing is not metaphorical. Pre-reform Vulcans killed to win a bride when necessary. Modern Vulcans, of course, abhor killing. But what happens when a woman doesn't want to marry the man chosen for her?

Spock likened *pon farr* to the homing instincts of the giant eel-birds of Regulus V, or the earthly salmon. But it is more than that—far more. Salmon die *after* mating. A vulcan dies if he *doesn't* mate. Even in a Vulcan, self-preservation is a primary instinct, especially when he has lost emotional control and is reverting to instinct.

A Vulcan desperate for his wife can be a raging animal. Spock says that *pon farr* "strips away our veneer of civilization." This savage instinct, a portion of Vulcan nature that normally is carefully buried, rises, and the Vulcan male reverts to the barbaric state of his ancient, pre-reform counterpart. It is a vital element in Vulcan culture, and just as crucial to the Vulcan individual psychological makeup. *Pon farr* is every Vulcan's unavoidable legacy. Spock says that "the ancient drives are too strong, and we are driven by forces we cannot control to return home and take a wife—or die!"

In other words, a wife to a Vulcan is life itself. Without her to cool the searing fires of his mind and soothe the raging demands of his body, the Vulcan male would cease to exist. Therefore, she is *his*—undeniably, unquestionably, irrevocably—and if someone gets in the way, he will kill.

Naturally, Vulcan society prepares the young for marriage, and the responsibilities they will have to uphold. A woman is taught how to help her mate through *pon farr*; and though Vulcans don't normally talk about the mating drive, it is only logical to assume that young persons are taught what to expect and how to cope with it.

The wide-ranging implications of a society which revolves around a drive such as *pon farr* are staggering to an individual from a society such as ours that is not based upon that kind of tradition. *Pon farr* must be dealt with and controlled at all costs—and at times, the price is counted in an individual's personal rights. If, in order to maintain the status quo, a man's or woman's preferences must be sacrificed, that is precisely what may happen. For if *pon farr* is not controlled, the very cornerstones of Vulcan society could be quickly demolished.

Marriage becomes a duty and a responsibility, and is not, by any stretch of the imagination, a casual relationship. The only divorce on Vulcan is the *kal-if-fee*—the challenge made at the time of marriage. Vulcans once killed to win a bride, and they still do when necessary. If the prospective bride challenges, the male in *pon farr* goes into *plak tow*, or the "blood fever." It is sort of a trance wherein the lust for mating is replaced by a lust for combat, and the male emerges from this condition only when (or if) he kills his opponent. The bride then becomes not the wife of the victor, but his chattel, to be used in any manner necessary to save the male's life. It is neither a pleasant nor a pretty picture.

Pon farr serves the specific purpose of mating and the continuance of the race, but it also serves another vital function: a release of suppressed emotion. Such suppression can have a deleterious effect on Vulcans, and the time of mating effectively releases those emotions. It is obvious that in the Vulcan male, the sex drive is closely entwined with the aggressive drives, and during *pon farr*, an enormous amount of pent-up violence can be released—either at an opponent, or during mating. Again, it is a mechanism for releasing all the negative emotions that even a Vulcan can harbor.

With the mental bonding, a woman probably does not have an easy time coping—without the bond, she could conceivably die. The point is that during *pon farr*, the male aggressively conquers and establishes dominance over his wife in a physical manner; just as on Earth, lower animals which experience a rut cycle thoroughly dominate their females.

The Vulcan male would, therefore, be reared to be the dominant partner, possessive of his woman, the master of his household. Still, his treatment of his wife cannot be totally ruthless, for she is an intelligent being and a person in her own right. *Pon farr* is the exception, for nothing else really matters except survival. Under normal circumstances, however, the Vulcan male treats his wife with the respect and dignity which is her right, and Vulcan tradition protects her. But the very nature of the Vulcan reproductive cycle establishes rules of its own which set the parameters for interpersonal male/female relationships—and puts the status of the Vulcan male as the dominant partner almost into the category of "matter of course."

Thus, the Vulcan male ensures his continued existence when future times of mating occur. It must be this way, otherwise the wife could conceivably leave her husband to his fate the next time, especially if their bonding is inadequate and she has no strong telepathic tie to her husband.

Therefore, a Vulcan must lay claim to his woman, making her his in a manner that humans cannot fully know or appreciate. The marriage ceremony is described by T'Pau thus: ". . . it comes down from the time of the beginning, without change. This is the Vulcan heart. This is the Vulcan soul . . . this is our way."

The very nature of Vulcan and the reproductive cycle argues a patriarchy, for it seems impossible for a matriarchy to be founded in circumstances where the physiology of the male places such a relentless demand upon him: Mate or die. One's wife is definitely one's life; and as such is to be cherished, protected, and kept.

Pon farr has formed and molded the present-day Vulcan and is the pivot of Vulcan sociological structures. It is central

VULCAN AS A PATRIARCHY

to the continuance of the race, and its control is central to the continuance of Vulcan society. Tradition binds all of Vulcan into a cohesive group, ready, willing, and able to do that which is necessary to preserve themselves and their culture.

They live within the bounds *pon farr* has placed upon them because they recognize that *pon farr*, and all that goes with it, is inescapable. A violent fight may pull a Vulcan out of *pon farr* for a time (it worked with Spock, though it may have been the shock of believing he'd killed his captain rather than the battle which actually snapped him out of it), but that is only a temporary measure. In the end, the Vulcan male *must* take a wife.

When T'Pring challenges, T'Pau asks, "Thee are prepared to become the property of the victor? Not merely his wife, but his chattel, with no other rights or status."

It sounds like a high price to pay for the privilege of marrying the man of your choice (if he survives!), but it really is not when you consider that the alternative to mating is madness and death. Causing the death of another on Vulcan is one of the most serious crimes against the reforms of Surak; therefore, the decision to challenge cannot be made lightly. And only in a patriarchy would such a penalty exist. No woman in a matriarchy would ever accept the status of chattel, no matter what the circumstances.

Now that it has been established that Vulcan custom points to a patriarchal society, and that the pressures inherent in *pon farr* also lead to patriarchy where does T'Pau fit in?

It is logical that a woman with unusually strong telepathic abilities would officiate at a wedding ceremony. After all, the female is not affected by the madness of *pon farr* (except when in a deep link with her mate), and provides his anchor to sanity.

The ritual mind-touch that T'Pau shared with Spock helped him to contain his roiling emotions until the proper time came to release them—in combat. No Vulcan male could handle such a link, as he would be affected by the fever in Spock's mind.

But what then of T'Pau's obvious political power?

Vulcan is sociologically patriarchal, but not necessarily politically so. We can draw parallels to twentieth-century Earth where two nations, India and Israel, are patriarchal in social structure, but have had women serve as heads of government.

This being true on Earth, it should not be so incongruous

that such a fiercely patriarchal—and logical—society as Vulcan could have a woman as an "Elder." After all, Vulcans are logical people, and are easily able to separate their personal lives and beliefs from their professional lives and practices.

No matter what goes on at home, it is illogical to waste the potential of a segment of the population—thereby denying to the progress of the race as a whole the benefits these people could contribute—solely on the basis of gender. To the ever-logical Vulcans, it would be unthinkable to repress women, just as it would be unthinkable to control another's thoughts by mental invasion.

Therefore, by the very nature of logic, T'Pau (or any other woman so capable) must be allowed to fulfill her potential as a primary force in the government.

In some respects, Vulcan society provides advantages to their women other societies do not. Since everyone is encouraged to reach his or her full potential, women do not have to fight for equality. As professionals, women are respected, and valued equally with men.

As wives, entrusted with the lives of their husbands, they are valued far more than many human wives, and are in no way considered second-class citizens. Males are possessive of their wives in a personal sense—and, as we have seen, they have excellent reasons for that possessiveness. They are what their biology has made them, a species unique among humanoids.

Vulcan society as a patriarchy? Yes indeed, it is only logical.

17.
A TREK INTO GENEALOGY

by Linda Frankel

The amazing success of Alex Haley's novel Roots *brought about a new fad in this country—a desire on the part of many people to learn about their ancestors and the events and forces that made them what they are. The characters in Star Trek are just as real to most of us as our own families, so it is not surprising that the search for "roots" would eventually include Kirk and Co. You will agree with us that Linda Frankel has done an admirable job of filling in the Federation family tree.*

If Star Trek is the history of the future, then it surely must have roots in the past that can be found with a little detective work. When this author began to explore the possible ancestries of Star Trek characters, some interesting and even amusing results cropped up.

Leslie Thompson's reference to an "ancestor raised by apelike subhumans in darkest Africa" in "A Brief Look at Kirk's Career" (*The Best of Trek #2*) is probably an exaggerated version of the career of Sir John Kirk (1832–1922), who did accompany the explorer David Livingstone on his expedition to Africa when it was still referred to as "the Dark Continent." Kirk remained with the famed Doctor Livingstone for five years. He was later appointed consul general of Zanzibar, where he became the sole representative of the British Empire.

An earlier Kirk was a rather successful privateer. (A privateer is a pirate considered a hero in his native country because he attacks ships belonging to enemy powers—ofttimes with the unofficial blessing of his home government.)

Sir David Kirk (1597-1655) was clearly a man of valor. He seized an entire French fleet, causing the previously impregnable French colony of Quebec to surrender. After he was knighted in 1633 by Charles I, he was appointed Royal Governor of Newfoundland until he was removed by Cromwell, who had little reason to like royalists.

A man of lesser integrity might have switched sides when the tide turned against the king. After all, Kirk was no aristocrat. His father had been a merchant. Yet if there is one quality common to all Kirks, it is loyalty. Sir David Kirk retired into obscurity, and never held any office under Cromwell's Commonwealth.

Traces of Kirks in American history can be found today. Still existing is Kirkville, Missouri, founded in 1841 by one Jesse Kirk. As pioneer life was not easy, founding a town was quite a feat. It shows the same tenaciousness we see in James T. Kirk, as well as explaining our captain's desire to go forward into "the final frontier."

And that same bravery and desire to explore in Jim Kirk could come from his British forebears. From them, too, he gets a skill in diplomatic matters—duties he always considers onerous, but performs very well.

Before discussing a possible ancestor of Mr. Spock, it first must be stated that there is absolutely no truth to the rumor that his mother Amanda was descended from Batman's youthful sidekick, Robin (Dick Grayson); or that her mother was a Hatfield (although it would explain her son's constant verbal feuding with a certain McCoy!).

One of Spock's more legitimate ancestors might be Cary Travers Grayson (1878-1938), a dedicated officer of the United States Navy. (If Amanda had naval forebears, she would not have accepted Sarek's disapproving attitude toward Starfleet.) To the Vulcan respect for life is added the compassion of a human physician, for Cary Travers Grayson was no less than the medical director of the Navy and the personal doctor of three presidents. If Spock strokes a Tribble now and then, we can understand why. It's a wonder he isn't trying to take over Bones' job!

As might be expected, Leonard McCoy has healing in his

blood. Nineteenth-century physician Simon McCoy probably wanted his son, Frederick, to follow the family tradition and become a doctor. Frederick did study medicine, but decided instead to enter the field of paleontology. We now remember Sir Frederick McCoy (1823–1899) as a noted expert in the field, and the founder of Australia's National Museum of Natural History. Did he find himself saying, "I'm *not* a doctor . . ."? Well, no matter what a McCoy may do, there's no escaping that association with bones.

There are some really fine Scotts to choose from in our search for Scotty's ancestors.

Robert Falcon Scott (1868–1912) was an Arctic explorer. He died with his entire expedition in a blizzard on a return trip from the South Pole. Tragically, the team was only a few miles from help. Scott's diary was later recovered along with the bodies, and it tells an incredible tale of hardship and courage.

My favorite Scott, however, was Percy Moreton Scott (1853–1924), the naval gunnery expert. Like our Scotty, he was very devoted to his own field. It was said of him that he seemed to believe that ships were merely platforms to mount guns on. He fought for his improvements in gunnery, and had continuous run-ins with the Admiralty.

Percy Scott was also a drinking man, but like our Montgomery, he never drank on duty. It would have interfered with his formidable command abilities. During the Boer War, a ship under Scott's command performed a historic rescue of a besieged town by getting its guns on the scene at the pivotal moment.

And on November 8, 1909, Percy Scott displayed a sharp vision of the future. Addressing the Scottish Clan Association, he predicted that air power would one day make sea power look insignificant. His audience laughed. Montgomery Scott would laugh also, but it would be with his ancestor. And that, lads and lassies, is the last laugh.

It is interesting to speculate how people reacted to the invention of the warp drive. Judging from historical experience of past innovators and inventors, it may once have been called "Cochrane's Folly."

Thomas Cochrane (1815–1860) was an unorthodox naval commander. Because of the unacceptable nature of his tactics, he wasn't even permitted to take credit for his victories. Instead, he was disgraced by being falsely accused of stock fraud.

As a result, he left the British navy in disgust and espoused colonial struggles. He commanded the Chilean and Greek navies in their wars for independence against Spain and Turkey respectively. The cause of Greek independence was highly fashionable in England, so Cochrane was finally able to return a hero, but he was still embittered.

Perhaps the same sort of early rejection explains why Zephrem Cochrane finally tired of his life and fled alone out into the uncharted galaxy.

Of all the causes that have been espoused throughout history, the idea of free trade among nations has been the least successful. Advocates of free trade must feel as if they are charging windmills when they consider the powerful interests that have always opposed it.

Sir Matthew Decker (1679–1749) was one of the earliest proponents of free trade, opposing the tax on tea long before the Boston Tea Party. As did many free-traders before him, he failed, and events eventually led to the American Revolution.

His descendant and namesake (Commodore Matt Decker) also failed in his attempt to destroy the Doomsday Machine. One hopes that both Matt Deckers are pleased with Will Decker's eventual triumph over an even more incredibly powerful force, V'Ger, by allowing himself to unite with the entity. It may seem like the "If you can't lick em', join 'em" strategy, but there comes a time when doing so isn't an act of cynicism at all. In Will Decker's case, it was an act of great courage, and a fulfillment of his long-held dream to achieve a higher level of consciousness in the eternal company of his beloved, Ilia.

You all remember Ambassador Robert "Popinjay" Fox from "A Taste of Armageddon." His naive faith in diplomacy in the face of a long history of hostility was shared by Charles James Fox (1749–1806), a British diplomat who attempted to the end of his life to negotiate a peace treaty with France. He failed in his efforts, but his descendant eventually succeeded after Kirk had undiplomatically incapacitated the war computer on Eminiar. Sometimes a soldier's decisiveness is needed to give peace a chance.

Probably the most astonishing thing about that remarkable lady Edith Keeler is that she had the vision to see that man would someday reach the stars. But she came by her preoccupation with heavenly bodies honestly, being a descendant of James Edward Keeler (1857–1899), the noted astronomer. Astronomy is not usually considered a revolutionary sort of profession, but Edith added her own natural optimism, and saw how the stars could transform our future.

I have mentioned the advocate of air defense Percy Scott. Another martyr to that belief was Billy Mitchell (1879–1936). In him we see what Gary Mitchell must have been like before the tragedy that destroyed him. Billy Mitchell was a far-seeing man who stuck to his principles regardless of the consequences. Because he spoke out publicly against his superiors, he was court-martialed and broken in rank. Later, he was forced to resign from the U.S. Army. By all accounts, he was a good man. Gary Mitchell, for all his brashness, must also have been one, or Jim Kirk would not have valued his friendship so.

During my researches, it occurred to me that Harry Mudd might have turned to crime to avenge an ancestor. Dr. Samuel Mudd (1833–1883) was subjected to a great injustice. It is usually agreed that physicians are not to be blamed for performing their function of healing regardless of circumstances (Kirk didn't accuse McCoy of conspiracy with Kahn Noonian Singh because McCoy treated Kahn), but the court that found Dr. Mudd guilty wasn't so reasonable. By their logic he should have known that the stranger with a broken leg was John Wilkes Booth, Lincoln's assassin. Dr. Mudd's name has since been cleared, but Harcourt Fenton Mudd might still have felt disgruntled. After all, it's nearly impossible to wipe Mudd clean.

It would be somewhat ironic if Lieutenant Carolyn Palamas, who nearly betrayed the *Enterprise* because of her love for Apollo, was actually the descendant of the monk Gregorius Palamas (1296–1356). That Greek mystic was so devoted to monkish virtues that he spent years in total isolation—or was it total?

Equally improbable is Cyrano Jones' claim to be among the fine family tree of John Paul Jones. When asked if he was making progress at picking up Tribbles at Space Station K-7, he replied with a sigh, "I have not yet begun."

An ancestor of Christopher Pike comes right to mind. Naturally, it is Zebulon Pike (1779–1813), who discovered Pikes Peak in the Rockies.
It is difficult not to believe in reincarnation when you realize how closely Chris Pike followed his ancestor's life pattern. Not only was he an explorer, warrior, and peacemaker, Zebulon Pike also had a fateful accident. Only in his case, it proved fatal.
Commander of a victorious campaign in the War of 1812, Pike was killed by a falling rock during the British retreat. For such a man as Pike, survival in a crippled state would have been worse than death. There were no Talosians available at the time to give him the gift of illusion. . . .

It was a delight to meet an accomplished woman in Areel Shaw's ancestry. Anna Howard Shaw (1847–1919) fought to establish herself in two professions: She won the right to become the first woman preacher and to study medicine. Later she met Susan B. Anthony, and joined the struggle for woman's suffrage. She was known as one of the most effective speakers in the feminist movement, and her descendant is no slouch as a speaker, either.

I will admit that Charles Warden Stiles (1867–1941) performed a service. His career was dedicated to eradicating the parasite hookworm. But it's rather a shame that his descendant, Andrew Stiles, decided to enter on a crusade to eradicate Vulcans, instead. The last description I would use for a Vulcan is parasitic.

Genealogy also sheds light on the behavior of Commodore Stocker. It is no wonder that he was unable to command the *Enterprise,* or any other starship, for that matter. He probably unconsciously subscribed to the idealogy of his ancestor Helene Stocker (1869–1943), who was a leader of the European pacifist movement. The last thing we need is a pacifist in the command chair during a Romulan attack. He should have stuck to his desk.

This article is by no means a complete study of Star Trek genealogy. Still to be discovered are notable ancestors for many members of the *Enterprise* crew, as well as the hundreds of characters that appeared in Star Trek episodes over the years.

And some of you out there are demanding to know if there is a connection between Pavel Chekov and the famed author Anton Chekhov. Frankly, I believe that the story of their being related was invented by a little old lady from Leningrad.

18.

ALTERNATE UNIVERSES IN STAR TREK

by Mark Andrew Golding

Mark Golding's articles examining the science and hardware of the Federation have been extremely popular with our readers, and with this newest article, Mark takes a daring step forward: He postulates that all of the voyages of the Enterprise *did not occur in the same reality. Disagree? You may not after you read this article.*

Although there is currently no solid scientific evidence to support the theory of alternate universes, it is quite conceivable that every time there is a choice to be made, two (or more) diverging alternate realities spring into being, one for each possible outcome of that choice. Thus, for example, you have a universe where you *did* do something, and a universe where you *didn't* do the same thing. Both universes are equally real, but you can perceive only one.

So one may theorize that *all* possible choices are made, and in each instance alternate universes are created. If this is true, then throughout the history of the universe, countless numbers of alternate universes have appeared.

The vast majority of these do not differ from our own to any great degree. An alternate universe in which your parents never had children probably would not be very much different from this one (except for you!), but an alternate universe in which John Wilkes Booth and his cohorts decided not to assassinate President Lincoln may be surprisingly different.

We see much the same degree of divergence in the alternate universes presented in Star Trek. Consider the alternate universe in "Mirror, Mirror."

It has starships of the same design as those of the Federation, and at least one with the same name, the *Enterprise*. It has genetic duplicates of Kirk, Spock, McCoy, Scott, Uhura, Sulu, Chekov, Kyle, Christopher Pike, and others, all of whom serve on the same starship as in our universe.

Clearly, the alternate universe of "Mirror, Mirror" could not have branched off from that of the regular Star Trek episodes very far in the past. We know that the history of the Star Trek universe was a fairly bloody one, and there are many instances where the wrong choice could have resulted in the degeneration of the ideals and aims of our characters and their commanders.

Thus, we can surmise that the universe of "Mirror, Mirror" diverged from that of Star Trek fairly "recently." For if the divergence had been too far removed, the majority of the characters would not have been serving on the *Enterprise*—if, indeed, they had ever even been born!

This episode is a perfect example of how a completely different universe may be created, while still having many, many things in common with our own, as is "Yesteryear," in which the mission of the *Enterprise* goes on without the presence of Spock, who, in the divergent universe, was killed as a boy.

(It is appropriate at this point to discuss *parallel* universes, which have also appeared in several Star Trek episodes. A parallel universe is one which co-exists alongside our own, but is not affected by choices made in our universe. Examples of parallel universes are seen in "The Alternative Factor," "Counterclock Incident," "Is There in Truth No Beauty?" and "The Tholian Web." Parallel universes may be similar to our own, but in most cases, they are wildly divergent, even to the point of having different physical laws.)

So while we have seen concrete examples of both alternate and parallel universes in Star Trek, there may be others of which we are completely unaware.

While it is quite possible for a starship to visit several dozen solar systems within a few years, it must be noted that in almost *all* of the star systems visited by the *Enterprise* in the live and animated episodes, extremely important and exciting events happen.

And certainly it seems logical that most of the missions of

the *Enterprise* would be routine and fairly dull, so that the actual number of missions undertaken by the starship must be several times the number seen in the episodes. That the *Enterprise* makes voyages that have gone unrelated is verified by the dialogue in many episodes.

So the *Enterprise* must have visited hundreds of worlds and star systems during a period in which Kirk, Spock, McCoy, and the rest of the crew seemed to age very little (if at all) in the course of what is referred to as "a five-year mission." That is, I think, crowding it a little.

And certainly the *Enterprise* crew has succeeded against almost infinite odds in the majority of most of these hundred-odd missions. In one episode, "Errand of Mercy," Spock estimates the odds against Kirk and himself making it to Kor's office as being more than seven thousand to one ... yet they made it.

If in each of the three filmed seasons and the one animated season, the total odds against success were seven thousand to one (and of course the odds were actually much more extreme than that), then the grand total of odds against the *Enterprise* succeeding in all missions over the four seasons would be 2,401,000,000,000,000,000 to one! It is hard to believe that even the crew of the *Enterprise* could succeed against such odds.

The order in which the Star Trek episodes occur is also uncertain. It may be that they occur in the order of their stardates, or the order in which they were telecast, or the order in which they were produced. There is also a fourth possibility: Perhaps they take place not one after the other, but roughly simultaneously, occurring in alternate universes.

After all, in many episodes you see Kirk making decisions about where to take the *Enterprise* next. And he must make a *choice*.

Thus there must be a vast number of alternate universes in which the *Enterprise* is not in the right place at the right time to be trapped in "The Tholian Web," or take a "Journey to Babel," as the ship did when it *was* in the right place at the right time.

We can definitely tie several of the episodes together, either through an episode being a direct sequel to a previous one, or through easily recognizable references to earlier episodes.

"Once upon a Planet" is a sequel to "Shore Leave." "Mudd's Passion" is a sequel to "I, Mudd," which was a sequel to "Mudd's Women." In "The Deadly Years," there is a reference to previous fights with the Romulans, probably those in "Balance of Terror."

In "The Survivor" and "*Enterprise* Incident," the Romulans are willing to take prisoners, a trait differing from Romulan practice in "Balance of Terror" and "Deadly Years." Reference is also made to Kirk's "habit" of accidentally entering the Neutral Zone, something which all Kirks of all universes must do with alarming regularity.

"More Tribbles, More Troubles" is a sequel to "Trouble with Tribbles," which is probably a sequel to "Errand of Mercy" (events revolving around edicts of the Organian Peace Treaty). "Day of the Dove" takes place three years after the making of the treaty, although it may take place in an alternate timeline from the Tribble episodes. Commander Kor in "Time Trap" mentions a previous conflict with the *Enterprise*, although it is not clear if this refers to "Errand of Mercy." The belligerency of the Klingons in some episodes would suggest that they take place in alternate universes in which the Organian Peace Treaty does not exist.

In "Turnabout Intruder," events similar to those in "Tholian Web" and "The Empath" were mentioned. Reference to "A Taste of Armageddon" was made in "By Any Other Name," and in that episode, Kirk stated that the *Enterprise* had been to the force field at the edge of the galaxy, although the costumes, equipment, and personnel of the ship in "Where No Man Has Gone Before" are quite different from those in the other episodes.

"Where No Man" might have occurred before all the other episodes. But in "Deadly Years," Sulu said that he had served under Kirk for two years. As it is known from several sources that Kirk brought Sulu to the *Enterprise* with him, this statement seems to be wrong, if "Where No Man" can be considered the "first" episode.

Also in "Where No Man," Sulu was a physicist, whereas in all of the other episodes he was a helmsman. Thus it seems likely that "Where No Man Has Gone Before" takes place in an alternate universe somewhat more removed from the universes of the other episodes (it may well be the only recorded instance in which Gary Mitchell existed!), and the encounter with the force field mentioned by Kirk in "By Any Other Name" was part of a different sequence of events than those in "Where No Man."

Lieutenant Sulu commanded the *Enterprise* in Kirk's absence in "Arena" and "Errand of Mercy," while in "Menagerie," Spock surrendered to McCoy as senior officer present and turned over operational command to Sulu, although Lieutenant Commander Scott had beamed him aboard. It would seem that in the universes of these particular episodes engineering officers do not have command rights by Starfleet regulations.

In the universes of episodes like "A Taste of Armageddon," "The Apple," "Gamesters of Triskelion," "Friday's Child," and several others, Scott did command the *Enterprise* while Kirk and Spock were away, indicating that Starfleet regulations do give engineering officers command rights in those realities.

Lieutenant Hansen is a relief navigator on the *Enterprise* in "Courtmartial" and "Menagerie." But in "Courtmartial," Starbase Eleven is commanded by Commodore Stone (stardate 2947.3), and in "Menagerie," the commander is Commodore Mendez (stardate 3012.4). So these two episodes are probably in different, but very closely related, universes.

In "Charlie X," the cooks of the *Enterprise* are instructed to make ersatz turkey out of meatloaf; in many other episodes mechanical food preparation machines can send food to any compartment of the ship. Apparently, the inner workings of the ship are much more efficient and comfortable in some universes than in others!

A good tipoff to which episodes take place in the same universes is the area of space in which the *Enterprise* is assigned duty. In "Courtmartial" and "Menagerie," the *Enterprise* seems to operate in the sector of Starbase Eleven. In "Who Mourns for Adonais?" the nearest starbase to Pollux IV is Starbase Twelve, and in "Space Seed," Kirk tells Kahn that Starbase Twelve (in the Gamma 400 system) is the *Enterprise*'s "command base in this sector."

Starbase Four is mentioned in "And the Children Shall Lead" and "Let That Be Your Last Battlefield." Starbase Nine is the closest in "Tomorrow Is Yesterday" and "Catspaw." Starbase Six is mentioned in "Immunity Syndrome," Starbase Twenty-five in "Slaver Weapon," Starbase Twenty-three in "Terratin Incident," and Starbase Twenty-two in "How Sharper Than a Serpent's Tooth."

In "Errand of Mercy," "Trouble with Tribbles," "Friday's Child," "A Private Little War," "Day of the Dove," "Ellan of

Troyius," "The Lorelei Signal," "More Tribbles, More Troubles," "Time Trap," and perhaps "Amok Time," the *Enterprise* operates near the border of the Klingon Empire.

In "Balance of Terror," "The Deadly Years," "*Enterprise* Incident," "The Survivor," "The Way to Eden," and "Practical Joker," the *Enterprise* patrols near the Romulan Neutral Zone.

These episodes are likely to take place in differing alternate realities than the Klingon episodes (although it must be noted that in many episodes, both empires definitely exist, sometimes as allies). And all episodes in which the *Enterprise* is assigned to duty on the Romulan or Klingon fronts are likely to be in alternate universes from episodes in which the ship is assigned to explore unknown regions of space. So in some realities, the *Enterprise* is a warship, and in other, somewhat more peaceful universes, it is primarily an exploration vessel.

The theory of alternate universes can also explain some of the distracting similarities and differences of persons appearing in various episodes.

Admiral Komack orders Kirk to take the colonists on Omicron Ceti II to Starbase Twenty-seven, but in "Amok Time," Komack's command area is sector 9. But "For the World Is Hollow and I Have Touched the Sky" takes place in the sector commanded by Admiral Westervilet, who looks very much like Admiral Komack. Perhaps in the time of Star Trek, people are free to choose the surname of any family they are descended from, and in the universe of "Paradise" and "Amok Time," this officer chose the name Komack, and in the alternate dimension of "Sky," he took the name Westervilet.

The same theory applies to the great number of *Enterprise* crewpersons that appeared in various episodes, then were never heard from again, or else reappeared with another name, rank, or duty.

The major characters also have differing backgrounds in the various alternate universes. In "What Are Little Girls Made Of?" it was stated that Kirk's brother had three sons, but in "Operation: Annihilate!" only one son exists. (In both universes, however, George Kirk is called "Sam" only by his brother.)

Perhaps Christine Chapel and the enigmatic Number One from "Menagerie" are the same person, having chosen different careers and hair dyes in different universes—although

Leslie Thompson's suggestion that they were sisters makes sense, and they could also be clones. It is likely that *all* of these explanations are true in varying alternate universes.

The theory of alternate timelines would also explain Kirk's habit of placing himself (and his valuable and almost irreplaceable command abilities) in jeopardy by beaming down to potentially dangerous planets and situations. Instead of having beamed down almost seventy times, he probably has done so only a few times in each reality, and therefore would not have to explain such recklessness to Starfleet Command.

In "Amok Time," "A Private Little War," and "A Taste of Armageddon," (to name just a few), Kirk played fast and loose with the Prime Directive, and made decisions in many other episodes that would likely have irritated Starfleet Command. If all of these episodes took place in differing universes, Kirk would be much less likely to be disciplined—or even court-matialed.

But perhaps Starfleet's irritation was tempered by the thought that nothing succeeds like success, as evidenced by the fact that Kirk and his crew managed to save the Federation (and sometimes the entire galaxy!) in many, many episodes. If all of these episodes occurred in the same timeline, the Federation would have probably created the special rank of Grand High Supreme Admiral of Admirals just for Kirk, provided he wasn't too busy to come back and accept it.

If the theory of alternate universes is correct, an infinite number of Star Trek television episodes, movies, stories, and novels could occur, even though the timelines in which the *Enterprise* encountered interesting events would be only a fraction of the total number of timelines in which Kirk, Spock, and McCoy voyaged on the *Enterprise,* and those alternate universes would be only a tiny fraction of the total number in which the Star Trek regulars served on various other Starfleet vessels, and those alternate futures would be only a tiny fraction of the futures in which the main Star Trek characters would be born at all, and those alternate timelines would only be an infinitesimal fraction of the total number of timelines in which the human race existed, and so on and so on and so on. . . .

An excellent example of this wide divergence of universes is found in Star Trek fan fiction. Alternate realities where Kirk and Spock are lovers, various crewmembers have their sexes reversed, characters either die or were never born, and hundreds more appear. But for our purposes here, let us examine some of the various Star Trek timelines in relation to our present timeline, and in relation to some present-day fiction.

In "Bread and Circuses," Spock states that 6,000,000 persons were killed in World War I, 9,000,000 in World War II, and 37,000,000 in World War III. Available sources list 8,538,385 soldiers killed in WW I (plus many, many civilians and over 5,000,000 Russians who starved in the postwar famine and 21,640,000 persons who died in the influenza epidemic of 1918 caused by the war), and anything between 16,000,000 and 54,000,000 in World War II (take your pick). It would seem that the world wars mentioned by Spock were very much less devastating than those experienced in our reality, indicating that he was referring to an alternate universe from our own. We have, as of yet, managed to avoid World War III, so perhaps things have a way of evening out.

Our first manned lunar orbital mission blasted off on a Saturday, while Apollo 11, the first manned moon landing mission, took off at 8:32 EST, on Wednesday, July 16, 1969. In "Tomorrow Is Yesterday," our heroes, back in the late 1960s, heard a radio announcement that the first manned moon shot would be launched at 6:00 a.m. EST on a Wednesday, date unmentioned. So except for a couple of hours difference, that Star Trek timeline could be the same as our own.

The launching of an orbital nuclear platform in 1968 as shown in "Assignment Earth" seems not to have occurred in our universe, although it *may* have, as the government would have been somewhat reticent about announcing that a secret launch almost crashed with nuclear warheads aboard.

Thus we see that the timelines of the Star Trek episodes have already begun to diverge from ours, although not too far in some cases, since Kirk mentioned the Apollo program in "Return to Tomorrow," and a Voyager spacecraft plays an important part in the Star Trek movie. It is probably safe to assume that in all alternate realities where humans developed space travel, the early stages were quite similar.

Star Trek episodes and novelizations ofttimes take place in alternate universes in which characters and situations from some of our present-day science fiction appear.

A Kzinti-like being was seen in "Time Trap," and the Kzinti were mentioned in "The Infinite Vulcan." The villains of "The Slaver Weapon" were the Kzinti, which Larry Niven adapted from his short story "The Soft Weapon." It would seem that Mr. Niven has implicitly stated that his *Known Space* series takes place in an alternate universe from that of the Star Trek series. Thus the laws of nature should be the same in each series, and some of the same intelligent races should exist.

Certainly, the histories of the two universes have been different, for in the *Known Space* stories the Kzinti wars occur between 2360 and c.2577; while the Star Trek episodes occur around 2200, and in "Infinite Vulcan," Kirk states that the last Kzinti war occurred a hundred years earlier, around 2100.

In his adaptations of the Star Trek episodes, James Blish made many changes in the format, most of them accidentally. He seems to have assumed that the episodes take place five-hundred years in the future, instead of two-hundred. So, one might think of the Blish adaptations as taking place in a different universe from that of the actual episodes. This is especially true when one considers that Blish had the Organians deprive the Klingons of spaceflight capabilities in *Spock Must Die!*

Blish also deliberately referred to events from other stories of his own in his Star Trek adaptations. In his version of "City on the Edge of Forever," Spock mentions Bonnar the Stochastic (who, in Blish's novel, *The Triumph of Time*, dies when the universe is destroyed in 4004 A.D.), although in the adaptation, Kirk states that Bonnar won't be born until after 2130.

In his adaptation of "Tomorrow Is Yesterday," Blish states that the region of space that the *Enterprise* is in was dominated by the Vegan Tyranny in the 1970s. In Blish's novel, *Cities in Flight*, it is stated that the Vegan Tyranny flourished from 8000 B.C. to 2431 A.D. Apparently in the Star Trek universe, the Vegan Empire was overthrown much sooner than in *Cities*.

In his adaptation of "Miri," Blish states that the planet where the episode takes place (in the 70 Ophiucus system) was settled during the Cold Peace some five-hundred years earlier. The Cold Peace began in 2022, and ended between 2027 and 2032, according to *Cities in Flight*.

In *Spock Must Die!* Blish tells us that Koloth had first

tangled with Kirk in the affair of the Xixobrax Jewelworm. In "This Earth of Hours" (in *Galactic Cluster*), a race of intelligent "worms" with jewel-like eyes are discovered living on Xixobrax. Therefore, the universes of Star Trek, of *Cities in Flight*, and of the shorts from *Galactic Cluster* must be in three separate alternate universes.

Many of the persons, places, events, and scientific laws and devices mentioned in the *Cities in Flight* and *Galactic Cluster* series are also mentioned in other Blish stories such as "The Star Dwellers," "Mission to the Heart Stars," "A Case of Conscience," "The Seedling Stars," "The Quincunx of Time," "The Hour Before Earth Rise," and other—stories in which there are also many differences from one another.

Thus it would seem that all these Blish stories take place in alternate timelines of one vast imaginary universe, one which is linked to that of Star Trek by the four common points mentioned.

As Allan Dean Foster added many details to his adaptations of the animated episodes, it might be well to think of his adaptations as taking place in a different universe from that of the actual episodes as well. For one thing, Foster places all of the animated episodes in order, one after the other, while by the theory of alternate universes, some would take place in different timelines than others.

In his script "Catspaw," Robert Bloch appears to have created an alternate Star Trek universe which involved the "Cthulhu Mythos," a series of fantasy, horror, and science fiction stories created by H.P. Lovecraft, and embellished by many others, including Bloch himself.

And it worked fairly well. It is then possible that the vast and complex imaginary universe of Star Trek, the imaginary universe of the *Known Space* series by Larry Niven, the many imaginary universes of James Blish's stories and novels, and the fantastically complex and ever-growing imaginary universe of the "Cthulhu Mythos" are all part of one vast "super universe" of fiction. If so, then the possibilities for meetings, given the capabilities of time travel and travel to alternate universes seen in Star Trek, are endless and intriguing.

If used with intelligence, consistency, and care, the concept of alternate universes for the different Star Trek episodes, and the relationship between the universes of Star Trek and the other imaginary universes mentioned, can be utilized to explain many apparent inconsistencies between episodes and to suggest many possible story, novel, and script ideas in the future.

ABOUT THE EDITORS

Although largely unknown to readers not involved in Star Trek fandom before the publication of *The Best of Trek #1*, WALTER IRWIN and G. B. LOVE have been actively editing and publishing magazines for many years. Before they teamed up to create TREK® in 1975, Irwin worked in newspapers, advertising, and free-lance writing, while Love published *The Rocket's Blast—Comiccollector* from 1960 to 1974, as well as hundreds of other magazines, books, and collectables. Both together and separately, they are currently planning several new books and magazines, as well as continuing to publish TREK.

TREK®

The Magazine For Star Trek Fans

Did you enjoy reading this collection selected from the best of TREK, The Magazine For Star Trek Fans? If so, then you will want to start reading TREK regularly! In addition to the same type of features, articles, and artwork in this collection; each issue of TREK features dozens of photos of your Star Trek favorites — all beautifully halftoned for the finest possible reproduction! TREK has full-color front and back covers, is fully typeset, and is printed on high-quality coated paper designed to last a lifetime! In short, TREK is the finest Star Trek magazine available today, at any price. Remember, if you aren't reading TREK, then you are missing half the fun of being a Star Trek fan! So order a copy of our current issue today — or better yet, subscribe, and be sure of never missing an issue!

Current Issue .... $3.00 plus 50 cents postage
4 issue subscription $12.00
8 issue subscription $24.00

TREK PUBLICATIONS

1120 Omar   Houston, Texas 77009